I0660541

Normalised Utopia

By William J Fraser

Second Edition

Copyright © 2022 by William J Fraser

William J Fraser

This is a work of fiction. Names characters, places and incidents either are the product of the author's imagination or are used fictitiously any resemblance to actual persons living or dead events or locales is entirely coincidental.

All rights reserved no part of this book may be reproduced or used in any manner without written permission of the copyright owner except for the use of the quotations in a book review.

Second paperback edition July 2022.

Copyright © 2022 by William J Fraser

Book cover design Copyright
© 2022 by William J Fraser

ISBN 978-1-7397032-4-0
(Second edition paperback)

ISBN 978-1-7397032-3-3
(Second edition eBook)

Self-published by William J Fraser

Normalised Utopia

Index:

0.0 Introduction.	v
01. Chaotic sanctuary.	001
02. Confidence interval.	039
03. Endogenous sigma.	070
04. Apostles of the Alternate hypothesis.	102
05. Error nodes, error terms.	145
06. Stochastic routines.	176
07. Spurious results.	201
08. An audience with Arima.	244
09. Exogenous nodes.	295
10. Unbiased inferences.	343
11. Bayesian optimization.	377
12. Madness of crowds.	407

Introduction.

State Utopia's capital, Primary_Sample_Space is a dystopian futuristic city previously referred to as London. The state is now governed by an all pervasive statistical totalitarianism, primarily in the form of the Economic Efficiency Act which forces all of the citizen nodes to adhere to strict, expected, normalised distributions of given, known, fixed, quota means, in every aspect of their lives; forcing them to think average, to think mean and be confident that they are adhering to the statistical quotas and its expected routines, thinking, behaviour and consumption quotas.

To always be rational and ruthless in choosing the highest payoff in their given, relative, constrained, game theory matrix, that they are presented with, each moment so they will constantly be within their normalised confidence interval, sigma caste. To always try to approach the mean, the average, to choose the most rational choice; to think mean.

Strict statistical quotas are given to serve the all-pervasive market Beta of the utopian state's economy so it will grow predictably, consistently due to complete control of the aggregate demand of the economy, resulting in all uncertainty within the market Beta being ironed out, a metaphor for Net Present Value. Statistical algorithm quotas directly control every aspect of the nodes' lives; routines, thinking and consumption which are enforced and expected, continually.

Every aspect of the nodes' lives is just a series of restricted options and normalised distribution of expected caste probability frequencies; constraining their choices, averaging out their routines and thoughts to fit into the utopian states' strict statistical regulation.

They continually adhere to acceting the rational choice; choosing the option with the highest payoff every time. Accepting the expected routines as the only rational way to pursue prosperity and a confidence in their security within a strict, ruthless society regulated by statistical algorithms, economic ideologies, embedded devices, artificial intelligence, database cluster supercomputers and emotional implied thought scanners.

The Sigma caste nodes are considered mere econometric variables; the population comprising of a divided caste system of citizen nodes within a normalised distribution of the standard deviations containing the different castes. The nodes' rank relative to their standard deviation from the given, known, fixed, mean of state utopia's current, quotas of each new monthly confidence interval.

The Alpha nodes are at the pinnacle of state Utopia's root down caste hierarchy with a positive three Sigma rank whose standard deviation in intelligence, societal and technological skills is in great sigma excess of the mean. Their privileged position in society is usually hereditary but can also occur through promotion from the immediate lower caste rank.

The endogenous sigma nodes live within the state Utopia's normalised distribution of economically efficient expectations and statistical compliance. The sample and population regression function; an equation used throughout this novel, is an economics model used as a metaphor for the endogenous sigma nodes and their environment within the utopian state.

The novel is written with econometric terminology taken literally, with in-depth intricate mathematical observations and also in a pseudo-science, philosophical, metaphorical, perspective which describes a constrained, statistical, totalitarian society. The hero of the book Bayes inevitably evolves to become statistically freer within his thinking and being.

The novel is written similar to a basic econometric text book with its description of a constrained, statistical, totalitarian state where mobile phones, big data science and crypto currency has not been invented.

When I began writing Normalised Utopia in 2011, I was not fully aware of those inventions as being commonplace or even of the term social credits. I solely intended to write the novel in purely basic econometric syllabus terminologies.

Econometrics is used as a metaphor for the more advanced contemporary big data science and as a mathematical tool to expand decisions choices; the binary expansion of thinking, self-determination and societal growth based on those methodologies. Econometric terminologies describe situations and concepts arising within a totalitarian society that is governed by statistical algorithms and expectations.

All political aspects of State Utopia's society are substituted with basic econometrics terminologies and concepts. Yet this narrative still imparts a societal wisdom that can be paralleled with many totalitarian societal conditions as mathematical systems and the evolution of biased weightings of binary decisions follows common trends, mechanisms and results, irrespective of the political brand name or individual restrictive ideologies.

The novel's main theme is the evolution of statistics; evolving from classical statistics to Bayesian statistics. This metaphorical evolution takes place from Harry Bayes' perspective and personal growth. He is an econometric analysis at the Ministry of Inferences who enviably rebels against the utopian state's statistical constraints.

At first he is aware of the fixed, known, mean which is given by the Utopian state's all present quotas and selection bias.

The Best Least Unbiased Estimator, dependent, independent and endogenous variables and all other variables and econometric measuring models and tools are first fit around the utopian state's given quotas data set unlike its antithesis, true econometric and statistical analysis. The utopian state creating the given, known, fixed mean and its official, contemporaneous, normalised distribution and confidence interval.

The Economic Efficiency Act creates quotas and statistical expectation around which the nodes form their routines, thoughts, perceptions and consumptions; all around the selection bias of the utopian state's expected result. This creates a fixed, known statistical mean. The nodes are also conditioned to be loyal to the state's apodictic, null hypothesis which is perpetually realised due to the selection bias of the state; making the state's null hypothesis biased.

In real econometrics, the null hypothesis should be rejected or accepted after inferring the data yet within state Utopia it cannot be rejected or questioned therefore it is apodictic, a paradox; apodictic and null hypothesis.

Bayes eventually through a series of epiphanies and an encounter with the unknowable, hidden, stochastic error nodes, where he becomes tainted with a lagged variable of uncertainty and randomness which coupled with other perspectives, leads him to becomes aware of a new societal reality, of an unknown, fixed mean, not given; that of classical statistics.

Bayes eventually becomes free of any given or unknown mean and is uncertain of any mean, unaware that he is even searching for it.

Bayes then becomes to realise the free floating mean, Bayesian statistics which constantly updates it's prior and mean.

Where there is no fixed mean, only a series of unknown, contemporaneous means based on observation and updated information, a relative chaos, based on limited sample data.

To an unknown, free floating, constantly updating prior of the Bayesian mean which is constantly morphing organically to a contemporaneous normalised distribution.

If the countless other endogenous nodes this would accept this Bayesian awareness it would lead to societal, "Wisdom of crowds" and a more natural free floating, constantly updating, statistical anarchy which is not biased to any particular hypothesis. As even an alternative hypothesis ideology is baised.

Within state Utopia there are large visible scanners mounted high upon tall poles which are strategically placed throughout the city to monitor the electromagnetic activity of each node's brain. The scanners analyse their contemporaneous, emotions then transform their data into their probable implied thoughts and expected routines; ultimately measuring each node's level of conformity at each moment, whilst awake.

Statistical algorithms, workplace targets, continual monitoring and subliminal advertisements, continually force the nodes to choose the rational choice; to choose the highest cooperative payoff. To always be thinking average, to always be accepting that they individually do not count only the collective averaged result, at each moment of inspection. They should think in multitudes of time and groups of nodes, not now, not me; but us, over that period. Not what I like or any node likes rather what we tend to like, statically, over a certain sample period.

The nodes are exposed to countless daily advertisements to mould their consumer trends; through a statistical control and enticement to consume within tightly regulated aggregate demand quotas which is used to service the all-important cash flow of the economy which is the primary role of the Economic Efficiency Act, to remove all inefficiency out of the economy, to maximise all profit predictably.

The node's lives are therefore perpetually constrained by a blatant, all pervasive, forced statistical conformity which is used to maximize the economic efficiency of the state.

All uncertainties in the financial markets and society are rendered to a net present value of zero, enabling the state to have complete control of the economy's aggregate demand which is a proxy for the nodes' free will.

Nodes that consistently fall outside the Economic Efficiency Act's confidence interval quota are classified as redundant nodes or outliers and are removed from society.

Statistical control is more ruthless than a stick of any dictator and yet more subtle than any carrot of a seemingly liberal controlled state.

Bayes is tasked with an econometric and applied statistical analysis role at the Ministry of Inferences. His main tasks involves analysing and amending the sigma nodes' monthly normalised variable result which directly affects the possibility of them being rendered a redundant node which would result in them being invited to travel to Arcadian which would ultimately result in their doom.

Inevitably the confidence interval quota becomes a personal issue to Bayes who slowly wakes from being merely a conditioned sterile detached statistical tool of the state. At the personal realisation of his neighbour, Mrs Whites' invitation to Arcadia and her predicted imminent demise which he is powerless to stop or even warn of.

He slowly develops a conscience and begins to feel a growing resentment towards the ruthless statistical driven state and guilt of his small role at the Ministry of Inferences.

As he becomes more despondent with the utopian state, he finds it harder to constrain his thoughts towards the official mean which are perceived to be perpetually monitored by the implied thought scanners.

Even though his aptitude is in introversion, being able to mask his true thoughts and routines more so than the average node, giving him an element of free thinking; he struggles to contain his emotions as his conscience grows.

After he is saved from a vicious attack by the hidden, unknowable, errors node vagrants, he decides to rebel against the state.

Yet he realises that trying to forcefully free the nodes' minds is futile, a momentary disturbance within the state's status quo and a minor turbulence in the great cash flow river.

He then finds himself journeying through the state and being confronted by different powerful characters; statistical realisations out of the probability ether, many are antagonistic authoritative characters trying to bend Bayes' will to the harmonised safety of the utopian state, for him to be a constrained endogenous node once again whilst other characters set him free with their insights and positive influences who talk about altruism and compassion and of the dangers of evolution; knowledge, mathematics, systems and computers which lead to perdition for any society.

For Bayes it is a journey of self-discovery; discovery of statically evolution and societal evolution.

Bayes searches for freedom and ultimate redemption for his part in the Ministry of Inferences genocide, this narrative is just before the rise of augmented intelligence; a connected, collective, harmonised, free society, augmented by a benevolent artificial intelligence and the population crowd of state Utopia.

Bayes is a catalytic agent or prophet of a new age in a time dominated by statistical efficiency and technology which are a natural prelude to the ultimate efficiency and statistical technology of artificial intelligence, augmented collective minds and tans-humanism evolution.

Normalised Utopia

"All systems tend towards an infallible, mathematical structure. Yet I am fallible therefore I am no system."

William J Fraser 2017

01: Chaotic sanctuary.

"Think mean, be confident!" said the red, blue and white poster, peeling off at both ends, as its cohesive forces succumbed to the erosion of inevitable entropy with a dutiful normalised symmetry whilst it remained fixed and known upon a tube station wall, deep underground.

I read the sign subliminally as I rushed past with the hordes of other worker nodes who hastily streamed through the insipid, dimly lit, narrow tunnel passageways; hurrying on to their endless punctual habits of expected normalised routines.

As the hordes of nodes rushed onwards, their senses were assaulted by unpleasantness from all directions; the dim flickering lighting illuminated the unpleasant view of the grubby tunnel walls, covered in dirt and used bubble gum; resembling a giant meandering scatter plot graph in need of, a goodness of fit linear regression function, to realise it's averaged value.

The continual screeching and deafening noises, emanating through the tunnel corridor network, indicated the presence of yet another dirty tube train; arriving predictably like clockwork, every few minutes.

The smell of bleach from the hastily cleaned floors intermingled with the smell of burnt oil from the antiquated tube trains; the feel of chaotic prods and pushes as indiscriminate passenger nodes jostled and brushed past each other.

Why the nodes were always rushing so desperately trying to catch the very next arriving tube train; resembling competing mice scurrying through the labyrinths of a, "Mouse utopia," maze? It still seemed so irrational to me; as there was a newly arriving tube train every few minutes.

Yet the utopian state's totalitarian Economic Efficiency Act tolerated the nodes' slight inefficient behaviour which was inferred as micro stochastic movement that was firmly restricted to only resonate randomly within a very limited fixed know sample space area within the nodes official standard deviation; within the sigma caste of their confidence interval, statistical quotas.

Their resulting chaotic movement and routines were considered by the utopian state as mere error terms; white noise within the contributing endogenous sigma nodes' commuting linear regression functions and redistricted economic models.

The nodes were classified as endogenous as they existed within the great linear regression model of the state and therefore contributed towards the great contrived apodictic null hypothesis.

They were referred to as sigma as their standard deviation was permitted a mere variance within which their thinking, consumption and routines were allowed to resonate around their societal Sigma caste mean.

Yet I like the rest of the endogenous sigma caste nodes continued on through the dimly lit, charmless, passages; carried on by the unstoppable mass of hurrying chaotic nodes around me.

Even though this great rush of endogenous sigma nodes appeared with the same regularity of a tidal surge, twice daily, six times per week, flowing through the underground corridors, like a flash flood; there was no need.

Any individual endogenous sigma node could easily catch the next tube. Individually it was irrational behaviour and collectively it seemed to be an inefficient routine yet the utopian state tolerated this, as individually the node was being selfish whilst chaotically prodding and pushing through the crowds.

Simultaneously, collectively they acted as a covariant herd which constrained their individuality and personal thoughts, especially within the chaotic melee of the seemingly unordered, unscanable, unpredictable, underground labyrinth.

The twice daily underground commuting melee was chaotic therefore was theoretically predictable, if all the initial variables were known exactly, prior to the process beginning, unlike true randomness.

State Utopia used the chaotic rather than random perspective to justify tolerating a certain degree of marginalised freedom within the chaotic undergone unscanable commuting labyrinth.

The seemingly endless stream of processioning nodes hurried on through the underground tunnels of Primary_Sample_Space tube station whilst they were bombarded with deafening loudspeaker announcements from semi-illiterate, Delta node tube staff who would announce endless, trivial travel information.

"Passengers walk carefully, please yeah!" "The District line has some delays and the Northern line has no stopping at St Pancras, yeah!"

On and on, the never ending deafening drivel was pumped out into the labyrinth of passageways, echoing out from the countless, strategically positioned loudspeakers; only outnumbered by the amount of facial recognition CCTV cameras which littered the underground corridors.

The facial recognition CCTV cameras were nearly as numerous as the chaotically placed bits of dirty bubble gum and randomly settled small sticky pockets of filth that clung to every part of the corridor walls.

Never ending emotionally inspiring advertisements played over the loudspeaker only to be broken by persistent deafening trivial time table announcements which implied continual adherence to the fixed, known, given statistical quotas.

As the screeching tube trains arrived and doors slid open, the entire sample set of endogenous sigma nodes waiting upon the station platform immediately, inconsiderately rushed onto the tube carriages, never considering waiting for the other sample set of endogenous sigma nodes to get off the tube carriages first. A correlated inconsideration, a social negative externality that the utopian state welcomed as it led to a lack of social unity between individual nodes.

I reflected upon this whilst I strategically stood back to let the selfish sample set, crowd on first, to let them fight and bustle against each other whilst boarding.

Once they had boarded the tube carriages, then the power games began; each node subtly fighting each other for their own minor selfish advantage, mainly in the form of different body positions and relative spacing whilst they stood crammed within the overcrowded, claustrophobic tube carriages.

Nodes standing next to each other were crushed even more by a new sample set of nodes getting onto an overly full tube carriage at each new tube station; these boarding events altering the temporary status quo at each new stop.

During the time interval between each tube station stop, the node's bodies were squashed against each other. They tried vainly to increase their standing in the temporary status quo by subtly moving their body at each opportune moment, trying to win a few extra centimetres of personal body space.

In the unpredictable micro meter sample space where the acceptable error term resides well within the regression function of normalised expectations but with an allowance for the event's positional error term to reside.

The small movement of moving a foot or an elbow in the overcrowded carriage was part of the node's subconscious power play. Each node selfishly taking a minor liberty with their neighbouring node's personal body space which in turn caused yet another node to move slightly, and so on; inevitably producing a chaotic effect upon the whole carriage.

Dominant, submissive body posture games were in play; node's constantly pushing against each fellow node or retreating away. Other subtle factors were used to gain or maintain some minor status quo upon the carriage; width of stance, a node's facial expression; the perpetual blank stare, that all endogenous sigma nodes where conditioned to adopt particularly upon the underground tube carriages; their most popular strategy to guard their personal privacy in passive form.

It was a predictable dominant strategy of selfish individuals surviving in a game theory sample space which resulted in a reduced personal utility and inferior etiquette. Their etiquette was to be expected of the endogenous sigma nodes, a symptom of a corroded culture; compensated with continual consumerism and a compulsory statistical conformity.

All the individual chaotic variables of body positions and spacing were subtle expected power plays resulting in a seemingly chaotic behaviour and positions influenced by other nodes, leading to an averaged predictable normalised expectation of positioning and societal conformity, only the micro meter sample spacing was not predictable on average.

I concluded this whilst standing sandwiched between a banker and a labourer whose filthy overalls were covered in random scatter plot of dried white paint.

I found myself analysing the endogenous sigma nodes that commuted between work, each day; whilst, simultaneously trying to blank out the unpleasant experience of travelling on public transport during the rush hour.

I like the nodes on the tube carriages never spoke to the stranger next to them, they hardly ever looked at each other, only in their peripheral vision; this way they retained their perception of privacy.

I pondered the situation, concluding that they did retain their privacy but it created an illusion that they had a sense of freedom; a self-determination in their crowded worker lives but without them realising, it made them weak and malleable. Their claustrophobic, insular, unfriendliness made them un-cohesive individuals in a covariant herd. It was a subtle disadvantage to them but a significant advantage to the utopian state.

Nodes desiring, to not communicate as individuals with each other was beneficial for the statistically driven Economic Efficient Act of state Utopia. As it decreased the individual's ability to influence their society, rendering them unable to gel, into a single unified independent organic crowd, which could momentarily or marginally alter the status quo.

The state encouraged the nodes to live congealed within large cities, like a proverbial, "Mouse utopia," whilst accepting their collective; fixed, known, given, mean of their sigma caste, expected monthly statistical quotas and routines yet remaining individually isolated. This was echoed by the node's acceptance of the utopian state's the great contrived apodictic null hypothesis that was socioeconomically engineered so it could not be rejected; nodes should accept only the utopian state's influence and not from individuals.

Through individual isolation there was a collective impotence and communal void. They had been subtly preened of their individual identity and collective unity. They were conditioned to accept that only the reasonable state utopia could fulfil their needs and objectives.

This was a derivative of the utopian state's great apodictic null hypothesis that the nodes should only look to the state for all solutions to their problems. Subliminal advertisements encouraged them to only worry about themselves and immediate associated nodes.

The chaotic underground tube network; a composite of perceived unpredictability; the chaotic nodes' individual movements and relative positioning, constituted randomness to the utopian state.

However state Utopia forbade randomness within its society as the Economic Efficiency Act was designed to eliminate firm specific risk within the great Beta market and to eliminate all uncertainty within the financial markets via the statistical quotas.

This was achieved by controlling completely the endogenous sigma nodes' aggregate demand consumption. This enabled the Centum Corporations to maximize their profits, lock in their internal rates of return, hold constant net present values and predict with near exact certainty their expected rates of return.

Therefore randomness was to be eliminated from the great Beta linear regression function of the utopian state as the endogenous sigma nodes contributed their work input dependent variable.

Religion and randomness were officially banned by the utopian state. The only transgression considered worse, was for a node to consistently fall outside of the confidence interval of the normalised probability distribution frequency of the state's monthly fixed, known, given, statistical quotas of expected consumption and routines. A more fixed and primitive derivative of classical statistics which has a fixed yet unknown mean.

Yet within the temporary, transient, sample space confines of the hurting tube carriages; the commuting nodes psychological positioning, governed by their minds yet were conditioned by societal expectations and experiences, compelling themselves to an expected given situation of predictable routines, positions and thoughts whilst remaining within an acceptable, controlled, fixed, known mean of expected probability.

All the while adhering to a societal compliance; their psyches all subconsciously, passively accepting the expected carriages etiquette of not making eye contact, of keeping their bodies in constrained postures, their psyche ultimately isolated from their fellow node only inches away.

Travelling deep beneath the bustling city of Primary_Sample_Space, I, a Beta node of unremarkable appearance and dimensions, stood enveloped in a crowd of fellow commuting endogenous sigma nodes within a noisy transient tube carriage.

I concentrated on fixing my stare into an imaginary void which existed inches before another node's chest, similar to an imaginary number plane realm hovering above a real number axis.

My perceptible vision, deep within the non-real, non-linear, polar coordinates of the imaginary number plane void; temporary free of the harsh, tangible, rational, linear, real number line existence of the three dimensional Cartesian coordinates of the inner tube carriages and of the correlated positioning and sentient perceptions of the game theory, power playing nodes.

My official occupation was that of a civil servant in the Department of Econometrics at the Ministry of Inferences, situated on the seventh floor of Senate house, Mallet Street, Primary_Sample_Space, State Utopia.

At first sight Senate house seemed to be an arbitrary government building, yet on greater inspection, it exposed an enigmatic intangible geometry; the building resembled a temple of antiquity that could rival many of the Seven Wonders of the World with its understated symmetry and intangible perspectives lines that tapered off into the void of expected intersections.

For the last decade I had worked my way up through the bands of the civil service; now a Beta node, one hieratical layer below the almost unbridgeable Alpha caste. The Alpha nodes oversaw the Ministry of Inferences which function was to continually monitor and constrain the nodes statistical routines with restricted economic models.

My fingers fumbled in my pocket as I felt the reassuring letter that I had unexpectedly received this morning at work. It had confirmed the Ministry of Inferences official acceptance of my probation to be possibly promoted to an Alpha node in the near future. I had worked my whole life for this possibility and now I may soon be promoted.

It was truly a chaotic day, receiving the most important letter of my life. A letter that I was not sure I would ever receive but now the extreme outlier event had been realised.

To me it was purely an unpredictable, chaotic event as the prior variables needed to create this extreme situation were exactly known but not by me, the recipient but only by the higher echelons of the Alpha domain.

To them it was a perfectly predictable; an augmented situation that they judged and engineered, this life changing event as with all socioeconomic events in state Utopia.

Yet to me it seemed an unfathomable chaotic, unpredictable, almost random event as it was so rare for a Beta node to receive an Alphaship promotion letter.

As I sat within the tube train carriage comprised of its Cartesian real number reality, I considered perhaps that the upper floors of the Ministry of Inferences where the Alpha reside whilst intermittently exercising their daily discretion; were the catalyst to a counterintuitive realised situation occurring, an absolute value transformation of a particular variable or situation by initiating the Fraser theorem.

Where a variable's limit is reached along the real number line existence, it transforms into a polar magnitude which then rotates through the imaginary number plane rotation; courtesy of the Lapse transform, through the complex number plane.

Yet unseen by the commuting nodes who dwelling upon the real number line plane whilst a sine wave begins its extradimensional existence in the third imaginary dimension with respect to time.

Resonating within a Fourier transformation; creating a seemingly chaotic, realised probability, situation resultant at the other end of the normalised spectrum of expectations.

Like most Beat nodes employed at the Ministry of Inferences, I had aspirations of one day bridging the unbridgeable; being promoted to the Upper Floors of the Ministry of Inferences; into the Alpha caste. And now it may happen. I felt a shot of adrenaline surge in my body as I stood in the crowded tube carriage.

Yet my posture remained statuesque as I held a slightly dominant position within the crowd of standing nodes not daring to move a centimetre or avert my gaze, to maintain my slight perceived positional advantage within the crowd. I had become a master of finding the right position and which node to position myself against, whilst commuting home.

I, like the commuting nodes, were now momentarily incarnate of the fixed, known, given mean as we stood there fixed and frozen within an expected standard deviation of the tube carriages even though our individual positioning was realised by chaotic processes and our subconscious nature.

Behind my fixed gaze I felt a warmth surging through my body at the novelty that I may become an Alpha node in the near future. I also drew solace of anticipating closing the door to my small solitary apartment and unwinding after another day of experiencing the overcrowded grubby Primary_Sample_Space coupled with the stress of working at the Ministry of Inferences.

I usually returned home tired, after spending the entire day and sometimes the nights, dealing with the many arbitrary tasks that the Ministry of Inferences econometric analyst role entailed. The job was mentally tiring, filled with tedious tasks, with only the rare occasion of more interesting projects.

My mind relaxed slightly as my fixed gaze induced a slight meditative state causing my conscious to go into an autopilot mode; nestled in the standing crowd of commuting nodes who were willingly crammed into an overcrowded tube carriage, deep underground. Yet I never really felt completely free to relax in any public setting; I was like most of the endogenous sigma nodes, always on guard to some degree.

I felt marginally safer underground, able to think and feel a little more freely; deep underground in the chaotic sanctuary of the transient tube carriages.

Without being subjected to the perpetual incessant bombardment of advertisements, that the average endogenous sigma node was continually exposed to, every waking hour, subliminally or not; through digital media and the countless advertisements that ran out intermittently throughout the day via countless technological mediums.

But I was temporarily free of those mediums whilst travelling deep underground on the transient, jostling, noisy, antiquated, tube carriages.

The nodes were also temporarily free of the all-pervasive emotions and implied thought scanner which measured the node's general emotions and therefore implied thought spectrum coupled with the ever watching facial recognition CCTV cameras.

Used in conjunction with specific advertisements and situations, nodes were expected to exhibit certain correlated emotions at specific times. If they did not, then the state would be confident that the node was thinking outside the expected norm.

It was originally developed by the United Statistical States of North America, to scan for any nervous terrorists in public places, just before a potential attack, by measuring the suspect's emotional correlations and reactions to contemporaneous environmental stimuli.

The technology inevitably evolved, blossoming in the corporate sector soon becoming the pre-eminent complimentary technology used in conjunction with advertising and marketing which relentlessly bombarded each node; every waking hour, analysing their correlated emotional reactions and determining their all-important marketing susceptibility.

Every waking hour was considered acceptable by the utopian state but mercifully subliminal sleep bombardment was officially banned after a few high profile suicides where linked to the emotional scanner marketing strategy.

Recently the state officially sanctioned that the emotional scanners be adopted by the Ministry of Inferences. The Ministry's public mandate was, "To monitor conformity of the state's official monthly statistical quotas; to regress wayward economically inefficient nodes back to the cooperative social mean, for the harmony of the Economic Efficiency."

"Think average, think mean, be confident," was the official propaganda motto used to encourage the nodes to conform. Did the message imply to think average or to think in a ruthless manner; most probably both?

The nodes were expected to remain within their given sigma caste, their expected standard deviation of the given, known, fixed, mean enveloped within a normalised variance of the confidence interval which acted as a socioeconomic parameter.

Their thoughts and routines were expected to fit the utopian state's statistical selection bias of its normalised statistical quotas. To constrain the nodes within a safe mean; that the utopian state had engineered for the sigma to perpetually gravitate towards, the given, known, fixed mean.

Fortunately for the nodes; a design limitation associated with the Emotional Scanners was that they were not able to specifically detect individual emotions and inferred implied thoughts, deep underground, let alone in moving steel tube carriages.

Unfortunately this fact was unbeknownst to the intermingling random nodes hurrying home, their bodies and privacy safely cocooned in transient steel carriages, hurling through the catacombs.

This fact that would have allowed them to take advantage of the situation whilst participating in the chaotic, unordered melee, of the rush hour, would have temporarily freed them allowing them to think and feel as normal; as before the implementation of the dreaded Emotional Scanners.

Yet I knew of the design limitation due to my position at the Ministry but most nodes were not completely sure of the rumour of the design flaw that was once leaked to the public a few years ago by the dissident, Pareidolia. But I was confident it was true.

Most nodes' subconscious individual inner voice concluded that even if the rumour was true, perhaps there was some newer technology that could detect their thoughts, even within fast moving steel tube carriages, deep underground. Most nodes were nurtured to be conditioned to the utopian state's will, they would not dare let their true, unrestricted thoughts be entertained in their minds for long, just in case the rumours were false.

Any unexpected emotions which could be implied as inappropriate chains of thought or opinion could be considered a subversive act by the state as undermining the economic efficiency.

Eventually the nodes had started to form thinking habits; purposely producing continual pseudo expected thoughts and emotions which ultimately became a form of self-brainwashing, referred to as, "Preening," by the Alphas; an altered state of societal perception and consciousness.

Each node's fear of being branded a subversive kept them constantly preening themselves, constraining their thoughts while remaining safe and being confident; accepting their monthly state sanctioned mean and statistical quotas.

I was privy to many state secrets whilst working at the Ministry of Inferences it allowed me to know many things that the general public did not, although I pretended not to know any secrets.

I momentarily contemplated this as I stood within the chaotic sanctuary of the noisy, steel rattling tube carriages as it made its way through the underground tunnels of Primary_Sample_Space.

Normalised Utopia

My finger subconsciously fumbled in my jacket pocket for an item my subconscious wanted to dwell on as my conscious then remembered the item's importance of that little piece of now crumpled paper envelope and the all-important letter within.

The realised expectations leap that I had been hoping for, possibly willing it into existence for many years to receive the news that I had been finally selected for a probationary period and possible promotion into the Alpha node caste category.

Soon perhaps I will no longer be a regular endogenous sigma node rather I would be beyond the endogenous sigma node classification, beyond being merely a contributing independent endogenous variable of state Utopia's linear regression model.

I am fairly confident that soon I would be an observer, an inferer of the linear regression function, soon I would be setting the criteria of the confidence interval and be free of the common endogenous existence, if I am finally promoted into the Alphaship of State Utopia.

I would be beyond reproach, at the very pinnacle of society. A position desired by all Beta ministry civil servants who were nurtured and conditioned to covert.

The Beta Ministry of Inferences civil servants managed the statistical quotas which ranked the nodes; keeping the nodes as mere endogenous variables, within a continual procedure of contribution. A never ending process of a socioeconomic system that kept the nodes trapped within their statistical quota procedures, classification and caste expectations.

I finally made it back to my apartment block. I opened the entrance door; reluctantly leaving the fresh chaotic intermingling mild temperate evening air behind as I entered into the cold concrete body of the utopian state's apartment block foyer. Its austere atmosphere, a by-product of the state's statistical quotas and of the Economic Efficiency Act's engineering policy.

I had left behind the chaotic; practically unpredictable, stochastic realm of the public commuting network and was once again regressed back into the ordered, non-stochastic realm of the state's infrastructure of perpetual monitoring and normalised expectations.

Where our movements, behaviour, emotions, implied thoughts and intentions were expected to be non-integrated, homoscedastic and morph around a contemporaneous given, fixed, known, mean of my assigned sigma caste; satisfying the statistical quotas of the utopian state's apodictic null hypothesis.

The lights in the hallway turned on slowly somewhat begrudgingly as they flickered, growing slowly into an insipid yellow dim glow; illuminating the grubby carpeted stairwell.

With a resigned athleticism I quickly made my way up the stairway, up to my small apartment situated on the third floor.

I knew that I must move uncharacteristically quickly as the hallway lights would cut off predictably at exactly thirty seconds after opening the grand foyer's glass door which was a stark contrast to the pokey stairwell that I now found myself racing up.

My haste was due to the term, "Quanta," which was accepted by the conditioned Sigma nodes decades ago; everything in State Utopia and Zhou Pingjun was, "Quantized," every commodity was broken down into its smallest commercially acceptable unit, to satisfy the Economic Efficiency Act. To further quantify and control the aggregate demand precisely in the guise of blatant rationing of the Sigma nodes during this engineered recession.

The Economic Efficiency Act, a statute of law, kept the nodes working to a perceived maximum economic efficiency so the Centum Corporations could maximize their profits, factoring in their internal rates of return and net present values.

State Utopia conveniently also used global warming and virus pandemics as an excuse to construct monthly statistical quotas, control aggregate demand precisely and ultimately augment the economy and society towards the great apodictic null hypothesis of the utopian state which insured know, fixed, predictable, consistent, non-linear returns of the great market Beta.

The Economic Efficiency Act was the reason the apartment foyer lights flickered duly and turned off so quickly. The dull flickering lights were in direct contrast to state Utopia's propaganda, referring to itself as a, "Shining beacon of statistical excellence and efficiency," whilst boasting of its first world ingenuity and economic success; superior to the lesser developing states.

I made it to my apartment door just in time as the dim light abruptly vanished.

Now plunged into darkness, I waved my wrist next to the door; a one hundred and twenty eight bit code appeared on a small screen on the door. I then fumbled in my pocket for the old brass key which I used to unlock the door.

Suddenly the lights blinked back into life, the narrow dimly lit hallway showed up the unsightly tacky carpet, just then Mrs White came out of her adjacent apartment.

'Hello Bayes,' she beamed, she was lonely as most biased nodes were in the new society. Friendliness amongst neighbours was a dying etiquette but I had known this harmless neighbour for years but had not muttered more than a few syllables to her at a time.

'You are looking smart this evening Mrs White,' I said with a contrived smile, even though I was tired, I continued to play my part as the polite neighbour even if only for a brief moment as I empathised with Mrs White who always seemed so desperately alone since she had retired a decade ago.

'Oh yes, I must get ready for tomorrow, I have just received a letter inviting me to Arcadia, tomorrow morning.' She paused then looked around as if to see if anyone was listening, lowering her voice to a whisper, 'It says in the letter I must not tell anyone, for security reasons but I trust you,' she beamed proudly with an unbiased mannerism. As with the baised nodes they start to shift to a state of unbiasedness.

My smile dropped momentarily, even with my mastery of masking my emotions, I could not stop my face from dropping. I immediately regained my smile but inside I was devastated. I knew all too well what happened at Arcadian and there was nothing I could say or do.

I wanted to say something such as "Oh enjoy," but I knew what awaited her, like the countless other nodes who travelled to Arcadia each day. I could not warn her but I would not stoop so low as to patronize her with sarcasm.

I said nothing but just smiled slightly to maintain the friendly atmosphere whilst I made my way to my apartment door.

Mrs White called back saying, 'Harry, I am going to celebrate my invitation to Arcadia, I have some old now banded alcohol. Please take this; I have already poured myself some. I know you don't drink but take it anyway.'

She produced from behind her back, a small bottle of alcohol.

I walked over to her and diplomatically yet reluctantly accepted the bottle.

As I walked back to my apartment door, she called out in a worried manner, 'Have you seen Monty?'

'Oh, I think I saw him in my peripheral vision, down stairs, on the first floor landing; he may have been scratching around in the hallway near the three apartment doors there, I am not certain which specific residents door he was at but I am sure he was at one of them at least,' I replied.

'Ok thank you, I will try to find him, he's probably doing the rounds again at other residents' apartments trying to get extra titbits of food,' she let out a sigh of frustration.

'I would be so upset if something happened to Monty. You would look after him if something

29

happened to me,' she asked, looking at me with almost pleading eyes.

I was stunned but I did not show it. How prophetic she was, I thought.

'I will,' I mumbled after years of conditioned small talk situations with her always trying to politely get away from this lonely biased binary next door as quickly as possible, like every other node in the apartment block.

I tried to walk away from her before she continued the conversation as she was always so desperate to continue the conversation whenever she could, to feel connected to her neighbours. The majority of the unbiased population were in a similar position to her, lonely, cut off, vulnerable.

The eighty year old Mrs White, overweight yet deceptively frail body, timidly felt its way down the stairway to search for her beloved Monty. Like a vulnerable unbiased, learning to walk and explore once again.

I courteously banged on the light switch to afford her an extra time allotment of, "Quantized," light even if this would approach an, "Unacceptable level," of light usage on my personal confidence interval monthly report.

I turned around and walked through the doorway of my small Spartan apartment making my way into the tiny hallway.

From this minute on, everything I did in my apartment was transformed into statistical activity, continually recorded and automatically uploaded to be stored on state Utopia servers, hidden in official nondescript bunkers deep below which were scattered amongst the quiet unassuming countryside. Every Sigma node's information stored would be analysed instantly by the state's statistical algorithms.

Any node's personal routines, emotions or implied thought variables that deviated from the official given, fixed, known, mean of the Economic Efficiency Act statistical monthly quotas by more than their expected standard deviation caste would have their personal data red flagged.

Their data would automatically be uploaded to the Ministry of Inferences for analysis of their Personal Routines and Implied Thought Deviations.

Each day, each night, each movement, each moment, each decision, each thought, was a struggle to keep within the statistically acceptable confidence interval. At every moment a node could be guilty of not towing the line, being outside the confidence interval of acceptable individual trends and therefore could be accused of producing a minor temporary negative externality that could affect the economic efficiency of society and the repayment of the public debt burden deficit.

I entered the compact living room which was dark, broken only by a dim street light ambiance, radiating up through the lower half of the balcony window.

Three lamps automatically switched on and slowly proceeded to increase in brightness, reaching a dull, homely, restful light. The living room was almost Spartan but was filled intermittently with retro, art deco style furniture. The near Spartan, clinically clean interior, indicated my single status and solitary lifestyle which was not uncommon amongst the Ministry of Inferences employees.

Suddenly the television buzzed into life, as the sensors detected my presence. The television monitor mounted on the centre of the wall dominated the room with its size, luminosity and loudness.

As the television warmed up a booming irritating voice came out.

"....and on tonight's show we have a host of unbiased hopeful talented nodes!" the image of a good looking dapper announcer appeared, as the television had reached its full power, by now the television was dominating the room, blasting out its non-stop incessant trivialities.

The television programs served only one purpose; to perpetually keep the audience's attention so at unpredictable times the advertisements could come blasting out of nowhere and the viewers would be lulled into a sense of complacency, prepared to watch each mindless advertisement after another, until they had forgotten what they were watching.

Just when the nodes collective aggregate average attention span had been detected as dipping below a certain Advertising Council Attention Ratio, just when the average node felt they could no longer stand another advert, the television program would came on again and the nodes would be hypnotised into another dubbed down trance until the next round of advertisements.

The scanners would monitor the emotions and implied thoughts of the audience analysing their real time emotions and concentration spans of the collective audience, deciding when to stop the adverts and continue the show.

The television monitor played the latest live popular television show, "the talent factory," a mindless, trivial talent show that most nodes were conditioned to watch due to its time slot. The show was just a reason to hold the audience captive so as to subject them to the many annoying advertisements that blasted out at unpredictable times during the show.

I stood in the kitchen in slight shock; I could not get the horror of Mrs White's position out of my head. I wanted to vomit in the sink but I kept cool. What a nice biased binary Mrs White is, she does not deserve Arcadian, I concluded.

I turned on the tap, some water poured into a glass for precisely three seconds.

Even the tap water was now, "Quantatized," at home when a node washed their hands; the tap only afforded them a quick stream of water, for a few seconds.

This was the state's officially recognised basic quanta for tap water. A node may only wash their hands for three seconds at a time. The node may push the tap head for another three second burst of tap water but this would be recorded on their Personal Domestic Usage database as an infringement of the mean; a deviation from the desired official State expected average usage.

Nodes who continually abused their quanta quotas would eventually end up becoming outliers, confidence interval criminals; redundant nodes.

That is what probably happened to Mrs White, she most probably in her frail bumbling way had started to be economically inefficient with her utility usage, I speculated.

If only she had told me a few days ago, I may have been able to pull some strings, I considered in frustration but on a deeper level I knew that was untrue. I would have been powerless to do anything to save her, I may work at the Ministry of Inferences but I was only just an analyst; a civil servant of the state.

A ruthless statistical state yet I accepted it. I never felt such guilt or distress before for anyone else. My parents had died when I was young and I had never felt close to anyone. But Mrs White's frailty and decency, her simple affections for her cat, had touched me as well as my empathy for her lonely, vulnerable position.

Miss White receiving the letter inviting her to attend an official census at Arcadia was predictable. She was an economically inefficient node yet I was living in denial of the state's ruthlessness and my guilt of contributing towards it.

Of course it was inevitable that she would get a letter from Arcadia. Her chaotic routines were considered as stochastic by the state's implied thought scanners, each time she produced a slight deviation in her expected routines; each time her new unexpected routine, starting point variable deviated more and more from the expected norm; from the fixed, given, known mean of the her sigma caste, normalised confidence, interval quota with an ever more complicated, unpredictable, chaotic regularity.

Miss White's newly received letter and my letter informing me of my Alphaship potential promotion seemed to be some sort of moral zero sum game theory event.

Normalised Utopia

I was expected to be promoted in the near future but now I see for the first time in person that I indirectly would have blood on my hands, my neighbour's blood as Mrs White will be sent to Arcadia. The seriousness of a statistically constrained society and of my role at the Ministry of Inferences had finally struck me.

I started to fall asleep, alone in my arm chair; my last waking thought was not of the great utopian state and its great achievement such as the soon to be completed underground transcontinental monorail network. It was rather that of Mrs White's fate tomorrow and of my impotence to do anything.

As I lost consciousness I tried to think of any patriotic thoughts to humour any prying implied thought scanners but Mrs White's plight left me feeling disgusted with State Utopia.

Suddenly, abruptly, all advertisements and forced announcements from the television and surrounding embedded systems went silent; now the ordeal of the twice daily tube station commute and the rigid statistical conformity expected by all endogenous nodes was just an unpleasant memory in my subconscious; only perfect silence reigned now.

The interactive television monitor had sensed my reduced sentience levels and that I was asleep, it switched itself off, in accordance with the law.

I was now free to dream my own thoughts as the scanners were banned by law to scan a node's dreams; the endogenous sigma's last freedom. The law was amended due to the fact that a node cannot control their subconscious therefore they were legally allowed to dream freely within the variance free statistical dream ether.

02: Confidence interval.

Mrs White antiquated alarm clock rang out, echoing into her small, apartment which was dimly lit by the awakening morning dawn. The stillness of the apartment compounded the emptiness of the desperately lonely atmosphere.

She was already up fettering around in the kitchen, carrying out her default lonely daily routine of making cups of tea to pass the time while she attended to the only object of her love and affection; Monty, her cat.

On hearing the alarm clock ringing she hurried over to turn it off, always considerate of her neighbours. In her consideration to cease the noise she had left the tap water running, it could not switch off automatically as she had absently minded left a teapot in the way of the tap's water stream detection beam. The water started to pool up in the sink.

She was becoming more and more like an unbiased, as she paradoxically aged. Her fallible node nature was becoming more predominant with each new day as it shone through corroding her expected routines and given, known statistical quotas, creating chaotic results; ultimately resulting in unpredictability.

She was far in excess of her daily stipulated and predicted kitchen water quota. She was rapidly becoming an inefficient economic node within the economic efficient society.

She was already dressed, as old lonely biased have always done, in a floral dress with a large hat that looked decades out of place, her expired once attractive form replaced by an understated modest respectability in the form of a faded light blue floral dress and a large ludicrous straw hat, she looked odd and vulnerable in her decades out of place dress sense and weak overweight posture.

She took one last look at Monty with a worried expression, if only she could take Monty with her to Arcadia, to meet all the cast of the famous Arcadian soap opera but she must be a good node and follow the law and attend the Arcadian consensus; she had even baked a cake for the cast she hoped to meet.

She hurriedly put on dabs of respectable makeup and sunscreen cream. She picked up her train ticket to Arcadia that she had bought online and placed it in her old fashioned handbag along with her prised official letter of invitation to Arcadia.

She hurried outside the apartment block and was met with a cold blast of morning air, the street was quiet and still, the cold morning air numbed her exposed body parts simultaneously. She braced herself and immediately started ruffling her jacket to protect against the cold.

She made her way down the almost silent street as the sigma nodes conformed to the excepted time patterns of waking and sleeping. She hailed an electric cab which was expensive but due to the time and importance of the day she would sacrifice later in the month to offset the cab fare; that only Beta and Alphas could usually afford.

She sat nervously in the back of the cab fidgeting around to relieve the stress of such an important day, to be a guest of the state and possibly meet the stars of Arcadian.

Finally she made it to platform ten of St Pancreas underground station.

She hurried down stairs where she was stopped by an underground official who looked better dressed and held a different posture than most underground workers. He asked abruptly for her ticket yet not mentioned the destination of Arcadia.

She proudly pulled out her ticket, the inspector looked at it and ushered her through.

She eagerly boarded the new looking tube train carriage, it looked slightly different from most monorails she had travelled on during her life but she was no expert on tube trains. She had been brought up, an unbiased binary in the utopian state therefore was conditioned to believe tube trains were solely a node's interest, not for unbiased binary's to pry into.

There was a broad spectrum of nodes on the extremely clean and modern tube train, unlike most public tube trains, that were always covered in grime and intermittent graffiti.

There was a broad spectrum of age, class, race and other node variables but she noticed quite a few biased nodes. Most unbiased nodes were not so bothered about the caste of Arcadia she thought, forgetting that the passengers on the tube train were not there by choice.

A burly looking official, tube train inspector dressed in an unfamiliar underground uniform that was impeccably clean and pressed, blew an ear piercing whistle.

The tube train carriage door slid then folded in towards the carriage giving off a hydraulic steam noise as the doors closed air tight, hermetically sealing in the passenger nodes.

The tube train started to accelerate down into the dark ominous entrance hole of the underground tube tunnel network.

She felt some anxiety as the tube train accelerated, too extreme for comfort.

The lights dimmed down a bit and an automated voice on the intercom peacefully asked passengers not to forget to strap their seat belts tight.

After a few minutes she and the rest of the nodes started to feel tired and light headed. Soon passengers started to flail around desperately trying to undo their seat belts that would not unfasten.

She felt nauseous and confused, she started to become very concerned yet her only thought was of Monty her cat. What would happen to him, if?

She mercifully blanked out as the air was slowly sucked out of the hermetically sealed tube train carriage while the lack of air was commensurately being substituted with gas.

Soon all the nodes had quietly suffocated to death in their sleep. After a few moments the tube train had transformed from a public transport system to a rolling mortuary.

The nodes were now cadavers, sitting upright in their seats; lifeless. Suddenly the light intensified to a high voltage and extremely high pitched alarm bells resonated with flashing LED lights.

An electric shock pulsed and resonated through the metal tube train carriage floor mercifully testing to analyse if any unfortunate node was still alive, in order to save them the final ordeal that lay in wait for the cadavers ridding the Arcadian express.

Then an extreme low pressure invaded the carriages as the on-board computer dutifully dropped the carriages to an almost partial vacuum, killing any possible remnants of life.

The carriage air was slowly replenished to normal atmospheric pressure. All solely done by an automated on-board computer embedded in the tube train; there were no guards or drivers on-board.

Eventually the tube train emerged from the underground secret tube line, far from Primary_Sample_Space. It accelerated to very high speed along a specially constructed South East coast railway track, passing through the beautiful countryside.

The passengers of the tube train; now cadavers, suffered one final assault of the carefully controlled atmosphere on-board the tube train carriage; flames shoot out from different positions, from hidden nozzles, under the solid metal seats, the cadavers where efficiently incinerated; the nodes were no more.

The tube train reached the apex of its proximity to the coast, valves automatically opened on the coast facing side of the tube train carriage as a computer controlled the negative pressure, sucking the ash and other debris out; leaving them to fly through the air, plummeting and drifting silently, secretly onto the rugged coast line and rough seas below, efficiently covertly, eliminating every trace of the nodes, their incinerated clothing and possessions.

Finally disinfectant and water gushed down into the automated carriages, removing every last stain and scent of the now non-existent nodes. All traces of the secret automated mass murder that just unfolded were washed away.

Simultaneously, all official records and big data analysis of Mrs White since her birth that had been stored over the decades on the state's databases were whipped clean. Mrs White no longer existed, she had officially never existed.

She had been a redundant node; as she aged, her crime was to let her essence, her natural instinct and inclinations slowly supersede the utopian states' will. Her individual actions and fallibility had been at constant odds with the statistical quotas' expectations.

She had been removed from the great statistical model; the utopian state minus Mrs White.

The Economic Efficiency Policy Algorithms where recalibrated, no longer running with Mrs Whites presence or lagged past big data just as the other nodes on the Arcadian express that morning where removed from the algorithm.

The Arcadian express ran like clockwork, every day, many times a day. No node ever suspected the truth and if they did, what could they do apart from end up on the Arcadian invitation census list.

Normalised Utopia

The Ministry of Inferences building comprised of just nine floors situated in Mallet Street, central Primary_Sample_Space adjacent to the enigmatic, imposing Senate House.

I sat at my desk on the seventh floor of the Ministry of Inferences' middle floors, reading the newly published official statistical quotas for the following month. Even the national news channel had published state Utopia's official expected quotas for the following month. The quotas contained the expected population economic aggregate demand and the sigma node caste sample consumption quotas.

Yet my attention was vacant as I moved my eyes from side to side pretending to read whilst I tried to calm my disposition over the concern of Mrs White's certain demise which I found deeply concerning.

The most sombre statistical quotas were dealt with by the Ministry of Inferences which included the previous month's stealth confidence interval quotas results which was my department's responsibility to process.

The stealth confidence interval quotas were distributed amongst the middle floors section of the Ministry of Inferences and processes by the Beta node civil servants. These stealth confidence interval quotas were more subtle and differed slightly from the publicly known caste specific confidence interval quotas results that all the endogenous sigma nodes were informed of each month.

I browsed through the statistically significant results searching for newly classified redundant nodes which I had been tasked to analyse and possibly amend.

The monthly redundant node list consisted of nodes that consistently fell outside of the stealth or personal confidence interval region of acceptable conformity. Redundant nodes transgressing the statistical quotas each month accounted for approximately 0.08 percent of State Utopia's population.

The confidence interval was calculated by the Ministry of Inferences statistical algorithms which were used as a tool to regulate the exact amount of aggregate demand within state Utopia per month. Ultimately controlling the nodes' personal consumption and defining an official spectrum of expected routines allowed by the state; all to insure the economic efficiency of the state Utopia's economy.

The confidence interval was the epitome of a fixed, known, given, mean of expected results even before the result had been realised. Yet each month the confidence interval mean shifted very slightly to compensate for stochastic macroeconomic exogenous shocks to the great population linear regression function of the economic efficiency act produced beta; the market price, free of firm and node specific uncertainty .

These confidence interval quota expectations unfortunately caused innocent nodes to be officially categorised as redundant nodes even though most were respectable complaint nodes that raised families, paid their taxes and continually thought within the politically correct opinion range their whole lives.

Yet they could be sent a letter of invitation to Arcadia at any month for being slightly outside of the new monthly expected confidence interval consumption, routines or implied thought standard deviation. Yet in their countless previous decades' acceptable statistical results were irrelevant only the current month's results mattered.

Ironically the fixed, known, given, monthly sigma caste specific means and its corresponding confidence interval depended on many stochastic variables that determined the monthly shifting of the official mean or the fluctuations of the variances.

Stochastic ratios such as the birth to death ratio and current exogenous shocks to the great Beta linear regression model as well as the Alpha nodes' discretion.

I had to deal with these sobering statistical facts every month, making sure these statistics were completely accurate as compliant lives were at stake.

Most of the newly classified redundant nodes were innocent law abiding compliant citizens who merely fell outside of the expected current confidence interval quotas. They were no longer part of the statically insignificant 95% majority; their crime being statically significant having a P value of less than five.

Yet an individual node's performance was partially stochastic therefore an element of luck maybe involved.

It was luck for an innocent endogenous node to consistently survive living in a statistical matrix of expected quotas that shifted dynamically and unpredictably each month.

What constituted whether an endogenous sigma node was innocent or guilty of the statistical transgression of falling outside of the current fixed, given, known, confidence interval quotas, condemning them to the secret category of redundant node; a few fractions of a standard deviation which ironically was influenced by stochastic exogenous shocks?

Blue walked past with his newly assigned recruit which he was tasked to show around the department. The recruit looked too young and naive to have passed the Ministry of Inferences analysts exams. Yet now he was an official Ministry trainee, ready to start work on the Middle floors.

Blue informed the newly joined recruit, 'the state now controls every aspect of the nodes' life by using different techniques but mainly with applied statistics and time series econometric algorithms coupled with behavioural psychology.'

He pointed to a computer terminal, 'these algorithms can be understood in layman's terms as partial derivative calculus equations,' he said in an official tone.

'You were taught at Ministry of Inferences' Academy that each node is an economically efficient variable that can be affected directly and indirectly by a small change in an associated node.'

The new recruit smiled eagerly while nodding his head.

'It could be an animate node, like a citizen node or a sub-node like a pet animal or an inanimate node such as an embed kettle or new routine such as taking a different tube to work,' Blue said waving his hands around patronisingly with an air of importance.

'An infinitesimal change in one of the target node's variables or in an associated node could affect directly or indirectly, the actions and thoughts of the target node.

'By controlling each specific variable in the spectrum of allowed variables within a node's life, we have created a set of partial derivatives; a ratio. This ratio will create a small change within an endogenous variable and will in turn produce a disproportionate change within the resultant variable's disposition and productivity.

'By merely changing an associate node's disposition for the day, we can affect the target node's productivity and routines.

'Microeconomics and behaviour analysis all rolled into calculus and applied statistics and time series econometric algorithms. That is the nature of the Economic Efficiency Act, to control aggregate demand from a microeconomic and macroeconomic level; bottom up, social engineering, for the efficiency of the normalised state.'

The new recruit thought for a moment, then concluded, 'So total partial derivative ratio manipulation of a target node affects its probability distribution function with a disproportionate subtle weighting, affecting the node's work routines and other nodes around him.'

'Correct,' confirmed Blue in a slightly patronizing manner, his eyes shifted to the right for a split second as he was shocked at the level of insight and articulation of the new recruit.

'Distributed lagged variables of difference equations can also be used to guide the node. Each variable of a target node has previous time period values. So by exposing a target node to certain situations or matrices of a particular variable set, we can mould the target node very subtly.

'When a target node moves from one situation to another, such as moving to a different job or neighbourhood, the node will retain a certain percentage of the previous environment and mind set which influences their new set of experiences.

'The target node will progress through time, intermittently changing their circumstances but at each new time interval, previous lagged time period variables are still being carried over, to different degrees of weighting, all affecting the node,' continued Blue.

'Whether the Ministry is directly or indirectly influencing the target node with infinitesimal changes to their personal utility or productivity whilst using the total partial derivative algorithms, we can also influence the target node through the accumulation of previous distributed lagged variables.

'Which will affect their current routines and behaviours, with previous perceptions, from their past, without the node even being aware,' added Beta interrupting Blue's speech, showing his enjoyment of stealing Blue's spot light.

Beta enjoyed making new recruits, nervous alluding to the extent of the state's control.

Blue glared disapprovingly at Beta who walked away smirking.

'Wow,' said the young new recruit 'that is impressive they did not teach us the distributed lagged variable algorithm at the Academy.'

'These techniques are only used to catch terrorists,' replied Blue trying to give a look of genuineness.

'Yeah right,' mumbled Beta who was now sitting nearby typing a report.

Blue gave him another glare.

Bernoulli looked on; I sensed his stone face expression hid a depressed disdain for the amount of manipulation carried out upon the nodes.

Blue became more stressed as the new recruit was being privy to innuendo regarding information that he would not be cleared to learn of, for many years to come.

The recruit face had an expression of concern at Beta's innuendo but he did not want to question these techniques which he now considered could possibly be used on ordinary nodes as well.

'And for outliers,' added Bivariate who could not help joining in the fun by walking past Blue and the recruit to add a bit of dark humour, enjoyed seeing Blue embarrassed in front of the new recruit.

'Oh and outliers as well,' said Blue, softening the transition from terrorist to outlier node.

'You've heard of outliers?'

'I did pass the Ministry of Inference exams,' replied the recruit with an uncharacteristic sarcasm, letting slip the submissive facade that most recruits feel obliged to perform when training at a new office.

'Of course you did,' replied Blue trying to regain his composure, taking charge while trying to calm down the situation.

'Well as you know,' fumbled Blue.

'An outlier is a node who is reclassified as a redundant node, a statistical transgressor, an economic criminal because they fall outside the Economic Efficient Act Confidence Interval. It can be a series of emotional; implied thought deviations. Or subconscious implied routine deviations or even financial transgressions such as having a permanent subpar credit score.

'Punctuality to work, regularity of bill payments, work productivity, the trend of television programs viewed, travel patterns and routines of a node.

'Any reason that a node deviates from a certain degree from the norm or the average, that node is no longer in the Economic Efficiency Act Confidence Interval. They are no longer normal, they are a deviant, an outlier, a redundant node,' said Blue, trying to add emotional conviction to his speech as if to justify the sentiment.

'If a node fell outside the confines of what was officially classified as normalised, then the node was no longer, a non-stochastic variable, they become stochastic; random, harder to predict, which is undesirable in the Economically Efficient Society.

'As a node's routines and consumption approached randomness; this led to unpredictability in the cash flow revenues and internal rates of return of the centum corporations and the Central bank's balance sheet.

'Ultimately it made the monthly and quarterly economic projections unpredictable and therefore undesirable.

'All because a small certain percentage of nodes won't remain within the Economic Efficiency Act Confidence Interval, this added additional risk to the internal rates of return of investments.

'Therefore it is better to terminate unpredictable nodes from the Economically Efficient Society,' concluded Blue.

''It's statistically more efficient for our society,'' Blue quoted the latest catch phrase of the Ministry of Inferences.

Blue continued, 'A statistical algorithm driven society can better monitor the nodes who exhibit expected behaviour. Expected facial movements, eye movements, blink rate, breathing rate, perspiration rate, heart rate, head movement rate, speech pause rate and frequency, expected tone of voice , expect smile ratio to conversation content.

'Expected emotions, expected brain map activity, expected daily movements and predicted routines, expected intranet usage, expected telephone usage, expected dietary intake, expected conversation duration, expected conversation topic trend, expected friend and workmate daily interaction.

'If the node falls outside of the confidence interval of 95% or more than 1.96 standard deviations of the quota variables mentioned, then that node would be red flagged and monitored by us at the Ministry of Inferences. They could well be the makings of a persistent Economic Efficiency Confidence Interval outlier; an economic criminal, a redundant node,' concluded Blue.

I listen whilst pretending to be absorbed by the data upon my computer screen, I knew this was not completely true as there were two Confidence Intervals; the stealth confidence interval which was analysed by the state and the visible caste specific personal confidence interval which every node was conditioned to be excited about and take pride in.

The Confidence Interval had been transformed into contemporary, computer generated, surreal graphs, providing surreal almost intangible information about the nodes' relevant variables, multi-dimensional patterns and dynamic shapes and shades of colours. It was the new trendy contemporary graphical way of representing information and the nodes loved it.

All the quantitative inferences and analysis, all to achieve statistical control of the population space of the utopian state and its nodes within. Yet not primarily by a political control as there was no official big dictator but something far worse, something infinitely more ruthless and controlling; statistical algorithms, the cold ruthless efficiency of quantitative methodology, root down hierarchies of ministries and corporations, economically efficient ideology: condensing, analysing, transforming thoughts and ideas about fairness, governance and the economy into cold hard numerical representations, devoid of pity or the irrational animal spirit.

The great statistical liberation and its economic efficiency philosophy was nurtured by universities throughout the utopian state and the Null Hypothesis Union; even within Zhou Pingjun and the Nodes' Republic of the Harmonious Mean Union; I knew this but remained silent as Blue continued to school the new recruit.

Blue continued, 'Are you familiar with the eGraphs?

Without waiting for the recruit's response, Blue continued, 'nodes self-analyse the shades of colour, of their personal eGraphs for hours hoping to get darker colours, nearer the middle of their surreal eGraphs. They hoped to have less pasty, almost shadeless colours, nearer the convoluted borders of the graph.'

I considered that the e-Graph where more ominous, it meant that the average unbiased impressionable node could even analyse other node's e-Graphs; a socioeconomic strategy for elevating the near omnipotent monitoring of the state.

I knew the state supported nodes taking time and pride in their e-Graph fashion accessory. It was an ingenious strategy by the state, to augmenter the e-Graph as a fashion accessory and status symbol which was eagerly adopted by the young nodes. The e-Graphs were viewed with pride on their embedded keychains.

They regarded their e-Graph rating as a status symbol, in the same regard as financial credits or a new personal fashion accessory or even an electric automobile which were rare now a days as most nodes had been weaned off personal transport and onto efficient public transport. Apparently to save the environment and to control the citizen's movements who were perpetually constrained not to travel in crowded busy environments; to be subjected to continual advertisements and travel routes all at the state's discretion.

Blue continued, 'The nodes called each other shade or shadeless; this referred to the fact that nodes had fallen out of the confidence intervals that were allowed to be known to them, the visible confidence interval; more subtle and sophisticated graphs presented in a new computer graphic orientated manner.

Surely graphs with different shadings represented different variables and relationships that ultimately allowed the reader to draw inferences about their level of conformity to general popular trivial expected boundaries that the average node should adhere to.

I carried on my chain of thought; the state propagated a competitive loyalty between nodes so that nodes would be proud of their different shades of colour in their e-graph. The richer the colour the further away it was from the boundary.

The boundary was the end of a transformed confidence interval on an average nodes' e-graph. The e-graph resembling a portion of paint splattered on the floor with different colours and shaded overlapping each other mixed.

The closer they were to the mean of the public confidence interval the richer the colours of the e-Graph grew, the more average they were the more proud the nodes felt.

It was impossible for all the diligent nodes who tried hard to stay within the boundaries of acceptability on their e-Graphs, no matter how hard they tried, some would inevitably fall outside the boundaries, their shades rendered transparent.

Blue and the recruit exited the office to view a room filled with database records. Many of the Beta node colleagues glanced at each other, letting out a series of sniggers after witnessing, "Uncle Blue," initiate a new recruit into the running of the floor.

If only the recruit knew the other half of it. Yet surely he will slowly be exposed to the truth, over the next few years. Once he is sufficiently desensitized and indoctrinated. It was all part of the process of turning an innocent recruit into a complicit Beat sundry responsible for the administration of the Confidence Interval.

Beta shouted to Blue and the obliging recruit, 'If you work hard, you can even win a ticket to Arcadia!'

Blue scoured back at Beta, his eyes pleading him not to mention too much to the recruit. The recruit's eyes lit up at the thought of a free trip to the famous Arcadia.

A series of further roars echoed from the Middle Floor as the Beta sundry realised the joke. While the recruit looked perplexed but slightly honoured that he may receive a free trip to Arcadia.

I understood the joke that Beta had made at the expense of the new recruit, that the Arcadian Express was extremely subtle, seemingly innocuous. It reflected the clever, ruthless and micro-statistical manner in which the state viewed and dealt with its nodes.

Nodes that consistently did not adhere to the stealth Confidence Interval quotas were classed as confidence interval criminals, outliers; redundant nodes.

These redundant nodes persistently produced subpar results which meant they would be classified as unacceptable, statically significant, standard deviation from the official mean. This negatively affected the statistical harmony of the Economic Efficiency Act.

Outliers, stochastic nodes; redundant nodes who fell outside the confidence interval of the utopian state had to be removed from society permanently, rehabilitation was not cost effective. Removing the redundant nodes from society would be a costly endeavour.

Bundling a known outlier, redundant node into the back of a van, to be killed in a concentration camp would be too laborious when faced with the never ending new collection of redundant nodes each month.

There were too many variables; possible guilt stricken utopian state kidnapers and potentially thousands of escapees on the run, spreading stories of mass terminations. Therefore the Ministry of Inferences had devised a much more refined and cost effective method of dealing with newly classified redundant nodes; an infinitely more efficient and subtle level.

Unaware outlier nodes were secretly reclassified as redundant nodes and were then sent an official letter, inviting them to report in person to a community hall in Arcadia.

When arriving at Arcadia they should present their official identity documents and answer a few important official questions; an unexpected individual census.

Most nodes were aware of the fact that one day they may be summoned to attend the Arcadian census; similar to jury duty. They also knew to keep their invitation a secret for state security reasons.

However the town of Arcadia did not exist. In reality it only existed in fiction; on all the official utopian state maps, found in government departments and in state school geography books.

There were even intermittent regular bogus breaking news stories, apparently emanating from Arcadia.

Stories such as a flood causing havoc or a heart-breaking, "Missing unbiased," headline.

There was even a popular soap opera on prime time viewing which was set and supposedly filmed in Arcadia; called simply, "Arcadia," but in reality the town did not exist.

The exact GPS coordinates of Arcadia, was just a collection of vacant farming fields, in the county of Cambridge. All the roads and footpaths leading into the area where it was believed that Arcadia existed suddenly stopped. Electric fences and patrolling guards stopped nodes from physically entering the area.

Security was increased during the school holiday season when there were a lot of holiday makers and school unbiased running around the countryside. Conveniently there was usually some breaking news story about a catastrophe emanating from Arcadia during that time.

A breaking news disaster story gave the guards a reason to erect permanent roadblocks and close off extra fences which they claimed were erected a few hours earlier for the purpose of containing the catastrophe.

The irony was that in the collective minds of the nodes, who witnessed each, breaking news, focused all their empathy on the poor suffering residents of Arcadian when actually there was no Arcadia.

These continual news stories reinforced in the minds of the nodes that there was actually a place called Arcadia when in fact there is not. All designed to condition the nodes so if one of them transgressed the statistical quotas when they were sent an official letter summoning them to attend the secret census at Arcadia, they felt they were going to a familiar place, a place where they have empathised and identified with.

Some binaries even baked cakes to bring with them to give to the poor locals of Arcadia or excitedly believe they would meet a famous Arcadia soap opera star when attending the census.

There were even full colour brochures attached to their official letter, implying that the nodes may even dine with the famous, beautiful stars; their amazing reward for keeping secret the perceived necessary official census.

The chartered public, tube train travelled to Arcadia direct; the, "Arcadian express," also known as the outlier express, to the informed minority of Alpha and Beta, Ministry of Inferences civil servants.

The redundant nodes were instructed in their invitation letter to report to platform seven and to board the only tube train there, the Arcadian express but to come alone; early in the morning.

There was strict security there due to the current perceived calamity at Arcadia but it was to just make sure they were the correct nodes, the redundant nodes.

The Arcadian express ran like clockwork every day sometimes many times a day. No node ever suspected the truth and if they did. What could they do?

03: Endogenous sigma.

Blue was matter of fact as he manipulated the bureaucratic statistical quotas, coldly reassigning a node's social status, even re-categorising innocent statically significant compliant nodes that were just within the confidence interval; rendering them as redundant nodes as he amended the dynamic confidence interval quotas. Different nodes, moved around to different fates, all done with an unbiased indifference.

Perhaps he rationalised that even though he may be destroying a node and family's life for statistical efficiency he was being unbiased and devoid of any malice therefore that did not make him bad.

This was not an uncommon mentality of the new generation of neutered, non-violent, office psychopath. Office managers were devoid of empathy, indifferent, they exhibited many qualities on the checklist of a non-violent office psychopath which state Utopia and the Ministry of Inferences encouraged within the Beta node ranks; as ruthless nodes excelled at achieving work targets and were loyal to total statistical conformity.

Blue was a prime example whilst he orbited the upper region of his compartmentalised work environment he considered himself trapped within the utopian state's hierarchy caste system yet his ambition was to rise to the Alpha level a position far above the regular endogenous sigma nodes.

Yet he was loyal to the state's propaganda of hard work and was completely obedient to the monthly statistical dynamic quotas, therefore he was quietly optimistic that he may be promoted into the Alphaship one day.

He approached me, asking, 'Are you going to celebrate your successes in receiving your Alphaship probation letter by coming to the bar tonight and watch Autarky's speech tonight?'

I politely replied, 'No.'

Blue's psychopathic nature boiled with jealousy inside. He was my supervisor, I was his subordinate, yet I had usurped him; by being chosen to be given the chance to be promoted into the Alphaship.

Now I was in the limelight which shone down directly from the upper floors of the Alpha, shining on me, not him. I would most probably be promoted into an Alphaship in the near future and he would be left in my shadow, an obscurity.

To a psychopathic personality like Blue this was unforgivable. But he had to play within the parameters of office etiquette.

So he beamed a false smile at me, a big Cheshire cat smile, 'Come now Bayes we need you to celebrate,' he said. I noticed his subconscious aggression and jealousy but I played the submissive role. A reverse psychology trick I used to deal with Blue.

'Oh no, sorry Blue, I am far too busy for that,' I replied modestly.

Blue's eyes started to glare, 'Too busy?' he questioned.

'Yes you will work even harder now to secure that Alpha promotion,' he rationalised; perhaps if he was not socially engineered to be non-violent he would like to have reached in and pulled my heart out.

But Blue remained focused whilst he glared at me with his trademark Cheshire cat smile yet his forceful mannerisms gave away what he really felt.

Even though he felt hatred for me due to the jealousy of my success, his psychopathic nature's one trait was grandiosity compelled him to feel the need to ingratiate himself with the contemporaneous flavour of the moment, namely myself.

As did most of society; that social media feed off and mainstream news was only interested in who was in the contemporaneous momentary spotlight. Nodes cared little about the past. Besides the past was filled with lies to make the present status quo of the utopian state and the Alpha, seem squeaky clean.

Blue wanted to bask in my light, to be a part of my success or at the least to be seen even momentarily as partially contributing to my success. Yet secretly deep down in his bowels of his psychopathic psyche he wanted to plunge a knife into my back for usurping him; I surmised.

'Come and speak to me in my office, I want to hear all about it,' boomed Blue so all the office sigma could notice his close association with the centre of attention. I put on my jacket while a few of the office sigma started to leave their office cubicles.

I would have preferred to have just went home and relax with a newspaper, read an old paper book or surf the intranet and indulge in a mindless comfort of familiarity within my daily routines and consume quantized food rations which I would hastily make from the nutritious mush in the Manifestor.

Yet the state expected me to join the endogenous sigma of the Ministry of Inferences to congregate at the, "Crowd bar," and listen to Prime Minister Autarky's quarterly budget speech then afterwards celebrate the utopian state's new quarterly budget plans.

I never really enjoyed socialising or celebrating within Primary_Sample_Space; especially at night as it usually entailed a cold, wet walk to some arbitrary tube station close by.

I sat in the tube carriage staring off into my imaginary plane of the imaginary numbers which hung inches over the real number plane of a random arbitrary passenger node, who stared with an equal intensity, his gaze fixed perhaps on the less mathematical pure imagination of his mind.

It was not confident as to where his consciousness was at this time possibly reliving a past memory or replaying a work conversation where this time his ego got the better of his boss only in his personal hidden imagined fleeting world, inches from my chest.

As I sat there staring at a point, inches from the chest of fellow passenger nodes whilst the tube hurtled noisily through the underground catacombs of Primary_Sample_Space's never ending passages.

My mind freely considered the meaning of state Utopia's statistical totalitarianism, of the Economic Efficiency Act and how it affected the socioeconomic positions of the state and nodes within.

I conclude that everything was a number of sorts. Everything organised; into sets and categories, ready for storage or distribution, sold at the expected profit. Everything quantified and labelled with its barcode category and unique security identity.

Everything, in its place: Its place was a temporary, contemporaneous space, simultaneously transformed into a projected future expected value; to offset the cost of borrowing and the ever increasing competitive economies of scale. To also serve the expected internal rate of return and remain, net present value neutral, in the

Economically Efficiently Society; constructed to have no uncertainty.

The Economically Efficient Model, its equation, a long river of computations, dynamic variables and probabilities; meandering, subtly, pooling and enveloping, invading each area of the state and the nodes within.

Ultimately cording and shaping the nodes' minds, its sediment forming their perceptions and ambitions, the fluid permeating into every convolution of their thinking.

Everything has its price, everything its cost; everything financial correlated to balance on the highly strung Economically Efficient Model.

Even inanimate nodes and corporations that exhibited negative net present value projections could be positioned to offset hedged positions or tax deductions.

All probabilities are calculated; only a certain probability frequency was allowed to happen within the state within a contemporaneous period, only rational choices falling within the confidence interval that tended towards profit maximization were allowed. All other possibilities falling outside of this range were eliminated from the model.

The Augmenter's state embedded algorithms which were even connected to the Central Fractional Reserve Bank, the Centum Corporations. Private Investment banks, pension funds and insurance companies all trading on the Efficient Economic Markets; all confident that their net present values were fixed and that nothing unsettling or uncertain would jeopardise their financial positions or the great economically efficient Beta.

That the great cash flow river like the river Nile which every year bursts its banks letting precious alluvial fertilising dividends soil soak into the corporation's investors pockets and into the pension pots.

Uncertainty affected negatively the investors' contemporaneous confidence in the great cash flow which was highly leveraged due to investor avarice and the states desperation to smooth each evitable recession period and business cycle positions with continual marginal positive growth in each financial quarter.

Investors were forbidden to search for any arbitrage situations. The utopian state controlled aggregate demand and eliminated firm specific risk yet hypocritically allowing a dangerous amount of leverage to entice the investors to invest in the tightly restricted markets with predictable Net Present Values but punishing any market manipulator or alpha seeker, like the despicable Berkshire and Miller. Yet long term growth, compounding returns, tax shelters and leverage were considered acceptable by the utopian state.

Their positions so leveraged that if the markets were to move just a few percentage points out of their expected range it could spell disaster for the entire Null Hypothesis Union's economy, if not the entire global economy.

State Utopia's Null Hypothesis Union and Zhou Pingjun's Nodes' Republic of the Harmonious Mean Union both practiced a unified dichotomy; each trading with one another, in a vicious circle of leveraged financial derivatives, collateralized debt obligations and sovereign debt which perpetually churned out profits from bond coupons and dividends derived from an ever expanding productivity and financial efficiency.

Perpetually compounded nonlinear returns were expected of each Null Hypothesis Union state's individual great Beta; irrespective of their current financial condition of their economies GDP.

Their long term Betas were expected to grow perpetually with a subtle marginal compounded exponential trend and therefore was by that definition unsustainable if the time frame was to be extended indefinitely.

The state Utopia tried to over compensate for this future possibility by continually deferring such as fall of its financial markets and fractional lending reserves fiat currency, huge trading deficit and national debt to the central banks by preaching that ever increasing economic efficiency and more specific individual and sector aggregate demand regulations and working hours.

Using the river metaphor of, "The great Beta river meanders up the valley and the hills, always upwards; its ripples, white noise of the firm specific risk."

Large swells and breaking waves, the alpha returns which were non-existent, just a smooth river flowing, counter intuitively upwards, slowly, subtly,

William J Fraser

meandering upwards with its tiny ripples roaming upon the surface, their naturally occurring firm specific risk, correlated in their unfathomable chaos of pulses and inferences all affecting each individual circular ripple pulse; some were magnified slightly, others phased out, yet all acceptable, natural organic motions of the complex financial markets and even more complex society.

A dynamic fluid strict of the state where all white noise, micro, marginal moments and forces, that even the great statistical economically efficient controlling state could not iron out entirely yet eventually the white noise residuals where smoothed out by the least quarters equation to an average of zero, then the net present value of each specific firm's financial returns eroded to zero, the great equation of the model up.

"Beta up, Alpha flat equals a strong economy," was another one of state Utopia's great mottos.

The state's great fear was that continual growth, each financial quarter, every year would enviably dissipate; then a dreaded recession. Even though officially there was permanent recession which was used as an excuse to marginalise the nodes utility and consumption quotas.

The economy could not expand forever; central banks could not create unlimited fractional credit forever. Central banks, lending the utopian state officially accepted fiat currency an almost counterfeit credit washed with a respectable veneer in the guise of government bonds and terms such as quantitative easing.

The smaller local retail banks could not provide unlimited credit to local businesses forever in a floundering debt ridden economy that provided very little that was tangible apart from the countless incarnations of the individual's manifestation which in many cases were short lived and where soon tossed back down the mush pipes.

Even the great Centum corporation based Beta could not produce a perpetually compounding growth indefinitely.

State Utopia, after many decades of fighting Zhou Pingjun, became envious of the consistent rapid growth of the flourishing Zhou Pingjun economy. State Utopia began imitating the Zhou Pingjun by slowly assimilating many of their economic and societal agenda.

Many of the Zhou Pingjun agendas were adopted by state Utopia; it was their blueprint for many of their new policies; escalating the utopian state's strict statistical regulation to become a subtle all pervasive totalitarianism ether. Both blocs were influenced to the point of total control by the cold impartial rational statistics of Economic Efficiency Act of the administrators of these efficiency quotas the Ministry of Inferences and the artificial intelligent Augmenter.

State Utopia was now rumoured to be even more ruthless than the Eastern Zhou Pingjun Bloc which still suffered totalitarianism under its socialist indoctrination and ideology.

Yet state Utopia was devoid of compassion it had been substituted by the cold ruthlessness rational of the Economic Efficiency Act forcing the nodes to choose the most rational choice or the most cooperative dominant strategy, to maximise their individual pay off each moment as well as the invisible murderous hand of the confidence interval that preened society of inefficient nodes directing society in, "The right direction," towards the utopian state sanctioned mean and it's acceptable sigma variance.

As I drew a conclusion to my thought rambling whilst upon the tube carriage my thoughts were disturbed immediately by the overly loud announcement that the tube station had arrived.

I jumped out of the imaginary plane; back into the Cartesian coordinates of the real world and automatically began to process out of the tube carriages as all the other nodes did, without thinking.

I made my way down the main road and met the Ministry of Inferences Beta work colleagues at the entrance of the foyer of Section Sigma shopping mall.

It was filled with the middle to upper sigma caste of the endogenous sigma castes; mainly Gamma and Beta nodes with a few fortune Delta nodes that were groomed on their probationary period as they were on the verge of possible promotion to one rung higher social status.

The middle and upper spectrum of endogenous sigma, devoid of the lower Sigma nodes sat around the busy restaurant tables chatting or hastily finishing off some overdue work whilst they stared intently into their laptops.

A small percentage had regressed to a passive insular voyeuristic role, sitting alone or in small groups, scrolling around on their embedded devices, intermittently looking up to steal a few fleeting glances at their preoccupied neighbours, observing the latest aspiring Beta fashion and gossip.

Binomial shouted out to the group as we entered the dimly lit bar aptly called, "The crowd." We walked towards Binomial's crowded table which was full of moderately important Beta nodes of the Ministry of Inferences.

We all greeted each with some genuine affection but also because it was the expected emotional response to a given official social gathering by the statistical algorithms, even though most of them hardly communicated with each other on a daily basis as we were in different departments.

Binomial offered us a round of drinks all paid for by the Ministry of Inference bonding petty cash account.

Binomial's bold cheeky character was now in his element, at work he was cheeky and cheerful yet was careful to limit his emotions and chatter, to stay within the confidence interval of the strict statistical expectations of the Ministry of inferences implied thoughts and expected routines.

Now he felt slightly more relaxed but still conscious of the continual monitoring and statistical inferences of all their current actions and emotions implied thoughts and words; compared to the restricted model of the expected implied thoughts and routines of what a Beta node's etiquette should be in a given situation.

Binomial's constant loud contagious laugh resonated throughout the bar and reverberated amongst the Beta around the tables. His contagious laugh, a tool that got him out of most embarrassing questions or situations.

They all sat around chatting, becoming more obnoxious as a new round of alcoholic beverages appeared. Soon the conversations had split up into different camps as each group of colleagues found different conversations more interesting.

'Do you know what I hear? That the Augmenter likes to stare at mice when it not doing its calculations for the normalised state. Its hobby is to observe mice and rats in their mazes and containment. It analyses and inferers their movements for hours,' said Bernoulli.

'Perhaps it sees the statistical movements and routines fascinating,' I replied half interested.

'Perhaps?' he replied ominously.

I watched out of the corner of my eye as the patrons moved around the bar. I was always fascinated by the sigma nodes behaviour and routines in general as I had studied statistics and econometrics.

Just then some patrons shouted for the waitress to turn up the volume on the monitors. The bar manager realised what was happening and turned off the music whilst simultaneously all the patrons regressed back into their default mode of compliant endogenous contributing sigma nodes.

The busy bar, normally loud with chatter and music went remarkably quiet. As all the nodes stopped what they were doing and stared transfixed at the breaking news on the monitors.

A reporter began his dialogue, 'The confidence interval criminals being judged in their absence today at the Courts of Justice where that of Berkshire and Miller.

Normalised Utopia

'These two great manipulators of the financial system who selfishly tweaked the financial markets to their favour, who selfishly produced one of the greatest sins that a node could commit, worse than treason. Manipulating the macroeconomic properties of the economically efficient state.

'Their heinous actions renders any mere economically inefficient node who relative to their personal situation, naively becomes a confidence interval criminal, outlier via a series of aggregate demand transgressions pales into insignificance in comparison to these great macro outliers who concocted a poisoned chalice of financially engineered synthetic options, to reap returns from manufactured financial inefficiencies.

'They wickedly conspired and constructed a great financial scaffolding that reached high into the economy's stratosphere. This great ambitious abomination precariously swayed in the random breeze of international buyers' liquidity, which even the great state could not control.

'The selfish greed of these protagonists produced consistent microeconomic Alphas; abnormal returns far in excess of the sacred Beta. The sacred Beta which hedges the state's accumulation of positive averaged capital gains; free of firm specific concerns, bringing consistent growth over the ages of posterity.

'These two great charlatans consistently manipulated the market's position by producing economic and financial inefficiencies, unpredictability, abnormal positive returns relative to the beta's return; breaking the sacred Beta up into fractions of its great self, into mere multifactor models. The sacrilege of perverting the very life pulse of the state's great Beta.

'These two were the worst transgressors of the state; selfish macro manipulators without limits, yes confidence interval criminals to the nth degree.

'Who risked the very fabric of the economically efficient state by manipulation and speculation, playing up different sides, engineering financial inefficiencies, creating financial turmoil in the great cash flow river.

'They even amended code in the state's financial servers, to alter the high frequency rhythm of the economically efficient state's ebbs and flows of the economic trading harmony.

'Shame on them, shame on these great transgressors who with every advantage, with every privilege, wilfully and shamelessly brought inefficiency into the great economically efficient state which protects and nurtures each vulnerable node in the cumulative average by averaging out every transaction, every movement, every thought; into a safe mean.

'A mean devoid of extremes; extremes that brought harm, chaos and change. Why change the great economically efficient state, why alter the perfect safe harmony?'

The crowd started to boo when pictures of Berkshire and Miller where show on the screens, under their pictures scrolled the provisional date for them to face capital punishment.

The crowd began to excitedly shout, 'hang them; hang them.'

If only they could be found? They had escaped prior to a warrant being issued, running off into the preverbal night, with their ill-gotten gains, the state so enraged by the duo they had begun the criminal proceedings without them and had found them guilty in one afternoon.

Then the breaking news program cut to a close up of state Utopia's Prime Minister, Autarky. His face created a montage on all the monitors and embedded screens.

All the nodes within the bars shouted praise at their benevolent leader who exuded humility which was his brand image.

He was no more moral than the average sigma node, he just appeared to be. Irrespective of his moral standing, his hands were tied; he was just a puppet of the Alpha as were all the political parties who acted as their rivals in alternate official parties. Even though they ruthlessly fought each other, to a hopeless draw of opposing political opinions; right into the expected mean which was set by the Alpha, as per usual.

'I hope the nodes are as proud as I am of this great state,' stated Prime Minister Autarky.

The crowd in the bar cheered, accentuated by distant cheers from other bars situated further down the mall.

'I think we should move forwards, towards greater freedoms for the nodes, disproportionate rights, and opportunities; greater empowerment for the previously marginalised nodes.

'This great utopian state allows such freedoms, such tolerance, unlike Zhou Pingjun.

Two decades ago, our party the Freedom Party, legalised recreational drug use. I personally believe in increasing the boundaries of liberalism, to one day, having no boundaries,' he concluded his statement shouting, 'a progressive society,' whilst raising his arms in the air.

The crowd applauded to engross in the liberal sentiment, momentarily forgetting the rigorous statistical control of the state and its restrictive effects on their lives.

Autarky was oblivious to how far gone his liberal agenda had become. It was perhaps a deluded, futile attempt at substituting moral decay, in the form of liberalism, to counterbalance the ridged statistical control of the economy and state.

The Alpha were not concerned about a node taking drugs or being promiscuous as long as they consumed the correct amount of drugs and remained within a quota of promiscuity, then they cared not about immorality, only statistical control, the cornerstone of their power.

It was easier for Autarky to believe his own propaganda than face the truth that he had no real power over the state which ran like clockwork always to the tune of the Alpha and their statistical quotas. He was only aware of five percent of the state's affairs.

He was even unaware of the Arcadian express. The Alpha regarded Autarky as a harmless fool, their puppet, who they allowed to rage on about liberalism while he attacked any node who opposed their values while all the time the confidence interval and the state's mechanism oppressed the nodes with a statistical stranglehold on their lives, thoughts and actions, even their future predicted actions.

The ever increasing liberalism was a corrosive thought virus, comparable to any extremist or fundamentalist beliefs, responsible for the breaking down of a society's moral fabric. Yet it was nothing more than a futile hypocritical illusion of freedom, a facade hiding the true nature of state, the contrary; the cold, ruthless, statistical efficient control by the state and corporations.

Autarky was compelled to add a statistical message at every speech that the Alpha's Economic Harmony lobby group always requested.

Autarky boomed out his speech, 'Before the great Economically Efficient Statistical revolution; a billion nodes starved a day on earth.

'Do you know why? Because of democracy!'

The crowd murmured at the concept of democracy.

'Populations especially in developing states; they had the right to choose their own governments and their own economic destiny; they had the right to democratically elect who they wanted to run their state.

'But they were ignorant, they were uneducated, they were crippled by their own archaic cultures, religions and perceptions; their thinking cointegrated with their antiquated inferior cultures, histories and perceptions of persecution from invaders.

'Therefore they chose stupid governments; inefficient governments and therefore they ended up starving,' Autarky paused then boomed out again, 'starving!'

'Suffering; thinking that they were free. Free to choose but they chose wrong.

'Or perhaps there was no choice; perhaps there was a dictator on either side of the fence. Or perhaps they were too ignorant, too sectarian, too culturists; too whatever.

'Look at the history of the western states; they are forever morphing and changing, shaping over the years. Look at the map of the old western continent, Europe. Over a hundred years, two hundred years, five hundred years; its borders morphing, pulsating, enveloping and overlapping each other.'

He paused again then boomed even louder, 'There are no states: there are no cultures; just the one state, the glorious statistical state Utopia! The utopian state that takes away freedoms and the liberties!' Autarky then paused looking around, looking for any opposition yet he found none.

He continued, 'but replaces them with an efficient, cold, ruthless statistics, yet it brings prosperity, law and order, to even the mindless, to the uneducated, to the lost; the nodes!

'Who previously had to rely on their own will, their own opinions; their tainted opinions, their biased opinions, their ignorant opinions, their old opinions!

'Democracy doesn't work; we need totalitarianism, a subtle statistical totalitarianism; all-pervading yet all accepting, completely unbiased!

'Just judging you, the nodes on your current data, your contemporaneous data!

'Your contemporaneous results; your adherence to the quotas, your adherence to the normalised cast distribution, that you are given!

'That is all that counts my dear nodes, not your ideals of democracy, of freedom and free will; those are all illusions!

'Individually maybe they are good but collectively they are corrupt, they are inefficient, they lead to a weighted, skewered, deviation from the efficient path; the most rational path, the most normalised path, the average path, the mean path.

'No the path that is skewed because of an individual's baised tainted past thoughts; their tainted beliefs, their cultures, their religions, their histories, their nations, their perceptions, their incorrect ignorant sample of opinions and knowledge: it all leads to suffering.

'That's why a billion nodes starved in the world.

'It's not because of the banks, it's not because of the colonist, not because of all the slighted feelings of past anger, of past frustrations of slavery, of colonialism; there has always been slavery and colonialism long before the slavers and colonist.

There has always been suffering, there has always been trouble, there has always been.'

He paused, 'inefficient thinking; inefficient direction!

'There has always been a weighted negative externality, forcing down subtly and blatantly upon the sigma, upon the nodes, the kings and queens, the monarchs and religious leaders; all skewering, tainting, guiding and augmenting into the wrong direction, instead of a free flowing direction that tends toward the known contemporaneous mean, given, by the great utopian state.

'But we are the state: we are the ones, who guide, generously, guide the nodes of the different caste, who are predominantly ignorant in their individual sample knowledge and perceptions of the state, predominantly, individually inefficient, like unbiased; lost unbiased.

'But we guide them; to the fixed known mean.

'To a mean that we set: a mean of harmony, of statistical bliss, where you the nodes you are forever safe; within the mean, within the average, never too much, never too little, always just enough,' concluded Autarky proudly.

The announcer then said proudly, 'the Fraser theorem; expanding a liability hypothesis. By expanding a liability to its limit it immediately transforms into an absolute value, the opposite, therefore an asset, Ceteris Paribus.

'Any idealistic relative variable expanded to the limit, transforms immediately to the opposite magnitude of the imaginary number plane, the absolute value.

'Therefore military conflict pushed to the maximum limit, immediately creates peace. Nuclear weapons create a cold war; peace.

Millions of nodes conforming to regulated statistical quotas, pushed to the limit; create freedom for the individuals as millions of other nodes are producing goods and services to the benefit of the individual's needs and utilities.

'So it sounds like a contradiction, it sounds like propaganda but it is not, it is a fact according to Fraser.

'Therefore statistical quotas are freedom. The individual nodes' personal egos and ambitions realised within their extreme sigma monthly residuals are stochastic, directionless, inefficiencies.

'Yet through statistical quotas all the nodes are unified within State Utopia. Their random individuality and combined will is averaged out by the cumulative sum total of all nodes activities and intentions. To produce a harmonious non-stochastic, stationary, know, mean of this great unified state Utopia.

'Obedience is mastery! Which state would challenge the great unified Null Hypothesis Union or state Utopia? Countless millions, even billions of nodes, all marching to one tune, one frequency, one monthly quota. All obedient to one statistical direction yet individually we are insignificant yet unified we are strong, we are the masters. Therefore obedience is mastery!

Normalised Utopia

'Privacy is perverse! Privacy leads to secrets which lead to bad habits, inefficient non-stationary thoughts, intentions and routines. Privacy leads to a Cointegration devoid, uncorrelated association with the great regression function of state Utopia. Regressing into an almost exogenous redundancy unified with the contribution endogenous nodes.

'Reduced disposable income due to higher taxation leads to greater wealth for the average sigma of the statistical state Utopia which nurtures and guides us all,' concluded Prime Minister Autarky.

'Income minus tax, domestic autarky minus foreign influence. Minus ourselves; our selfish will, to minus is positive reduces the turbulence, the societal chances of failure and inefficiencies.

"Yes, vote yes," flashed some subliminal words very quickly at the bottom of the screen.

"Poorer equals richer, think average sets you free; free to follow the efficient mean derived by a collection of superior minds and calculations which surpass the individual working node," flashed more messages.

They all saw it but were not completely sure not it did not matter, they all believed it, they were all behind the speech, all behind the state.

Autarky then lowered his tone, looking right into the television camera and said, 'Nodes you need to strive harder to be average, to work towards an Economic Efficiency Society, to bring it to full optimisation for the good of the state and of the unbiased of tomorrow.

'We should be thinking in terms of us, of others, not of ourselves, we should be working together, for the greater good, not for ourselves as individuals. 'Individual pain and suffering is irrelevant; only the collective harmony is the concern.

'Cry, bleed, work, for us; for the future for an improved tomorrow. Today you, I, pain, sorrow, loss; it's irrelevant, in the grand scheme of things.

'Statistical is fair, it is us, it is over all time, collected, and averaged; instead of a selfish me, now, one instance, one fleeting moment of self-gratification, one moment of narcissistic introspection. Forget about the self. Think of us, together, not just now but over time, in the future, in the now, in the past.

'Think average, think statistical, think unbiased. Be confident,' concluded Prime Minster Autarky.

The crowd clamped ecstatically in the bar then the screen when blank, the music started to pay again.

Autarky added, 'It is also imperative that you report outliers who are economically inefficient nodes in the economy.' Autarky then finished again booming out the state's catch phrase, "Think average, think mean; be confident!"

Even though Autarky was a morally corrosive political, a well-meaning imbecile, a mere tool of the Alpha and a parental figure for the unbiased voting nodes he was a great orator and rabble-rouser. The Alpha knew that he was perfect for his role and they continue to support him every election.

04: Apostles of the Alternate Hypothesis.

The next morning, as I made my way towards the grand foyer of the Ministry of Inferences, Senate house building, Mallet street Primary_Sample_Space

I passed a crowd of official protestors who were waving placards and shouting passionately about more rights and inclusion for the ambidextrous nodes, why should there be only left handed or the right handed nodes having all the opportunities?

They shouted, 'Be proud to be ambidextrous!', 'The Ambidextrous have rights too!' and 'Not just rights for the left handed and right handed on either side of the normalised distribution tail!'

As they protested their voice shrieking with emotion; this was their only outlet against the restrictive, totalitarian, statistical utopian state that controlled their every intention and consumption.

They could not protest against the utopian state itself or the confidence interval quotas yet this was their one small outlet. They were officially allowed to protest for trivial social rights; so trivial it was even amusing to the elevated Alpha nodes who resided permanently upon the upper floors of the Ministry of Interferences and other Ministry departments.

As I sat in my office at the Department of Applied Statistics and Confidence Interval Inferences; I began to read Pareidolia's blog which was posted on an underground dark web forum dedicated to the, "Alternate Hypothesis," which was in opposition to the utopian state's, "apodictic," null hypotheses of the Economic Efficiency Act.

Pareidolia's thesis: "State Utopia's economic efficiency null hypothesis leads to a perpetual diminishment of the nodes utility."

I hunched over my desk with my shirt sleeves rolled up whilst I started to become engrossed in reading this.

I focused sternly as if I was appalled with what I was about to read, to appease the ever present state's sentience; the cameras and scanners which always was processing my expected routines and emotions at each instance, to infer my probable thoughts and intentions towards the normalised utopia of the state and it expected quotas.

The perpetual monitoring, always present, always observing, constantly analysing our implied thoughts. Perhaps the Emotional scanners could even sense my heated forehead as an indication of my frontal cortex's emotions which would imply that I was outraged. To the expectations of the monitoring algorithms that required this reaction from a loyal Beta, Ministry node; soon to possibly be promoted into the Alpha caste.

Yet unbeknownst to the algorithms, cameras and scanners, I was focusing my outraged emotions which I subtly struggled to subdue after the most probable demise of Mrs White after she received her invitation to Arcadia.

As I read through this thesis, I generated a pseudo outraged expression, ironically mimicking the corresponding emotion which I felt internally about Mrs White. This allowed me to mask the emotions from the emotions and implied thought scanner.

I could mask my disgruntled emotions against the utopian state's confidence interval cull whilst reading this subversive thesis; where I was expected to feel such outraged emotions.

Normalised Utopia

In Pareidolia's defence I respected his courage in rebelling against his nurtured, non-stochastic caste which had immersed him within the state Utopia's apodictic null hypothesis yet he had blossomed into a stochastic subversive follower of Apophenia and the Alternate hypothesis.

It felt uniquely liberating; to momentarily empathise with Pareidolia's perspective which I was conditioned to never do. But now perhaps some tiny latent speck of random free will had emanated from within my animal spirit which not even decades of state conditioning could factor out of me completely.

Pareidolia's thesis read: "The economic efficiency of the null hypothesis with its constrained normalisation in the form of state controlled confidence intervals produced a statistical totalitarian ideology yet was just a sample set of the Null Hypothesis Union and its supposed eastern rivals of Zhou Pingjun.

"Yet together they are merely economic trading partners which have a global control over the world's resources.

"They perpetuate their global strangle hold by accepting each other as convenient enemies even professing to hate each other yet they both continue to trade with each other.

"This dichotomy of global power was born out of competing for natural resources, maximising their individual market shares; ultimately spreading globalization which now envelops the world completely.

"Bringing together a single unified statistically augmented economy guided by the ruthless statistical Economic Efficiency Policies which are taught in all universities.

"The Economic Efficiency Act is now more of a negative thought externality to our societies, its processes enslaves the nodes for life within a mundane, minimum wage, unfulfilling employment whilst the Alpha live in luxury without the need to toil in the fields or factories.

"This illusion is perpetuated by both sides of the Null Hypothesis Union and the Zhou Pingjun, both profess to be ideologically different yet there is no real difference whilst they propagate their propaganda to their respective worker nodes that their null hypothesis and unique economic ideologies are the righteous side and the other alternate hypothesis is the culprit.

"But it is a lie; to solely reject the other's null hypotheses as both sides have the same capitalist Economic Efficiency Policies both states would compromise their laws and ethics to keep control of their nodes.

"Each side is equally prepared to enslave their own nodes, to feed their Economic Efficient Society that consumes nodes and states alike with an unbiased ruthlessness whilst perpetuating the idea; that the other side is morally corrupt," stated Pareidolia's written thesis.

I knew this as I see into the randomness of the societal ether; I see into the nodes, I see into their patterns, their meaning, I see in their faces whether in person or upon the CCTV screens; I see their facades which they present to the state as obedient endogenous sigma nodes.

I see their expected emotions yet I see their eyes. Their eyes cannot hide their intrinsic nature, their sub consciousness that cannot be tamed or dampened; there is an intangible glimmer of the animal spirit, an intangible glimmer of the irrational where the eyes of truth are always watching.

No amount of lies or conditioning can corrode away completely, this glimmer, this spark of consciousness or sub consciousness. Yes it can be rationalized away by the obedient nodes' conditioned psyche but somewhere deep down the nodes surely feel or know instinctively the unnatural containment of their artificial statistical society.

Their eyes lead to their hearts which I can feel through the randomness of the oneness of the universe.

I see their pain and unhappiness, they continue to process within the non-stochastic, harmonised, normalisation of their society; wearing their expected facial expressions. Feeling expected emotions, ultimately adhering to merely process their existence and lives within the statistical algorithms' expectations.

To always be obedient to their individual expected routines which collectively is the process; the great Beta function. A process that was supposed to augment and nurture the nodes yet ultimately it controls and corrodes them to merely serve.

I caught a lift down underground to the $-n^{th}$ floor where the offices officially did not existent. In reality they were just a series of large dark nooks and crannies of open plan rooms filled with countless computers and huge wall mounted monitors. Their screens sub divided into many CCTV camera views around Primary_Sample_Space.

A few large wall mounted monitors presented dynamic graphs, their contemporaneous data shifting and morphing continuously representing the Hidden National Confidence Interval Quota.

Each computer terminal had a civil servant observing and analysing individual nodes of interest whose recorded movements on CCTV were transformed into statistical data, testing the node's levels of societal and statistical conformity.

I walked through the general analysis area proceeding deeper into another large dark open plan room which housed a similar assortment of computer hardware and large all mounted monitors but this room was dedicated to apprehending only the most serious of outliers.

I was handed a metal safety deposit box which was securely locked; a nameless expressionless, security node wearing glasses which contained a camera, recording everything he saw to deter him from ever observing anything that was in any of the boxes, he took me to a secure room where I could sit alone and open the box.

A separate security node approached me with an equally detached expression and handed me a small metal key to unlock the box.

Upon the locked metal box were handwritten ink words in bold capitals, "Utterly confidential: Apoehnia-16-08-2048."

I sat down as the door closed behind then I heard the noise of it locking as I sat in the secure metal viewing room.

I tentatively opened the box which contained as I exacted a transcript written on the antiquated medium of paper. This transcript which was apparently recorded by an undercover agent of state Utopia was far too dangerous to be held as a file on a computer database in case it may be hacked.

I was secretly curious as to what was written on this piece of worn handwritten paper. But I was equally honoured to be given the clearance by the Ministry to open this utterly confidential box and read its contents.

The Ministry must trust me; it had nurtured me and would soon perhaps promote me into the Alphaship therefore they must be confident of my loyalty and my impeccable discretion.

I started to read the transcript from the node the Ministry referred to as Apophenia. One of the most wanted dissidents of the state yet considered a spiritual leader by his followers.

Pareidolia used the number eighty four to signify the belief held by a small growing group of subversive called, "Stochastics," that a prophet called Apophenia was preaching that the end of ridged statistical control within state Utopia would begin in 2084, this year. Pareidolia was loosely categorised by the state as a follower of Apophenia.

Apophenia's real name was not known and did not even have a personal security identity number. He was not official an exogenous node nor a redundant node he was some irrational term some emanation of the countless small regression functions creating this statistical analogy.

A sigma far in excess of any normalised or categorised sub four standard deviations. It's as if he emanated from far outside of the confidence interval, far within the $(+a/2)$ of the z-value, of the murky, intangible, statistically significant not allowed statistical ether.

Within the realm of spirituality; a term considered a residual term, never used only when it was used immediately before the word, "Superstition," in old propaganda videos.

Only a handful of nodes within the utopian state did not officially have a security identity or name. He had been given the code name, "Apophenia," by state Utopia which viewed religion as a form of apophenia. Apophenia's followers also adopted the name and referred to their prophet as Apophenia.

Apophenia preached against society's heavy reliance on technology which he referred to as, "Techism," and warned against the spiritual dangers of societies being strictly controlled by soulless statistical algorithms.

Apophenia's location was classified as uncertain but somewhere within a dynamic normalised distribution within his own separate probability wave function, around the mean of the Cornish coastal hinterland area, roaming chaotically whilst preaching his subversive spiritual teachings.

Mainly within caves by the sea, where his Stochastics followers were known to congregate and process their functions; in the fractal curves of the near infinite coastline hoping to find a glimpse of the spiritual ether, via his preaching.

This is the written transcript of Agent X, "I finally found the entrance to the hidden cave which was nestled on a small secluded beach behind a series of low undulating grassy hills in the Cornish coastal hinterland.

"I was stopped by two burly Stochastics, followers of Apophenia. They asked me, what I wanted? I replied with the expected correct response, 'Salvation from statistics.'

"The burly Stochastics looked at each other; then ushered me in.

"I entered a shallow bell graph shaped entrance to a large, dark cave, littered with naturally occurring crystal encrusted stalactites, hanging from above and below, like statistical graphs, frozen, incarnate from both directions; averaging their difference points out, at each inflection point of random stalactite points.

"Nature's own cathedral filled with a small congregation of Stochastics followers; free spirits and disgruntled redundant nodes all standing around Apophenia listening to him answer questions.

"Apophenia stood on the alternate cave wall, wearing his white robes looking like a religious leader whilst he spoke of statistical freedom and intrinsic goodness.

"So many countless subversive statements and concepts were spoken by the congregation and Apophenia, too much for this one report but all comments and intentions were firmly against the state's null hypothesis of statistical conformity.

I had just enough paper to write this transcript of Apophenia," wrote agent X.

Apophenia had started his sermon with one word, 'Choices.'

He had then continued, 'The state is too rational, too statistical, too systematic; too ruthless. Nodes are only given certain options to choose from.

'They are trapped in a proverbial, "mouse utopia," of their neighbourhoods and workplaces; all controlled by the statistical state. The state only cares about one thing and that is efficiency; maintaining its Economic Efficiency Act quotas.

'Always the cold, rational, payoff; the payoff given is the one with the greatest economic efficiency creating a perception that the state always provides with aid of the superior cooperative dominant strategy; a cooperative nirvana were the nodes are safe.

'Safe from hunger, safe from extremes, safe from the irrational; safe from themselves.

'But it is our nature, our individuality, our animal spirit, our irrationality; to love, to dream, to share kindness from our hearts. Altruism!

'It is illegal to give beggars credits; it is illegal to show kindness where it is not appropriate where the rules and laws and quotas say, no. You must not, under threat of punishment.

'I learnt years ago about the confidence interval and how the state is perpetually pigeonholing the nodes into their little sigma caste slots, their little routines of existence. But where is the option for altruism?

'Where is the option for the irrational moment, a moment of individuality, a moment of kindness, the option to self-sacrifice, to offer a disproportionate payoff, completely irrationally, against the grain of society. Where the intangible, the animal spirit lives; the altruism, the irrational. Even the madness and the genius.

'I am no expert on statistics but the confidence interval is symmetrical in its distribution, therefore there is a negative region as well, yes.

'Maybe that negative region of a normalised distribution quota is not good, perhaps it contains the opposite of altruism, the opposite of kindness, residing within the negative region. Harbouring perhaps a negative externality such as madness which is not to be encouraged but perhaps madness spawns genius maybe adversity spawns character.

'All I know is that the animal spirit and altruism would reside within the $+a/2$ outside of the official normalised confidence interval sigma. Residing outside of regulated choices and routines demanded by the state.

Normalised Utopia

'Outside in the statically significant sigma variance; within the intangible realm of above the $+1.96$ or even $+2.045$ standard deviations. Outside of the confidence interval within the murky, unpredictable, chaotic realm of the unrealised probability; relative to the state's restrictions on thinking and routines.

'Outside the confidence interval; lies the intangible goodness. Maybe extreme evil, resides on the negative side of the confidence interval, $-a/2$.

'But I am certain, a form of evil rules deep within any confidence interval where only restricted choices are allowed.

'The spirit, animal spirit, altruism, synergy, they all exist outside of the confidence interval, within the intangible.

'In a statistically controlled society, the average, the given, known, mean and its normalised distribution is the only thing that counts.

'Where the nodes are forced to conform to a mechanical, emotionless, strategic way of thinking and routines.

'There is no place for extremes; therefore no place for the intangible, no place for the animal spirit, no place for good or even evil.

'There is no place for the good spirit in the regression models of an unnaturally forced, non-organically evolving society.

'The good spirit is intangible, only existing outside of the confidence interval where the nodes true intrinsic, irrational nature and the spirit exist.

'Our minds are mere decision machines; all they do is make choices based on perceptions and calculations of their sample data presented to them by the utopian state.

'When the utopian state restricts our choices, they are restricting our individually, our very souls.

'The spirit can jump and spread from variables, it is independent of correlations. It cannot be controlled, be manipulated or die.

'The spirit is the cornerstone of all thinking, like a frequency or ether, in the atmosphere, permeating throughout everything, soaking into all thinking and leading the way to intentions which lead to thoughts, words and actions.

'But be careful of the negative frequency. The nodes make the subconscious choices whether to accept the spirit at each decision process; their thoughts and actions are a direct indication as to their intentions, what they think about and what spirit is at the root of their thoughts.

'Just by reverse deduction you can conclusively see if you are thinking with a tainted bad intention. The negative spirit will make a node rationalise, to be angry, to justify wrongdoing. This will lead the node to carry out a perceived righteous harm.

'A node with the good spirit in them however will have love and good intentions within them; their binary decision structure of thoughts and options will lead to a good thoughts and good choices.

'The spirit supersedes all the nodes' variables and attributes, it is the connection to God.

'Rules, superstitions, code, conduct, protocols, mystics; are all irrelevant only the spirit is needed.

'It permeates through all thinking and is higher than the combined might of all the states' servers and infrastructure contained within.

119

'Tune your spiritual frequency to find the good spirit, but remember there are different frequencies, bad and good. Just open your heart and you will find the good spirit,' preached Apophenia.

Apophenia continued, 'I have meditated within these caves trying to find a reason, an answer to all of these situations and the existence of this restricted totalitarian state.

Then one day, out of the thoughts, out of the statistical ether, like a seven sigma event, I saw an infinite chain of numbers and symbols then one stood out; the plus sign, the great plus sign then I knew immediately what it signified.

The greatest religion, the greatest faith that has been banned for decades; that now is only mentioned once in a blue moon in cryptic mumblings.

Now I see the connection between spirituality and of the antithesis of the cold rigid fixed utopian state engineered to be devoid of any spirituality or connection to the statistically significant great plus sign that resides far outside of the $+a/2$ confidence interval, far beyond the four standard deviations sigma.

The great plus sign.....'

Agent X had written please refer to the other piece of paper.

I looked in the box but I could not find any other piece of paper. My hand frantically fumbled in the dark processes of the box as I now desired to know more of this great plus sign.

But unfortunately I could not find any more paper.

Perhaps that precious piece of antiquated medium lay imprisoned anonymously within one of the other safety deposit boxes in the vault. Yet unfortunately I did not have the leys or permission to open the other boxes.

As I put away the paper back into the box, I considered the fact that I was aware of finance principles such as there was no positive net present value in financial instruments and of the strong markets hypothesis. These principles eliminated arbitrage opportunities or free easy profits.

Before the great statistical revolution before the implantation of the Economic Efficiency Policy when profiting from the financial markets was encouraged and legal, financial traders performed technical analysis trying to find any return anomalies or some profitable trends.

They had faith that there were some arbitrage opportunities within the markets even though they had been taught that there were no recognisable non-stochastic patterns, autocorrelations or predictable trends; merely random walks.

When religion was legal, religious nodes also had faith even though there was no rationale to their belief.

However some traders did consistently make profitable returns.

So maybe Apophenia was correct, perhaps altruism was where economics met spirituality.

I called the guard; he came and collected the box, double checking that all the paperwork was in it.

I realised that was a very profound deep truth that I had just read and that the state hid these extreme thoughts and variables to protect itself.

I then remembered seeing all the countless other boxes in the safety deposit box vault there were countless other boxes perhaps filled half with lies and half with truths or perhaps only filled with truths. I suppose it is rational that a totalitarian state hides the truths and propagates its lies.

The correct result or truth can damage the state's statistical quotas driven society filled with biased lies of the given known mean, constructed by a statistical bias foundation which was too flimsy to prevent damage from the truth.

Whilst the lies need to be continually propagated by the state the truth only needs one fleeting glimpse to do its damage and to resonate within the observing nodes indefinitely changing and corroding their contrived assumptions of the state's null hypothesis.

The countless boxes all contained possible truths, possible treasures, just like Apophenia's great sermon, the life changing sermon, that could turn the nodes against the state by waking them up from their sleep induced statistical conformity.

Each box a possible truth, a truthful mean, correct mean, an unbiased mean, not a given mean but just being, just existing, within the murky ethereal probability cloud of the unknown; not known until the box is opened and analysed.

The hidden mean, a mean that is true and unbiased, unplanned and most probably inconvenient to the state and the observer but a truthful mean of the data, of the situation, of the reality that its distribution wraps around itself, around a true, unbiased, unknown probability of an event or circumstance.

But the state needs to hide such truths, such inconvenient probability realisations as to protect itself and the great Beta of constant, predictable returns, smoothed out variances and dividend streams with consistent marginal growth.

So the state hides, restricts and locks away every truth, every unbiased mean; every classical statistic realisation; with a biased, skewered, contrived, selection biased of its own official given, know, mean substitution.

The data and nodes must wrap themselves around the given, known, mean of the self-fulfilling prophecy of the state's guiding hand, the current monthly state quotas and personal confidence interval expected sigma distribution realisations of the great mean.

To think rationally, think mean, to choose the most ruthless choice, the highest payoff at every given event.

The collection of hidden means locked away in their boxes all collectively together forming one great mean, one hidden mean that emanated in this letter transcript being read.

Perhaps the greatest truth lay in this box? Or perhaps it lay within one of the other safety deposit boxes. Perhaps the greatest truth regarded the statistically significant, mysterious great plus sign?

Possibly the greatest truth of all the hidden means contained within the locked hidden boxes; a deterministic incarnation by the all-pervasive probability ether wave functions, resonating and culminating far in excess of the constrained vault walls, pulling me in towards it, so I a recently disillusioned Ministry analyst with a minuscule of potential power would be privy to the great truth.

As if the very fabric of the universe, reality and probability had conspired to bring me here today, to this heavily secured isolated monitored room to read the truth which was now set free, within me, within my very observance and inference.

Or perhaps I am seeing patterns that are not there, merely a superstitious observer acting within the random chance of life, perhaps I am becoming an Apophenia too?

But from now on I will no longer think in fixed known means rather fixed, unknown, means.

I felt the unknown, fixed mean enter my body, my mind, my thinking, no longer my psyche governed by a stagnate fixed, known mean, of the statically state's quota driven ideology.

No now, a slightly freer node, able to accept that there was a true mean, a truth, at each instance, in the probabilistic ethereal reality.

1 realised that I would have to work to find each mean, each distribution; that there was no given, known, mean.

Only an unknown, fixed mean, I felt a little freer and more confident with my new frame of mind which I hid from my emotions and frontal cortex.

I remained as stale and clam as possible to the expectations of the scanners after this significant experience where I had just read such a subversive paper as Apophenia's.

'They caught Pareidolia!' shouted Bernoulli excitedly over the encrypted satellite communications.

'Great, take him to the Information Agenticity Agency building,' said Blue.

I felt a sudden shudder of terror at the thought of the Information Agenticity Agency's methods of extracting information. It was on a different level to the more moderately sadistic methods of the Ministry of Inferences.

The utopia state, even with its all-encompassing malevolence had an air of fair play, a marginalised, autoregressive, distributed lagged remnant, of their past empire. But the predators at the Information Agenticity Agency were from a different state, they had less restrictive limits on their treatment of interrogated nodes.

Which they meted out to any perceived enemies of their state; domestic or foreign. They might even fly the poor Pareidolia on a rendition to some non-Null Hypothesis Union state for a more extreme inquisition.

A stranger's voice was heard over the communications channel, it must be one of the officers, barking orders at him in a domineering, patronizing manner as the now apprehended suspect was treated as guilty from the onset.

In a state where nodes are terminated just for being a few shades of violet from the norm on their eGraph, a perceived persistently, successful political agitator was worthless, less than nothing, a negative variable to the overzealous and psychopathic officers who were now all-present in every state.

Pareidolia took a deep breath as the hood was whisked away from his head, the small stuffy claustrophobic integration room air seemed like the sweetest flesh air that he had ever breathed compared to the suffocating old sack that had been used as a hood for the last few hours.

The dimly lit rooms seemed as big as St Paul's cathedral compared to the confinement of the smelly old hood.

He sat there focusing on breathing in as much oxygen rich air as possible to let his body make up for the lack of if for the last few hours.

'Good evening Pareidolia,' said one of the integrators.

'Did you enjoy your rest?' asked another.

Pareidolia concentrated on breathing whilst his head and torso bent forward; he started at the desk that he careened towards. It sheltered him from the bright spotlight that shone onto his now hunched silhouette.

One patronizing guard shouted, 'Wakey, wakey.'

I watched the scene unfolding even though I was not an official integrator but had been allowed to witness the interrogation because I had helped apprehend him.

Pareidolia raised his head slowly as he grimaced, he tried to peer over the incessant glare of the high powered lights which bleached his silhouette, making him appear almost in an all-white resplendence, befittingly white, that of a saint or deity; radiating the reflected light into the rest of the dim room.

'I am not Pareidolia,' he replied, 'you have the wrong node.'

'We have all you're online and embedded data there is no sense trying to lie this time,' continued Delta-two.

'Lie?' replied Pareidolia, 'the whole economically efficient utopian state is built on layer upon layer of lies.'

Delta-one slapped him saying, 'The utopian state nurtured and fed you, treasonous variable.'

'Yes you were privileged to receive a Beta level education then you betrayed the state's guiding hand that nurtured you,' continued Delta-one.

'The state is not free or fair, it traps the nodes in a fixed, given, know contrived mean corrupted further with its corresponding standard deviations, which we are forced to exist in.

'It discriminates against the lesser sigma caste who have a lesser normalised utility to exist in. Forced to reside closer to the repugnant negative Z-values, perpetually constrained near the subpar, lower standard deviations, bordering on just being outside of the confidence interval within the wretched tails of the $(-a/2)$.

'Condemned to an engineered lesser utility; to lesser prosperity, to a more menial existence whilst the Alpha enjoy the fruits of the lesser sigma's labour,' Pareidolia relied passionately.

I found myself secretly stirring inside by his response.

'The economically efficient state functions perfectly but each node must follow their quota to allow the great iterations, calculations and expected values to create perfect efficiency,' reasoned Delta-two.

He then gave Pareidolia another crack with a rubber baton.

Pareidolia screamed out in pain.

I began to sweat as I was confident the situation would escalate into violence. The only uncertainty was how long would Pareidolia hold out for until his inevitable breakdown and submission to the state's integrators.

Both the Delta guards seemed the usual psychopathic integrators, predictably enjoying their professional methodical beating of Pareidolia.

There was even a statistically significant probability that Pareidolia may even be killed during this integration if he held out too long. His body would then most probably be thrown into the Information Agenticity Agency's incinerator on the basement floor of the pyramid.

'You think you are both free individuals?' Pareidolia spewed out spittle into the lights whilst his blood dripped down the side of his mouth.

'Of course we are free,' shouted Delta-two then cracked Pareidolia again with his rubber baton.

Pareidolia let out a piercing scream, his body frantically moved while his mind tried to deal with the shooting pain, he resembled some possessed creature whilst he screamed and mumbled some undecipherable angry, frustrated words.

However it did not seem a scream for mercy rather a scream of hatred because the integrators were not showing him any respect.

'Do you still think the state is imperfect?' shouted Delta-two, ready to strike Pareidolia again for insolence and for stubbornly holding on to his convictions.

I began to shield his eyes, predicting another round of violence and sadism.

Delta-two was about to swing his rubber baton again at Pareidolia but then suddenly like a quantum fluctuation apparition, a third node appeared from the shadows of the room that I had not noticed on the grainy commutations receptions.

He had appeared from the shadows his facial features resembled that of an officer, unlike the stocky heads of the integrators.

He held back Delta-two's arm; Delta-two turned around momentary glaring with at the third node with hatred, for stopping his violence but then his eyes glazed over in a submissive acceptance of the third node's authority.

The third node was dressed in a dark trench coat; he almost resembled an Alpha.

Pareidolia looked at him with two half closed, bruised eyes. He was looking now at a non-random face yet seeing randomness through his bloodshot eyes within the dark interrogation room. This paradox; Pareidolia seeing randomness in a non-random shape could signify his inevitable turning and capitulation to the utopian state.

The third node offered him an e-cigarette which he gladly took, even if it was just to stop the beating and emotional trauma for a moment; to feel like a respected as a full ranked, endogenous node, once again.

They both remained calm and silent whilst they took long pleasurable drags on their e-cigarettes.

The third node then questioned Pareidolia assertively, 'Pareidolia you can't deceive us, are you not one of Apophenia's disciples? Are you not a derivative of the Apophenia; "Pareidolia," that sees patterns in randomness, in particular, seeing faces and meaning within random shapes and even clouds?

'Do you not think in redundant randomness? Do you not merge you thinking with stochastic forms and any shapes, inferring some convoluted appearances that seduce you into thinking subversively; finding meaning outside of the official confidence intervals within the statistically significant stochastic thoughts, intentions and routines?

'Just like Apophenia who sees meaningful patterns of rebellion against the state, against the utopian ideals, against the great economically efficient, risk free economy.

Apophenia; the ultimate transgressor against this statistical harmonious bliss that rejects the non-stochastic; a subversive who is against the great apodictic null hypothesis of the utopian state!'

inquired the third node then paused and smiled, softening his voice to a clam, empathetic tone.

'Come now, it does not have to be this way. Are you familiar with game theory?' he questioned.

'No,' replied Pareidolia.

'Well we have a classic, "prisoner's dilemma," game theory situation here. We have another one of your political agitator colleagues in another integration room,' stated the third node.

Pareidolia looked up at the third node frantically examining his eyes searching for some glimmer of a clue as to who he was referring to. Who was it they had in the other room, a loved one perhaps Pareidolia speculated?

The third node predicated this response and smiled whilst continuing, 'The good news is, if neither of you refuses to confess; you will only get a small custodial sentence.

'However if both of you confess, then both of you will get ten years in prison. But the bad news is, if you do not confess but your co-conspirator does confess; then he will get only one year in prison but you will get the death sentence. And vice versa,' the third node paused, to let the full gravity of the statement sink in.

'Therefore the dominant strategy is to?' he asked Pareidolia patronisingly.

'Not confess,' replied Pareidolia, confused under the pressure of the interrogation.

'Incorrect. In that case you would both get ten years in prison,' answered the third node.

'It is better than a death sentence,' replied Pareidolia.

'Yes I suppose so,' the third node laughed, 'I never thought of that additional perspective to this game theory decision matrix.'

The third node paused as if thinking deeply he then leaned over and whispered into Pareidolia's ear, 'but not worse than you receiving the death sentence whilst your co-conspirator only receives one year.'

He stood up and walked towards the shadows nonchalantly, 'He gets rewarded for betraying you with a lighter sentence,' continued the third node.

The sentence cut through Pareidolia's bruised and bloodied head into his narcissistic ego; some other conspirator getting one up on me, he thought.

'The dominant strategy is for both of you to confess, in case the other betrays each other. You cannot trust anyone, not even your fellow righteous conspirators,' concluded the third node.

'No, he would not betray me,' replied Pareidolia.

'I hope you are right, for your sake,' replied the third node sarcastically.

'He will hold out for the cause.'

'Perhaps he nobly will? But would you bet your life on it,' finished the third node; similar to a master salesman?

Pareidolia thought for a moment with a look of concern; concern for a possible death sentence but also for the possible betrayal of the claimed, captive comrade in another room.

Pareidolia then looked up smiling and said, 'I chose the dominant strategy. You are right I can sit here all night and you can beat me to a pulp whilst perhaps my fellow conspirator would yield to his violent interrogation before me; then he would confess and I would no longer have that option to confess. He would have won a lenient sentence and I would be doomed to a death sentence.'

Pareidolia lowered his head, resigned to betrayal; the only rational choice, to accept once again being caught up in the limited choice spectrum of state Utopia's statistical tyranny and restricted binary decision trees of personal utility.

'Therefore I confess to everything, I am guilty,' he announced.

'Guilty?' questioned the third node, his tone enticing a more specific confession?

'Guilty of rejecting the state's null hypothesis, guilty of rejecting the confidence intervals and it's fixed, know, mean,' stated Pareidolia.

He then thought for a moment as if regretting being rash to confess straight away, his shrewd mind finding perhaps some space to negotiate, some small freedom or benefit, for his betrayal that should not just be given up on a silver platter, even if there maybe perhaps some loved one in an adjacent room.

'I am prepared to soften my views; I am prepared to work alongside your Information Agenticity Agency.

I am prepared to change,' stated Pareidolia solemnly.

His demeanour became calm as if he was a million miles from the interrogation room whilst sitting completely still, resided to submitting to the non-stochastic, imagination devoid state.

Yet strangely Pareidolia was wearing an enigmatic smug expression perhaps at the prospect of still being valuable; still being important, still rising above his designated sigma caste mean; before he was a subversive.

But now he was a traitor yet he still held an additional intrinsic value; allowing him to hover like an imaginary number above his birth allocated real number line, sigma caste. Pareidolia's ability to always be above his determined sigma cast, no matter the outcome or situation, made him like a superconductor in a quantum superposition; always hovering above some electric field track irrespective which side up he was.

'No way,' exclaimed Delta-two in disbelief and frustration.

'Silence!' shouted the third node.

'You are being prudent Pareidolia,' replied the third node calmly, even lovingly.

Even I was shocked by the unpredictable rapidness of the events unfolding within the small integration room deep within the pyramid.

'Can you turn that spotlight away from my eyes?' asked Pareidolia looking directly at the third node, now accepting his submissive dependant endogenous sigma position.

The third node looked at Pareidolia for a few seconds saying nothing, to remain in control. He then walked towards the light and repositioned its glare towards the floor.

'I think we can work together,' said the third node as he waved away the two integrators to leave the room.

I continued to watch transfixed by this interrogation, perplexed at how the once mighty Pareidolia who spent decades criticising the utopian state would turn so quickly.

Pareidolia continued to stare up at the third node as if bonding with him and the utopian state, savouring a new relationship where he still had an advantage, an economic rent, a star status, high above his ordinary sigma caste rating; high up in the imaginary plane, quantum superposition of political intrigue and celebrity.

'I will work for you; I am getting old and tired of being an aware outlier, always having to live outside of the confidence interval, always looking over my shoulder or up to a possible spy satellite high above, never trusting anyone fully.

'The higher caste Gamma sigma nodes of the who secretly consider themselves subversive liberals, whom I entertain with my preaching, will carry on oblivious within their comfortable lives; who once in a blue moon perhaps would indulge their curiosity in secretly meeting some famous outlier node who supported their trendy alternate hypotheses,' said Pareidolia resigned to his new caste as a professional traitor.

I switched off the communications channel whilst Pareidolia and the third node continued to bond; chatting and smiling like old friends.

Who was leading who? Did Pareidolia break due to rationalism or was he playing a game, stringing the third node along?

Then it dawned on me, Pareidolia has no convictions, he is merely an attention seeker, going against the utopian state not because he truly believed in subversion mainly because it made him feel special, it made him feel unique, it fuelled his narcissistic personality with attention and importance; he was nothing more than a convenient contrarian.

I suppose everyone wants to feel special and unique especially within such a statistically constrained society as the utopian state, especially a narcissist like Pareidolia.

I concluded that the small integration room had been full of damaged personalities; psychopathic guards and narcissistic dissidents, even my hidden, unique observing personality.

What about the third node, what type of creature was he that would have let the guards beat Pareidolia to death one second, then laugh and have an e-cigarette with Pareidolia the next moment?

After observing this, it fixed my view, that Apophenia seemed more spiritual than political. He seemed to truly believe his teachings, to truly believe in his convictions and I doubt that he would ever change his views or betray his followers; unlike Pareidolia.

Apophenia was a real spiritual figure, a real apostle of the alternative hypothesis; stochastic freedom, unrestricted aggregate demand, chaotic unpredictable free market efficiency.

As well as freedom to embrace spirituality; the ultimate imaginary number plane.

I started to feel concerned that such a seemingly moral and good node was considered such an enemy of the utopian state.

After reading Apophenia's truths coupled with most the probable demise of Mrs White and the reverberating epiphany of the unpleasantness of the state Utopia's confidence interval reality; all these contributing factors were leading me to despise more and more, my role at the Ministry of Inferences and my connection to the statistical totalitarianism.

But I had been nurtured and conditioned from the cradle to be a specific type of Beta node who dreamt of reaching Alphaship. I was trapped within my caste yet my thinking was changing.

Perhaps I would just continue to mask my thoughts whilst cradling a secret hope for an ideological revolution within the utopian state.

I had felt this earlier as I had left the vault, now I was concerned what would happen to Apophenia? Had he been secretly arrested by a snatch squad or was he still preaching to his Stochastics followers within one of the countless cave labyrinths along the Cornish coastline.

Hopefully Apophenia would be preaching his message of statistical freedom and of altruism whilst remaining free of the sample space scanners which continually searched every face that walked past, at each moment, in every sample space; for him, the most dangerous node. The utopian state's infrastructure's very own sentient paranoid, "Pareidolia," inferences.

05: Error nodes, error terms.

I walked out of the tube station, leaving the subterranean labyrinth of screeching noise and incessant, inane announcements far behind.

I walked out into the dark winter's night's air, engulfing me in a bracing chill, awaking me from my journey induced stupor which had seduced each passenger into a meditative state as they sat within the tube carriages; trying to blocking out the noise and uncomfortable close proximity of each other. Each node, forced to endure a lack of privacy during their journeys to and from work on the tube.

A short cut, through an alleyway, then a stroll along the garden allotments, which most endogenous nodes used who wanted to break free of the utopian state's concrete infrastructure for a brief moment; To reside amongst the seemingly chaotic pseudo random, pseudo nature of the utopian state's garden allotments.

Some allotment renters probably fantasise that they were living off grid yet never did. They spent a few

William J Fraser

free hours a week, scratching around on their rented soil; their little allotment of nature.

I made my way into the park, a more unbiased model of nature yet not quite completely random or free. It was a treat though, to be away from the relative chaotic hustle and bustle of Primary_Sample_Space's city centre.

I breathed in a few large mouthfuls of crisp evening air that seemed to sooth and invigorated my lungs, body and mind. The birds chirped high upon bare winter trees which collectively stood tall and regal.

Yet individually they looked hauntingly alone and leafless; the barren trees seemed to be the incarnation of partial derivatives within an unfathomably large collection of total partial derivatives, as they all randomly scratched and probed the dark night sky, with respect to time, a time weighted with a seemingly near infinite coefficient.

I was about to regress temporarily yet fully into a meditative stroll as I traversed through the near random hinterland of the park, indulging in a pseudo freedom from Primary_Sample_Space and its continual statistical aggregating of every node's actions and interactions.

Suddenly, a figure loomed out from behind a clump of bushes. As the silhouette approached I made out that it resembles an unbiased node. This unbiased youth looked tough; I noted by the way the figure carried itself in a deliberate ignorant, ostentatious manner. Trying to exhibit self-importance through its ignorant, menacing, over exaggerated body language coupled with irrationally positioned attire which hung from the silhouette in every irrational position.

'You got change, yeah?' demanded an unbiased node arrogantly, his malicious beady eyes beamed a glimmer of joy, his face held an enigmatic smirk, subtly revelling in the situation, where momentarily he would be in charge of another node's fate. He would most probably show no mercy.

I read the situation; the thug would launch a full scale attack upon me, a perceived simple harmless node. He was hoping perhaps to permanently injure me then rob me of my possessions. It would be a bit of fun, for this thug, he knew his rights, if arrested; he would probably be placed under the Dummy Node, Special Dispensation Act even when committing a senselessly violent crime.

His excuse would be that he came from a poor family, which although received generous welfare benefits due to the Dummy Node Special Dispensation Act and lived better than most working class Delta node families. He would plead that he was forced to commit this violent act out of cumulative discriminatory bias that had been accruing against his sample sub caste for generations.

The thug may be ignorant but not ignorant of the basic law of the state which he had learnt when probably being arrested many times before. The thug would be shrewd in dealing with any arrest. The thug was wise enough to follow me to this quiet park, before initiating his attack.

'No, I am sorry,' I replied smiling, trying to hide my fear; I had read about the many horrific violent muggings in Primary_Sample_Space, that the state deliberately turned a blind eye to; in doing so, helped to perpetuate.

Then the thug launched his attack, I tried to make use of some martial arts training I had once received, I was able to evaded most of the punches but eventually the thug's natural fighting instinct kicked in, I instinctively grabbed his sleeve, holding onto his arm and began swing randomly at his face.

For all of my training I was no match for the young, tough, athletic, malicious thug. I slowly succumbed to the relentless onslaught. As the punches rained down on me the pain built up then faded as numbness and disorientation seeped over my head.

I thought of the irony of these Dummy nodes, which always played the victim but when they have the upper hand, momentarily, they show no mercy. Carrying out gratuitous savagery, without remorse, yet they expect to be treated with kid gloves and special exceptions given to them by the state.

Just when all hope seemed lost, suddenly the beating stopped. Through the melee of distorted grey silhouettes that my brain desperately tried to analyse as post-concussion set in my swelling brain. I could see a silhouette, a pair of arms then another pair, whose were they?

I lay there, trying to regain a semblance of my former consciousness, dealing with the pain and disorientation.

As the silhouettes started to increase in resolution, into recognisable figures and objects of my past comprehension of reality, I could see a group of dishevelled vagrants standing around me.

They seemed to look concerned; one was pumping my legs backwards and forwards, trying to pump air into my diaphragm.

The vagrants were the lost nodes that did not fit into the great regression model of the state; categorized as errors nodes.

I had hardly given the error nodes, these embarrassing irritants; unimportant to the endogenous nodes and variables of the great regression model. Those irritants, that were usually normalised away; to a value of zero. When errors terms were realised, producing an R squared value below sixty percent, embarrassing any Ministry of inferences Beta node who had set and inferred their specific failed regression model.

I had never given the error nodes a moment's thought before but now they were my saviours. At this very moment, relative to my perspective, they were the most important nodes within the utopian state and they were not even sigma caste; endogenous or Alpha nodes.

Through a weather beaten face, one binary error node wore an expression of empathy as she applied a cold soda bottle against my swelling face.

Another error node who had a large rough appearance was sitting astride the now unconscious, badly beaten thug.

At that moment I felt guilty; I, like most endogenous sigma nodes had always looked down upon the errors, the unwanted nodes; the residuals of the great societal model.

Some errors, may have been, escaped redundant nodes who for some reason did not board the Arcadian express or had escaped as aware outliers yet most were just the error terms within the model or even the statistically significant who fell outside the confidence interval but did not threaten the Economic Efficiency Act.

My entire recollection was that the errors were conveniently discriminated against and discarded by the utopian state which no longer cared about the errors nodes, the hidden animate variables.

These error node variables where hidden from the model yet were always included and calculated by the sample data, their existence no mystery to the utopian state yet a conveniently hidden random homoscedastic, normalised, sigma variance that was weighted by an error correction, covariance matrix.

This matrix was filled with scavenging utility probability values that kept the error terms perpetually scavenging for marginalised constrained discarded refuge and reliant on spontaneous acts of illegal altruistic donations from passing nodes.

The error terms were allowed to manifest, their random movements within the utopian state's great regression model yet they were kept predictable with a series of time intervals by restricting them into a conditioned normalised, homoscedastic, time series range that was accepted by the state.

Relative to the states regression model, the error nodes where hidden error terms only becoming incarnate within the realised sample data once inferred as residual variables which was deemed officially acceptable. As long as the independent residual aggregate demand quota variable, influenced the targeted dependent variable with a high R squared value.

Then the normalised, homoscedastic, error terms were tolerated as an unavoidable part of a healthy regression model function; the only uncertainty within the great regression model, a sort of quantum fluctuation within the great financial economic mechanics of the great utopian state which was built upon the Economic Efficiency Act and its financially engineered certainty. Yet this uncertainty was managed within the very model by the Ministry of Inferences with the use of the Markov normalised constants.

But now they were attending to my welfare, an endogenous sigma caste node? It seemed irrational; the birth of some new irrational term or situation. A quantum, imaginary number, popping out to the unconditional probability ether to merge with a real number value; me or this situation; creating a complex number becoming real and realised with a "complex conjugate," to form a new unpredictable unimagined future, perhaps.

I was helped to my feet by a biased error, his face hidden almost by a long dark hood and beard. A face to be expected of the unknowable fleeting stochastic error node essence only realised when they become a residual term still hidden within the normalised aggregate value of zero. Yet I somehow instinctively knew this unknowable error node was called Anova.

Their fate even though individually free, was even more mundane and devoid of existence as their engineered mean would always be impotent, devoid of influence, set to zero. At least the constrained endogenous sigma nodes had a positive value expected mean which gave us some weighting, some importance, some existence within the utopian state's great regression model.

I mumbled softly, 'Thank you,' as my mouth was in pain from the many chaotic blows received from the thug.

I struggled to concentrate whilst trying to deal with the emanating pain, every few moments my eyes kept darting anxiously, towards the unconscious thug whom my brain still deeming as a potential threat.

The biased errors noted my fear, 'Don't worry about him again. He will not harm anyone again,' said Anova as the other errors laughed.

'What do you mean?' I asked drowsily.

Then Anova's eyes peered past his thick beard which permanently hid his true essence and presence. His eyes darted back and forth issuing a silent command to the large burly rough looking error node, I again instinctively knew he was called Mu, who was sitting astride the fallen thug.

Anova nodded his head which was obscured by his hood and thick beard. Then the burly Mu flicked open the partially obscured object which he was holding.

I rubbed my eyes trying to reduce my distorted vision.

The object flicked into a long switchblade, the burly Mu smirked sarcastically at me, then at the Bearded Anova; the other errors all stood around silent anticipating the next event with relish.

Mu as if ritualistically, removed his long dirty tramp jacket, revealing his physique composed with powerful muscle. This fact caught my attention not so much because an error usually had a poor diet but because of the many tattoos that cover his body.

Mu must have been a convict, I thought, as tattoos were illegal; apart from the state and Advertising Corporation Board, sanctioned tattoos.

The burly, tattooed Mu pulled back the unconscious thug's trouser leg then ripped off one shoe. Aggressively with one swipe, he cut through the thug's Achilles tendon.

The pain surged through the thug's unconscious body so much that it awoken him from his violently induced slumber.

As the thug started to awake to the pain, the other errors smirked whilst the tattooed convict raised his arms standing over the thug with his boot on the thug's body as if he was posing for a big game hunting photograph.

As the commotion of the active errors started to subside to a realised random homoscedastic normalised routine, a gathering of endogenous sigma caste nodes appeared and started to observe these residual node with perplexed inference as to the nature of these errors, residuals, animate nodes who lived within the model yet where outside of the normalised sigma caste, outside of the regulated regression model of endogenous sigma nodes and of the independent and dependant variables.

These bearded vagrants, hidden outcastes barely tolerated with the utopian state's great regression model yet my personal irrational saviours of this day; were truly error terms incarnate.

The sigma nodes approached looking to observe and infer the unexpected realised incident of the wounded thug lying in the park; an event that was far outside of their confidence intervals expected routines, for the day.

The errors sensing the attention, observations and inferences from the sigma nodes started to merge back within their hidden statistical ether, within the foliage and leafy obscured hinterland of the park periphery, out of view of the prying eyes of the inferring nodes, perplexed at the strange unusual realisation that the sample model of this situation had produced; a screaming bleeding solitary thug lying in the park path pleading innocence and expected victimhood.

I stood in shock at the extreme level of violence, I had just witnessed and experienced, for the first time I had never witnessed first-hand even though I had overseen statistics which related to hundreds of thousands of outlier nodes being sent to Arcadia.

The Sigma began to form larger pools of gawking crowds yet all keeping a discrete distance from the crime scene.

The thug began to scream in agony as he tried instinctively to get up and attack me again as I stood in shock.

But the thug's ankle nearly broke as his tendon tried to hold his body weight, snapping more as they tried to move.

157

The thug, a Dummy variable node yet still part of the official endogenous sigma node regression model society, fell to the fall screaming in agony not fully realising what was happening.

One minute he was stalking his prey; creating his predictions on the event as it unfolded, a form of selection bias; he was self-prophesying with an unproven prior.

The next minute, he was beating his prey with effortless ease; as if collecting data from a model, confident the independent variable, I the prey, would succumb to the dependent variable himself.

Yet the next minute he was battered into unconsciousness, waking up in searing pain. If he was educated perhaps he would have considered the realisation that his selection bias had become tainted by the hidden effect of the error terms incarnation within the sample data of that particular situation.

The error nodes had become realised residual terms that were only known when actually realised, when the sample data was realised and the residual terms appear, to the detriment of many an observing statistical analyst thwarted by a low R squared and the collection of distribute lagged variable engineered to thwart autocorrelations.

Normalised Utopia

I decided in that chaotic unpredictable surreal, even irrational moment, the moment an error term transformed into a residual realised term in that moment of shear confusion and panic yet perhaps a moment of pure stochastic unbiased clarity; in an instant I ran after the mysterious outcaste error nodes, to follow them back into their murky statically hinterland within the great regression model yet within the unknown statistically significant ether, incarnate within the park's foliage.

I would immerse myself with the unknown, hidden; different yet conjoined ethereal error nodes, far off the normalised confidence interval of expected routines of a Beta endogenous sigma node that represented the Ministry of Inferences.

I had seen a new character of node that resided within the great utopian statistical society even though on the very margins. Animalistic and violent, where there was perhaps no, right or wrong just the most savage was righteous. State Utopian was no different; it just hid its barbarity within the tunnels and catacombs beneath the sprawling conurbation of Primary_Sample_ Space upon the Arcadian express and on some far flung battlefield on the border of the null hypothesis.

As I unpredictably and uncharacteristically ran off towards the errors, in so doing, I had most certainly jeopardised my career and life.

I was acting now as an unpredictable outlier; I was exhibiting three standard deviations of statically significant behaviour, unacceptable for a node, let alone a Ministry of Inferences Beta node.

I ran after the errors that had seemingly ran off toward the top of a small grassy hill flanked by countless small trees. They stood there on the periphery, their hoods up, their beards and scarf covering most of their faces; they were only identifiable by their dress and their physiques.

Anova watched me as I ran towards them. The other errors kept an eye on the endogenous sigma; who were gazing from far away becoming more disinterested with the errors with each passing moment.

'What do you seek?' asked Anova as I drew near. He had a defensive hostile look in his eyes peering through the hidden bearded foliage of his face and hooded head, flanked by countless wrinkles and weather beaten skin. Perhaps they could easily turn upon me I speculated as I slowed with trepidation whilst I approached the ethereal, unknowable, error nodes.

Maybe they would melt and merge away into the foliage as I an observer approached.

But they did not, maybe because I was like them now, I had committed to leaving the endogenous sigma caste back in the park and now momentarily I was with them perhaps the ethereal error term lurking somewhere hidden within the model, only to be realised into a residual term when the sample data being inferred.

I was still in shock and not offended by their hostile innuendo and expressions. I mumbled, 'Thank you again. May I ask how can I help you?'

The other errors all looked at each other in shock.

'Help us,' laughed Anova, 'we are vagrants, outliers, error nodes, hated, cast out and intangible; hated by all the sigma. And by you I am sure.'

'I am sorry for my past perceptions of you and by my fellow endogenous sigma nodes,' I said acknowledging the statement.

The moment of honesty touched the errors nodes.

'You are sorry?' repeated Anova, trying to mimic my expression and tone, trying to feel what perhaps what I was truly feeling.

The burly tattooed Mu stood smirking at me with half-crazed eyes yet rationally enjoying the fact that one of the respectable endogenous sigma nodes were acting uncharacteristically; fraternising with the unknowable hidden errors.

A binary error implored with the group, 'Can't you see, he is in shock, we need to look after him.'

The group of errors paused, not knowing what to do.

'I suppose I could never repay you but you are very necessary to the great statistical model, I know. The sigma are not aware of your importance but the utopian state is,' I said truthfully yet meekly, still in shock.

There was a long pause then Anova replied, 'How do you know that? Who are you?'

Another error approached me and put his hand in my jacket; he took out a wallet and riffled through it. He looked at my ID card.

The errors then looked at Anova saying, 'Look he works for the Ministry of Inferences.'

At that moment Mu strode towards me and flicked his knife near my throat.

I stood there keeping my calm yet still in shock perhaps the errors thought I was exhibiting courage.

Anova said, 'No wait.'

Burly tattooed Mu glared at me momentarily then folded his knife and walked away.

'You could repay us,' said Anova.

'How?' I asked eager to repay the group for stopping the attack.

'We have an unbiased binary, she needs a medical prescription but we cannot access it. We are errors, we steal and scavenge feeding from society's covariance matrix to survive but even then, without proper identity chips we cannot buy the medicine. You could purchase the medicine; we will even give you some credits if you need,' asked Anova.

'No I will pay for it but I need an excuse to buy medicine. I will say that I was attacked and hurt in this park,' I replied.

'It will be difficult if she has a heart problem. How will you get her specific medicine?' asked Anova.

'I will have to switch medicines,' I replied.

'She needs to be on the state's database like all the endogenous nodes that get their medicine.'

'I will try to procure the medicine by tomorrow for her and possibly amend the medical database so she may receive intermittent prescriptions to successfully treat her,' I said.

'We would appreciate it if you could achieve that,' replied Anova.

'You are now an honorary error,' announced the Burly tattooed Mu, flashing an elusive smile.

I paused then said with reverence, 'I will endeavour most earnestly to procure the required medicine,' I sounded as if I was accepting an official award into the honorary error status but I was still in a certain degree of shock.

With that the group led me to the edge of the park.

'We presume a chaotic process will guide you throughout your new stochastic routines by helping us and therefore defying the non-stochastic, normalised utopian state after your immediate departure now but ultimately we expect to witness you at theses coordinates tomorrow,' said Anova.

'I am quietly confident that will be realised,' I replied.

As I was leaving, I heard one error whisper say, 'the endogenous always say they will be back but never do. He won't return once the shock wears off.'

This made me more determined to return and repay the errors.

As I made my way out of the park; slowly, methodically emerging out of the hidden foliage of the murky statistical ether where the realised, observed, residual terms hide, residing as unobserved error nodes deep within the linear regression model of the state and of this statistical reality.

I strangely felt that I had been somehow touched by the error nodes presence whilst interacting with them; I had somehow retained some of their residual term, intangible, random essence within me.

I had somehow become slightly an error term myself; I felt more stochastic, less predictable and more elusive than before the attack. Maybe it was just the stress of the day yet I felt myself retain some of the error's essence or subconscious mind-set.

Even though I was feeling more stochastic, more unpredictable, I realised that the error terms were controlled by the state's error correction model with its covariance matrix containing the scavenging utility variables. The error nodes' collective mean was normalised to be homoscedastic, having a mean of zero, as devised by a Ministry of Inferences econometric analyst, Markov.

The errors nodes; become incarnate within the inferred model of the great sample liner regression model of the utopian state as residual terms then they are minus from the model, from the utopian state; as a normalised average of zeros, through the Markov technique.

Yet I was not an intangible unobserved error node hiding within the murky statistical ether, I was not a realised observed residual term either; I was an endogenous sigma, a Beta node of the Ministry of Inference.

Yet now I strangely felt like I had slightly become an exposed realised, residual term of the fixed, unknown mean, of State Utopia's great regression model of the current, contemporaneous, realised observed data of this observed reality.

I felt like I was a realised residual term that was now being continually presented to an observing State Utopian model. My perceived very existence tainted by the residual term was observed and calculated into fruition within State Utopia, incarnate with the model as a glaringly obvious residual term.

My guilty perception grew with each foot step as I hastened almost burgundy back into the rigid real ether-less State Utopian society and infrastructure, once again as I was observed by more and more cameras, positioned high above on intermittent lamp posts, observed constantly by the state's sentient devices that littered the lane that border the quiet natural park and it's foliage that hid the murky statistical unknown within.

Where the error terms nodes reside but now as one camera detected my presence as I approached the high street I became a recognisable endogenous sigma node once again but secretly I felt slightly like a residual term who would be classified as a glaringly obvious residual term to the observing cameras as I would be observed emerging out of the murky foliage of the park's statistical hinterland.

Yet I felt strangely slightly stochastic, more free, more unpredictable, more intangible and fleeting perhaps it was just my new mind-set, altered slightly by this new extreme statistical event of being attacked in the park and momentarily regressed to a more primitive entity whist sheltered by the intangible error terms.

I considered that the error nodes mix with the endogenous nodes but they are separate yet both contribute to create the utopian state's monthly regression model. The vagrant, error terms are the white noise, the unaccounted for errors that the utopian state knows exist yet turns a build eye to. It would be inefficient to try to eliminate them, more trouble that they are worth.

The park where the error terms lived, was a constrained region, a collection of partial derivatives, where one axis, their acceptance by society was held constant as marginalised yet in every other axis, which their minds and lives inhabited, they reached full capacity. Maybe we all live in constrained existence, maybe we all have partial axis and variables held constant and yet we are not aware of it, whether it is financial, social or some other inhibition, naturally occurring or a state engineered function.

As I made my way back to the Ministry, I realised that if I honoured this agreement then I would officially become a subversive; issuing goods and medicine to the errors nodes.

Yet strangely enough the slight residual term I felt within me made me feel that I somehow reside partly outside of the confidence interval now within the murky ether, within the unrealised, of the 'not allowed' tail.

I now partly resided, realised within the statistically significant region of the utopian state model yet the intangible statistical transgression past the expected official confidence interval z-value within the deep; not allowed tails of the normalised distribution.

I felt the residual murky deviation of an error term, the murky ethereal statistical force with its intrinsic good spirit resonating somewhere within, magnifying my feelings of altruism and morals.

I now felt even more of a conviction to help this unbiased binary who was considered far outside of the mode yet ironically a part of the model; forever relegated to being nothing more than a fleeting realisation within the model, a residual term conveniently considered non-existent. Yet existent, an error term waiting to be realised, to be observed and inferred.

Yet she may expire before the chance to even be realised, to even be observed and inferred by the state, I felt more conviction to rescue this unbiased binary.

Perhaps a lagged distributed emotional variable deep within my psyche still futilely trying to save Mrs White even though she was already rendered redundant.

My statically significant, intangible feelings perhaps bordering on irrational; like an imaginary number hovering above the real number line of the ridged quantifiable utopian society. My emotions imparting an almost extra-terrestrial, inconceivable notions of altruism; morals which superseded specific situations and expected outcomes of the utopian state. My emotions becoming correlated with the good spirit.

All magnified by my new perception of partially residing within the murky ether of the intangible statistical realm of the stochastic error terms and now perhaps at least subtly residing outside of the narrow spectrum of the confidence interval.

My intention of trying to save this unbiased binary would mean I would be on my way to becoming a redundant node, instead of an Alpha.

I could just choose to forget the errors and return to my career. I then soon would be an Alpha as I helped catch Pareidolia. Pareidolia, that false weasel, I have no guilt in my part catching him.

But the unbiased binary error, what had she done? And harmless Mrs White eliminated for nothing. Thousands of nodes falling outside of the confidence interval every week who were mostly innocent.

No, I would honour my commitment with the errors, just this once.

Then I would accept my Alphaship or methodically plan a way out of the utopian state.

I made my way back to the Ministry of Inferences on the seventh floor.

'You are late. Where have you been, the quotas are piling up. This will go down on your attendance record. It will affect your eGraph rating,' said Blue smugly.

'I was attacked in the park,' I replied.

Blue's face dropped with frustration that I had a statistically significant excuse to use against my slight statistical indiscretion.

I knew it was true, I took a delight in frustrating Blue, that nasty piece of work. I continued, 'I need to freshen up.' As I pushed past him delaying my work duties further, to his annoyance.

Blue replied with a frustration edged on his face, 'I need your report by the end of the day. To stop the lateness report being logged against you.'

'No way,' cried out Bernoulli, 'Bayes was attacked in the park,' relishing in the excitement, escaping his mundane office routine.

Soon, many co-workers had surrounded me, demanding that I tell of the attack; again and again, until it had morphed into an epic tale.

I left out the part of the story containing the errors as I did not want to seem as if I had fraternised with a banned caste or that I intended to help them.

I had transformed this official minor punctuality transgression into a positive merit, there would no longer be a negative comment placed against my workplace routines rather yet another merit would be included in my monthly report, the other merit for helping apprehend Pareidolia.

Blue ground his teeth with jealousy, he was the supervisor; he should be the centre of attention, not me. I noted that Blue was side-lined out of my view by the gathering crowd of Beta Ministry sigma.

My expression was one of joy, being a hero, revelling in the attention, it was rational, it was to be expected by the scanners, my excitable storytelling to the office workers correlated with my official narrative.

My enjoyment and euphoria was now detected by the scanners yet I was happy to have deceived the system, thwarting Blue, relief from not being caught fraternising with the errors.

I was safe, I was untouchable, I would soon have a double merit awarded in just one month when most Beta Ministry sigma never received a single merit their entire careers.

I was on my way to being an Alpha, I knew it, they all knew it, so did Blue who had now decided to back off.

Maybe I would be his boss, Blue possibly reasoned yet he secretly hated me and anything that he perceived usurped him. He despised the lower caste nodes below him and was jealous of any equal Beta node bettering him. Only the higher caste did he respect, he worshiped them; that made him the perfect Beta Ministry sigma, a model node of state Utopia, the perfect employee.

I kept to my expected routines for the rest of the working day, bore the pushing and shoving in the overcrowded tube carriages, then closed the door to my subsided apartment.

I tried to mask my feelings of guilt, letting down the errors by not returning this night but I felt relieved at having a second chance.

I might just continue to be a small insignificant integral part of the state and not rebel.

Normalised Utopia

Why put myself in harm's way in being a subversive it was dangerous therefore irrational. But the residual stochastic term resonated and stirred magnify my intangible animal sprit within. I would honour my agreement with the error nodes and help the unbiased binary.

06: Stochastic routines.

Blue had issued a letter of concern to the Upper Floors, indicating that my expected disposition spectrum had consistently entered into three standard deviations recently.

An Alpha residing on the upper floors received the encrypted message. After reading it but elected to disregard the report, the data was considered white noise; a symptom of my recent exceptional performance and associated stress.

He typed a quick reply message on his computer, "Bayes overall stealth eGraph's confidence interval is deemed acceptable even though exhibiting temporary transgressions into the three standard deviation range."

The message was shared to a centralised database cluster warehouse situated in a grubby industrial estate on the city's border to be processed by the Confidence Interval Server Clusters, known as the Augmenter.

The Alpha kept note of his computer while waiting for final confirmation from the information infrastructure, the Augmenter; for the Alpha's discretionary veto request to be approved.

While waiting the Alpha thought that my performance had been extraordinary, I had produced three standard deviations of positive work by catching Pareidolia. He reasoned, conveniently, even hypocritically, that I had now entered into a negative three standard deviation range which was an acceptable balance in this specific case.

This balance regressed me back to normality, to my personal expected mean.

It was a form of self-augmenting my own behaviour and emotions, subconsciously or maybe it was by the very laws of the statistics and the universal laws itself, a natural regression of things; an Ergodic regression back to the average. An individual, version of the wisdom of crowds' scenario.

The Alpha immediately scrubbed the thought of wisdom of crowds, he looked around for a moment realising that even he was subject to statistical monitoring.

The Alpha knew that the utopian state encouraged the nodes to bob along their expected caste mean, predictably, reliably; their daily actions tainted slightly by a subtle unpredictable random white noise yet acceptable as minor momentary deviations from the expected mean.

But in certain cases there could be exceptions, he concluded.

Just then the Augmenter returned a message; the simple message masked the complicated algorithm codes of countless calculations, auto correlations of related nodes, causations and interrelations, to finally produce a short answer,

"Stealth_eGraph: Bayes_31428_Beta_Minisitry. Monthly_Standard_Deviation_Significant: Null. Invitation_Arcadian: Null."

The Alpha allowed a slight smirk to flash across his face. Soon Bayes would be one of us, he concluded.

This Alpha had saved me from an unnecessary doom. Those slips ups were only for the countless nodes, the statistically insignificant, that inhabited the population regression function crowd. The Alpha only took note of the endogenous nodes' general activity as they scurried to and fro, intermittently, at set times each day; to lunch, or back and forth from work.

Blue's report had confirmed to the Alpha, not of my statistical transgression but of what the Alpha already knew, that of Blue's borderline sociopathic personality. It made perfect sense to expect Blue to be jealous of me in general.

Now with my success, it was all predictable, all reasonable. No; the Alpha were satisfied with the current events, even with my current abnormal routines.

The Alpha also approved of Blue's report. Blue's jealous character trait was to be encouraged, to have the lower caste, especially the caste privy to the state's secrets such as the Beta nodes at the Ministry of Inferences betraying each other, it was good for the Alpha; it kept them divided and us in control, he concluded.

I received a message in my embedded device; I was scheduled to attend a meeting with the Alphas, on the Upper Floors.

I felt anxious, what was it for?

Did they already know about my meeting with the errors or was it because of my rebellious feelings regarding Mrs White's demise. Or was it the incident with Blue?

But these events were all too sudden for them to know?

After making my way to upper floor I sat in the impressive lobby of the Upper Floors, superficially noting the receptionists working away behind the large glamorous reception desk, intermittently an Alpha floated past, quickly yet confidently, too busy with important work to look up.

I had met the odd Alpha once or twice for a fleeting moment during my career but mainly never saw them, only vicariously on monitors. Once, an Alpha had shaken my hand when joining the Ministry but nothing more than that. The Alpha never interacted with the Ministry workers; they were too busy, too aloof.

I had heard that the Upper Floors were luxurious, now I was sitting there, on a large leather couch, engulfed by a shiny marble floor, all the while, the Beta receptionists typed away.

I was filled with anxiety which was heightened in some perverted way by the incessant background music of continual advertisements that ran out, "Jingo Jazz washes clothes brighter!"

I was feeling nauseous with anxiety coupled with the sickening antithesis of the overly cheerful music. The music seemed completely indifferent to my plight. I tried to stay focused, thinking positive emotions.

I had been secretly classified an aware outlier?

Was this how they got rid of aware outliers, in my position? Would I be overpowered when entering the Alpha's office, whisked away to some covert concentration camp?

'I do not know,' I let out a conscious thought, masking it behind an expected crescendo of the loud musical finale ending of the Jingo Jazz advertisement.

The scanners would not pick up unexpected emotional activity when there was loud music accompanying an advertisement. It would be regarded as white noise as it was directly related to a temporary sensory overload induced by the music.

I was aware of these facts as I had personally factored out similar emotional data from countess nodes' monthly statistical analysis to determine if they fell outside the confidence interval.

I slipped in, one last, masked thought before the music would stop; I must just sit, focused, feel happy.

I focused on feeling happiness. The scanners' invisible, all pervasive electromagnetic waves continually scanned the ether, monitoring the nodes brains, including mine, determining if their emotions and implied thoughts where statically insignificant.

If they were within the expected emotional confidence interval, the atmosphere of the advertisement, determined the situation to be fitted to the model.

The scanner's contemporaneous analysis registered me as "Happy". It was the expected autocorrelation; of emotions, the situation and the contemporaneous advertisement mood placement; I exhibited a perfect autocorrelation score of two. Durbin Watts would be proud.

The scanners however could not read intentions, or motivations; for my happiness. I drew on a deferred happy emotion, not from my recent success but from avoiding Blue's meddling. I sat there smiling, my anxiety lifted, content in my resignation to whatever fate arose.

'Akinien will see you now,' said an attractive receptionist, peering through a pair of glasses which privately recorded everything she saw and did. I smiled back at her knowing that I too would be recorded by her glasses. I entered the doorway to the Alpha's office as it made a swishing noise whilst opening automatically.

Around the table, sat three Alpha nodes, without moving or showing emotion.

'Take a seat,' said one of them, without making eye contact.

They all stared ahead, into the void without showing the courtesy of looking at me.

They were too aloof to look at a Beta Node, their civil servant; a glorified sigma node.

They were dressed impeccably, not a hair out of place.

The first Alpha began the conversation without introduction, just speaking in a formal monotonous tone, 'Mr Bayes, you have done a great service for the Ministry by apprehending the outlier, Pareidolia.'

'A thorn in our side,' said the second Alpha.

'An intolerable, viral, inefficient catalyst, of the state,' said the third Alpha.

'We therefore commend you, for your service,' said the first Alpha.

'Thank you,' they all resounded simultaneously.

Then all chose to look up making eye contact for a split second and nodding their heads in recognition. It was a moment of equality, of acceptance by the Alpha, for a split second; they almost seemed, like regular nodes.

'It also has come to our attention that you were recently in an altercation in a public park,' said the first Alpha ominously.

I felt a sudden rush of anxiety, had they found out about the errors, the medicine?

'We wish you a speedy recovery,' said the second Alpha.

'We also would like to inform you, that you have been placed on a pre-promotional observation period of three months, after this if you are seen as fit, you will be awarded the title of Alpha,' said the third Alpha.

'Do you have any objections?' asked the first Alpha.

A genuine smile broadened on my face, I had been conditioned my entire life to covet promotions. Not just any promotion; from Delta to Gamma. No rather a Beta node to an Alpha; an Alpha at the Ministry of Inferences, no less.

There was no need trying to muster an expected, pseudo emotion; I was genuinely proud and simultaneously relived. I was not going to be eliminated in a secret concentration camp but rather promoted into a position of near infallibility.

'No objection, sir,' I said relieved.

The Alpha made eye contact again, to witness the realisation on my face; that soon I too would be on their level, free of the sigma classification stigma. Soon I would be elevated, like them.

It must be their little joke, no node, could ever object to an Alpha or to the system. Who would object to a promotion into the Alpha's world, to escape the drudgery of the sigma's normality, the burden of their working caste?

'Good then, I am sure we will see you on the Upper Floors, in the near future,' concluded the second Alpha.

'What name have you chosen?' inquired the third Alpha.

Without hesitating I blurted out eagerly, 'Auger.'

They all smiled at each other.

'That is a good name for you indeed,' said the first, appreciating the relevance of the name relative to my role.

'Yes,' said the second.

'A well thought-out name; for a statistical node. I mean citizen,' said the third Alpha correcting himself, trying to hide his hidden bias towards the lower caste nodes; the non-Alpha, exogenous contributing nodes.

The first Alpha wanted to distance himself from the embarrassment of the slip, by bringing to a close the meeting, he concluded, 'Well Mr Bayes please do not let us keep you any longer from your important work.'

'Helping to protect out utopian state,' said the second Alpha.

'We all owe you a debt of gratitude,' said the third Alpha.

It was all patronizing pseudo praise, I knew it; they knew it. It did not matter. I was safe, soon to be promoted, I thought while still exhibiting a genuine happy emotion.

They all stood up immediately and simultaneously presenting their hands to shake my mine, they then sat down with the same rigid regiment as they had stood up with, immediately returning to their seats staring off into the void as if I was no longer there.

I turned around for the door, eager to leave the embarrassing void as the door swished close behind; I was glad to leave them. That moment of embarrassing void had shown more about their empty character and inhumanity than all the words they had carefully chosen.

The elevator made it back to the Middle Floor; I no longer knew how to feel inside but elected to support an enigmatic smirk etched on upon face, to appease the scanners and create a lagged expected prior emotion which the soon to be informed Ministry Beta sigma would take note of.

I made my way to my desk, taking a moment to reflect on the day and week's events whilst conscious of the emotional thought scanners.

I sat there calmly creating a busy attentive facade while endless data streamed past my screen, soaking my eyes in a luminous ether of information, soaking into my brain, data and words transformed automatically into ideas and thoughts in my conscious, the process, a result conditioned by years of education.

Lines, curves, graphs, nodes, information, data; relations, causations, autocorrelations, degrees of freedom, sample sets, estimates, P-values, stochastic errors. Downloaded, uploaded, analysed, dissected, logs and lags added, weighted, augmented. Then repackaged to different departments; to be added to the daily confidence interval eGraphs. Unfortunately this would result in doomed nodes receiving invitation letters but it was for the Efficiency of the utopian state, the good of the whole, I concluded. Half-awake as the data slid past my eyes effortlessly, seamlessly, continually; my mind started to switch off.

I started to regress back, to officially, the most important moment of my life. I began to think about the Alpha I just met; they seemed distant, subtle, supremacist, detached, yet when they made eye contact.

I perceived there was a small glimmer of normality, perhaps they too had been young unbiased once? Perhaps they too had seen the world through innocent, normal, eyes? Perhaps there was still a small glimmer of that, in them?

A tiny spark, a tiny connection between me and them but then there was nothing; they were more incarnate of the system than of the nodes. Just more subtle, more intelligent, more game theory aware, nodes; always taking the most politically shrewd option, to insure their perpetual elite existence, for them and their progeny, I reflected.

Even though they were arrogant, supremacist; at heart, they seemed to be just simple nodes? Perhaps I could not judge them. Most nodes would evolve into their mind-set or worse when given the option to inherit their power or nurtured into deluded perceptions of an equitable society; such as entitlement and superiority.

I considered this whilst trying to keep a happy emotional disposition and attentive work posture to placate the scanners and ministry Beta sigma.

As the data continued to stream past my partial dreaming eyes. My consciousness could not fully determine what world I was inhabiting? The office world or the world of the two dimensional screen. The screen; enticing me in, further and further, with each new bit of data and the anticipation of the next bit of unrealised future data.

Or was I in my own private world of thinking to myself. Or was I in the world of the near past, reliving the Alpha meeting, whilst still in my own current private thought filled mind. Maybe I was in all of them but not completely in anyone world, either; a partial relative consciousness.

Suddenly an epiphany struck with a subtle undetectable violence that simultaneously sent a sudden shudder that reverberated down my spine, momentarily, my stomach clamped up; soon I would be in their world, permanently, in the world of the soulless, the unreal, the false. I would be inheriting their power but what would become of me?

How would I act after even a few years of living that life? What would my soul be alike if it was not tainted already with the countless confidence intervals quotas inferences and amendments?

Now I realised that maybe the Alpha were not joking when they asked if I had any objections to being promoted. Maybe an Alphaship was not the golden ticket to happiness and contentment, far from it. Perhaps it was a burden, becoming an Alpha, I concluded whilst coming out of my partial dream state?

I considered; continuous change affects even contented nodes and situations; inevitably, change brings a less contentedness, a new existence for the current contentedness. Maybe the state tried to protect against sudden dramatic change and standard deviations, to protect against future discontent; future inefficiencies?

Sitting back in my chair, I stared up to the blank ceiling. Soon I will be an Alpha, unless Blue can interfere but it was too late for even him to corrupt my expected promotion.

No ministry, civil service, Beta node had ever failed the three month promotion probation period, I reflected.

It was strange that there was always some node or creature trying to undermine some similar creature; it seemed to be one of the great laws of the universes.

I am a hero amongst the endogenous Beta sigma nodes of the Ministry of Inferences; currently. I am held in such a high regard that even the Alpha stoop down from their lofty perches to make eye contact momentarily with me.

I concluded that catching Pareidolia was my inheritance of the elite world; damning another node's life was profitable. Was that not what I do every working day when amending the confidence interval quotas?

I caught an eco-bus from Mallet Street whilst sitting looking out of the window. I became aware of a group of unbiased, binaries traveling from school, sitting behind me.

One unbiased binary asked the others about their eGraphs.

'You should make sure your eGraphs are always a healthy, a rich bright shade of colour and not an insipid shadeless opaque colour; like the shadeless,' she smiled as the others giggled.

'Not like the shadeless,' said another unbiased binary. 'No!' they replied shouted hysterically.

They all agreed that being shadeless; deviating from the official quota mean was the ultimate social embarrassment for any prepubescent school unbiased.

They were conditioned to find it embarrassing and amusing at the thought of deviating from the social mean that the great utopian state had set as the benchmark.

They all strived to be part of the, "In crowd" as all unbiased have since the beginning of time but state Utopia had cleverly took advantage of the fiery, dogmatic, loyalty of the immature, ignorant, newly self-conscious teenagers by moulding their thoughts and identities with trendy celebrity ridden propaganda of how to dress, of what to drink, of what to eat, of how to act.

William J Fraser

The eGraph was the physical emanation of that peer pressure to be seen conforming, fitting in with the, "In crowd", not sticking out, like the shadeless losers.

The embarrassed, unbiased, transgressors of the eGraph would run home after school not sticking around to share their daily eGraph diagrams with the other unbiased.

The unbiased starving themselves, going to extreme self-routine modifications, sleeping early, eating only the expected food ingredients, overly dressing; all desperately trying to increase their eGraph colours.

So that next week they would have a glowing resplendent rich colourful eGraph that would make a cathedral proud to use their eGraph as a stained glass window.

Sometimes the state would modify the unbiased's eGraph knowing how susceptible and malleable they were to peer pressure.

The Ministry of Inferences noted the unbiased's fasting and acceptance of extreme routines as they desperately tried to increase their eGraphs' colours. The utopian state wanted malleable, superficial, dumbed down caste specific endogenous sigma nodes who would suffer; going to great extremes to conform to the utopian state's norm. These unbiased were favoured within the Ministry roles that state Utopia advertised.

The unbiased were conditioned to think it was shameful and amusing when other unbiased fell outside the boundaries of their eGraph which they were encouraged to openly accept.

If an unbiased's little surreal shaded graph mascot became shadeless it only meant they would have more tax to pay or have less credits to spend.

Not like the hidden covert confidence interval where each node was bound to adhere to without even being aware of it.

The hidden confidence interval was deadly serious where outliers would be subtly terminated. In both cases even if the nodes all tried hard to maintain an obedient compliant lifestyle; statistically some would fall outside of the acceptable region and would be publically shamed or subtly terminated.

I turned back around and stared out of the window again whilst remembering Blues' lecture to the recruit yesterday.

It's all about the BLUE; the best linear unbiased estimator of the population regression function. All castes', sectors' and industries', sample regression functions should try to replicate the great population regression function.

For the harmony of the Economic Efficiency Act, the great regulatory financial ether, the invisible hand that guides the covariance of different sectors.

To cohabit, cointegrate, amended and interconnection between the dynamic factors and variables in harmony, augmented by the augmenter, to keep the regulation and quotas intact, to the keep the efficiency of the sectors running smoothly with no significant autocorrelated white noise from the residual terms.

All variables lagged, to remove trends, autocorrelations removed with lags to achieve the great Durbin Watts value of two.

An artificially contrived harmony existing by constantly trimming the outliers of the inefficient, uncorrelated, non-cointegrated. The endogenous nodes approved, the exogenous and outlier removed continually until there is no unpredictably in the economy the net present value of everything is zero, no nasty turbulences, just seamless,

196

continuous, predictable profits for the state to feed off.

Workers even get in trouble for achieving too good a positive result; it breaks out of their expected mean result and interferes with the NPV and IRR of the Economic Efficiency Act's aggregate demand and the general cash flow of the state.

The bus passed into the Economic Efficiency Ambit of the Delta_Epsilon_Sample_Space; inhabited predominantly by Delta and Epsilon endogenous sigma nodes; the working class.

They had all been systematically moulded into continual financial vulnerability by the Socioeconometric engineering of the relentless statistical quotas, conditional social associations and its subtle correlations.

It created the illusion that their community was the result of an organic, biological self-selection yet their genetic and social destiny was the direct result of strict econometric models which presented to them a constrained maze of restrictive financial and social options to exist and breed within.

The Socioeconometric engineering, a contrived invisible hand developed to augment and guide the different sigma castes into genetic and social stagnation, segmented and dived, complacent, accepting sigma. Evolving towards an ergodic trend it's a mean, a perpetual state of mediocrity.

They were relegated to a permanent position of underachievement; destined to a life minimum wage, menial employment on temporary contracts with limited hours per week, in order to merely service their continual liability streams of endless bills and the expenses of life. Also they may carry out their noble, hardwired natural core process, that of raising a family.

These heroes, to their families, underappreciated by their neighbourhood and mere serfs to the great cash flow river, that cyclically, benevolently, floods the river banks of the consumer sigma homes, its metaphorical alluvial soil, the goods and services of sophisticated state Utopia.

Yet the state demanded the continual sweat of the endogenous sigma who were virtual serfs of the state who obediently toiled in the preverbal fields of expected statistical routines and work output.

So they may service their families liability streams which systematically drained back into the great cash flow river. The rivers binary liquids, state Utopia's economic output GDP and its correlated Beta market price composites which perpetually intermingled together like the hot and cold currents of a great ocean.

The Delta and Epsilon nodes reside near the border of the $-a/2$ lower tail confidence interval of -1.96 standard deviation was the neighbourhood at the lowest level of normalised utility.

They subsisted within the most polluted neighbourhoods where they perpetually toil with their mundane tasks relative to the higher ranked sigma nodes who reside past the fixed mean, nearer the $+a/2$ confidence interval boundary upper tail.

Their concentrated neighbourhoods contained significantly higher than average air pollution, containing countless heavy metals which pervades their neighbourhoods and lungs, pollutants working its way deep into their vital tissues.

Passing on their accrued toxins into their unbiased's bodies. Engineered prior locations were the lagged distributed variables that autoregressed a current node towards a mediocre biological mean.

Every aspect of society was geared towards complete economic efficiency and sigma caste categorisation irrespective of societal costs or negative externalities.

I considered this as my momentary partial reflection appearing intermittently like an apparition on the wet drizzly window while the partially obscured shifting insipid sunlight appeared momentary whilst the bus moved onwards.

07: Spurious results.

I tentatively opened the door of the grand foyer of the Ministry of Apothecary and handed the Gamma node my pseudo elixir prescription form.

He examined it with a reserved curiosity then he looked up at me and smiled. An expected expression by the utopian state statistical scanners yet the smile was more an enigmatic intangible expression as if he seemed to know of my bluff.

For once in my life I was cheating, handing an altered slip, one that was false but for a good cause, a moral crusade yet a spurious data variable.

It was the chain reaction of the stochastic routines that I have exhibited since I left the park after my unexpected interactions with the barely tangible error nodes.

'Even Beta nodes of the Ministry of Inferences,' he said.

I tried to maintain my Bluff and protect myself from embarrassment 'what do you mean?' I replied.

He looked at me knowingly, 'Anyway there you go,' he said as he pointed the scanner away saying, 'We all spin the rules sometimes.'

'You can turn off the scanner?' I said.

'We have to clean it,' he said smiling.

'I thought they could never be switched off?' I replied shocked.

'Well senior Gamma management are allowed to service the scanners if need be. A malfunctioning scanner could possibly present a fire hazard,' he said winking.

'You know I am a Beta civil servant,' I replied ominously.

'You won't say anything, not with your special prescription,' the Gamma said winking.

I knew well of the endogenous sigma Delta nodes but these Gamma nodes were a bit of a mystery to me; they were not as high as a civil servant Beta node or the highest ranking caste of the Alpha node.

Yet they were much higher and elusive than the common Delta and Epsilon endogenous sigma nodes that made up the majority of the 1.96

standard deviation of the endogenous sigma caste specific confidence interval of the utopian society.

These Gamma node professionals considered themselves upper middle class even when the middle class system had been replaced with the great utopian sigma caste system yet these Gamma seemed so confident within themselves not necessarily within their confidence interval quota compliance such as with the simple common Delta and Epsilon nodes.

It seems now I have been suspected of corruption; all fear and respect of my slightly superior Beta node position was lost.

'We all cheat,' he said pausing, 'and lie,' which he said with a smile, confident his facial recognition expectations did not fall outside the confidence interval as the scanner was pointed away from its prying observance.

I tried to rebut the comment but his gaze, stared into my eyes which glimmered with a newly found naivety; created by this situation where I was vulnerable due to the wilful dishonest transgression of the rules all to help the error node, unbiased binary.

'It's for a good cause,' I replied honestly yet tacitly admitting my guilt and trying to rationalise a defence.

The Gamma apothecary looked at me and said, 'I am sure. You don't look the type, too honest, too rigid; too submissive to the system.'

Another Gamma node, the apothecary's assistant appeared behind the counter, 'Switch this will you,' he then looked apprehensive at my presence.

'Oh don't worry about him, he's one of us now,' said the biased Gamma apothecary, almost laughing; enjoying my newfound position as a fellow corrupt node.

'Switch this to the P-value of six, so it passes,' said the apothecary's assistant.

'You nodes cheat and lie,' I said shocked at the blatant level of corruption.

'Well don't be so hypocritical.'

'I am sorry,' I replied, offended that a Beta caste node such as myself, would be accused of dishonesty.

I always thought of the endogenous Sigma nodes as simple, harmless common, cannon fodder, and stable yet now I see the endogenous sigma were aware of the statistical conformity yet they still managed to cheat and change the realized data, manipulate the results.

They still manage to play the system, adapting to the conformity, the constrained statistical social matrix they find themselves in.

'Well yes we have to adapt and evolve to find the highest payoff. But the payoff that is sometimes manipulated by our corrupt, spurious, realized routines and data.

'It is the nature of the nodes, our animal spirit we all know a little part of the system, our neighbourhood, our expected process perhaps even better than the utopian state and we merely tweak the system, it is our nature to do so,' said the apothecary's assistant.

'We can alter the model, through lies and corruption, we can minus any variable with our corruption,' the Apothecary said smiling.

'We are a part of the utopian state yet we still hide our indomitable node's will and intrinsic intelligence,' concluded the Apothecary's assistant.

I was shocked, I realized then that I had been living in my own bubble of the Beta node, the civil servant sigma bubble was only one sections of this society and the endogenous sigma was only a sample function on the entirety of the cumulative perceptions and whims of the node population of state utopia.

The endogenous nodes were far more intelligent and hardy than I had given them credit for whilst I and most Beta node civil servants sat in our lofty perches on the middle floors of the Ministry of Inferences.

The lower sigma cast endogenous nodes were just as intelligent, just as capable. We sat detached in our biased perceptions of the conveniently apparent inferior endogenous nodes.

This gave us justification to infer and amend the confidence interval data yet they were as intelligent as us.

In fact perhaps even more so as they were in a more restrictive less opportune environment within the endogenous sigma societal matrix of statistical conformity and quotas.

Yet they managed to find loopholes within the system without the education of how the system works within their microcosm of their pigeonholed societal positions and roles yet they still managed to outfox and hoodwink the system with all its statistical technology whilst the utopian state merely plodded on indifferently.

Ironically the most Sigma nodes who worked hard paid their taxes somehow fell outside of the confines of the confidence interval and were sent to Arcadia whilst these corrupt Gamma nodes and probably Delta nodes too, managed to circumvent the system; even when they are not privy to all the intricacies of the statistical algorithms of the utopian state.

It is amazing, it seems to be an epiphany to me, I felt less guilty of the apparent harmless nodes. Ignorant endogenous Sigma nodes constantly outside of the 1.96 standard deviations were sent to their doom on the Arcadian express but then my guilt returned.

Mrs White and the countless decent innocent endogenous nodes that perhaps never lied; never produced spurious results. They were still rendered redundant; no murdered, by the statistical genocide cull, every month.

But the utopian state is no different to these corrupt yet ingenious endogenous sigma as the Ministry of Inferences' Beta nodes amended their data every day to fit the expected contemporaneous targets. Is that not the same as the corrupt nodes producing spurious data result?

The state sets the great population regression function, the sum of the beta variables for the entire node population, and their cumulative total socioeconomic contribution.

The great unrestricted model is written; yet the great Utopian state cheats; manipulating factorizing and augmenting the confidence interval statistical quota data with distributed lagged variables, weighting, logged and compared against restricted models but as the monthly model is manipulated.

So are the variables; the animate nodes, their lives and existence cheated and moulded around the great monthly population regression function data which is alerted conveniently by the Ministry of Inferences.

Normalised Utopia

Whatever happens to the great regression function equation happens to a certain subsection of the population.

If a variable's data is alerted augmented with a distribution lagged variable then certain communities lives are changed to great extent; a negative autoregressive weighting will affect a certain aspect of their lives in the future.

If a certain viable is held constant to create a dummy variable or a restricted model; then the nodes maybe be rendered redundant and invited to Arcadia. So the utopian state cheats and lies about the data to fit the individual and cumulative nodes weighted average around the Utopian state's great Beta model.

This is how the economic efficiency policy is implemented with the stroke of a pen or with a few binary digits moved around in an unlimited sea of binary digits. This is how even the great utopian state cheats.

With the consent of the Alpha and overseen officially by the augmenter; a node can be slightly elevated or whipped out in an instant for no particular reason other than to affect the economic efficiency of a particular variable within a particular economic sector; to smooth out a derivative of an associated variable.

The node may even be far removed from the targeted economic sector yet the unfortunate node will suffer the upheaval of being manipulated into a different set of circumstances.

Is that not the same as the corrupt nodes producing spurious data results?

I took the elixir medicine whilst the two corrupt Gamma nodes laughed at my shock and hypocrisy. The biased Gamma apothecary turned back on the scanner and carried on working.

I now had the elixir medicine; it was corruption, it was a lie against the great utopian state. A wrongdoing against statistical efficiency, against the will of the state; of its statistical expectations, of the nodes, of me, the high ranking Beta node which the state holds in high regard.

So high that it wants to promote me into its Alphaship. What a credit I am to the state, to my forgotten family. What a righteous node.

No, none of that.

Normalised Utopia

What a controlled, submissive node I am. Who obediently, weakly accepts the utopian state's will and conditioned etiquette as somehow the logarithmic base of morality as if the great Beta trend line of state Utopia was the primary mathematical rule as to what the epitome of truth and righteousness was.

Being predictable relative to the utopian state's statistical routines, quotas and general etiquette; that does not necessarily make you good, righteous or respectable.

Adhering to the utopian state's contemporaneous mean, the mean of apathy; of no individual will.

It merely makes you devoid of a will; utterly predictable, non-stochastic; perhaps mean-less.

The very result that I walk with this corrupt, spurious, elixir medicine in my pocket even though I follow the pedestrian crossing etiquette, follow all the node's rules whilst commuting home, the very fact I have a corrupt, spurious, non-animate node variable medicine in my pocket means my routines and intentions are stochastic. I am exhibiting stochastic routines.

I am wilfully navigating into the spurious ether of lies and deceit yet I already am within its statistical ether of my limited perception bubble of the statistical rigid ideological subtle fanaticism of the Beta nodes of the Ministry of Inferences.

We judge and expect all the nodes to be as fanatical as us that they all be obedient, loyal, honest, rational and efficient to the maximum yet they lie and cheat to satisfy their selfish needs.

Yet it makes sense, they are organisms that make decisions based on payoffs as they are conditional set by the utopian state yet it is in their nature, in their very genes, within the very fabric of the universe. For the organism to strategize; to take the highest payoff even if it must by cheating or tweaking the system to its will.

The marginal technical rate of substitution; substituting truth with lies but the truth is a lie. Merely an official will, an official expectation of set quotas and etiquette perhaps there is no truth in society no right or wrong merely obedience to will; our will or the state's will.

My thoughts have become corrupt with this first step into the other dimension of the unreleased possibilities of deviation from the mean, no longer cointegrated with the stationary, non-integrated path trend lines of the state's expected dimension of non-organic direction.

I was now in a position where there were countless options of lies and deceit as long as I managed to manipulate the cumulative current expected actions and routines.

Yet it was not my nature; I was good, I was righteous but relative to what?

In this godless society what was right and what was wrong?

Most probably merely obedience to and acceptance of; the current confidence interval quotas.

Theoretically workers could not shirk with complete sentient monitoring there was no possibility of shirking as the confidence interval was their sole incentive coupled with complete monitoring compelled them to work efficiently with no shirking.

There was no unemployment in the utopian state which could lead to possible shirking. There was no chance for the nodes to shirk. The nodes could only work to their expected values set by the statistical quotas of the economic efficiency utopian state.

Yet the nodes, in particularly the Gamma, lie and cheat all the time. I was shocked; I thought the little nodes were so innocent, so hard done by relative to the Utopian state and the Ministry of Inferences but up close the nodes were clever, cunning, resourceful, adaptive and wilful.

Too tweak the system; to hack the odds against them, they manage to balance the books, to cook the books, barter and trade on the black market.

Trade by playing up each other, each side, bend the status quo by having hidden false cooperative dominant strategy by having secret agreements by having consumption yet conforming.

They consume mixed products, consume by using complementary and substitutes by taking advantage of the sticky price variables that the state allows for.

Nodes are allowed to amend their positions relative to a confidence interval or quota shift the nodes are allowed as certain leeway as with most market prices there is a sticky price or overshooting of the trend lines but eventually it settles down at the correct price or position.

Yet the nodes know this and all it takes is one clever node to spread the information which they follow deviating from the strict statistical quotas, these seemingly hard done nodes yet aware to certain extremes of the crooked arbitrage that they live momentary within; the sticky prices changes that they trade and consume commodities even though they had reached their limits of consumption quotas.

They learn to blend in, to lie, to be strategic, to remain hidden, to just follow the patterns, the prerequisites yet within that lays another universe, another world; a world of lies and deception.

The state knows of this situation, laying at certain extremes, they know of traders who follow technical analysis who always change their trades at certain trend line events, such as with the fallacious yet fabled Fibonacci ratios.

The state knew the way they thought but allowed it as within its society. It knew the nodes were strategic players, assuming the nodes to always be rational and to always be taking the highest payoff.

Therefore it was rational to expect them to cheat; cheating produced the highest individual payoff not necessarily the highest expected or averaged payoff. Spurious cheating routines and bogus variables were still added into the great Beta equation and averaged into a pseudo harmonious normalised summation.

The nodes lived in and around the payoffs; in and around the limits yet the utopian state allowed this to happen. It was too much work to control every nuance; it would be statistically inefficient to go that deep.

As long as the masses, the population or the significant sample set analysed, in each variable category, in each sector; conformed and produced a cumulative statistical obedience.

The utopian state would turn a blind eye as long as each node at the end of the month had their eGraph colours in the rich beautiful colourful centre and not in the shadeless border then they would be considered to be statically significant; no invitation to Arcadia would be sent.

I left the Ministry of Apothecary trying not to look too guilty as I held the medicine bottle firmly in my pocket. I had acquired this bottled elixir with the pseudo prescription with the altruistic help from the dishonest Gamma nodes of the Ministers of Apothecary who perhaps were more purveyor and alchemists of spurious data than medicine; the endogenous sigma nodes' individual spurious data was the bitter medicine that the utopian state despised so much.

I hurried on through the crowds of intermittent nodes who indifferently jostled and prodded through the cloudy drizzle soaked day along the bland grey streets and towards a random bus stop.

Strategically avoiding my direct route home; via the expected tube train as my guilty intentions were incarnate in my now stochastic spurious actions and routines.

Through the random trickles of raindrops and running rainwater through the blurred steamed up Perspex bus shelter I saw what looked like a biased looking Delta node approaching.

As he came into full view he stopped as if sensing a sentient being nearby observing him showing interest in me, observing him from behind. A collection of shapes and shades merging from behind the chaotic drizzle saturated dynamic microscopic chaotic world of the Perspex window plane of existence.

He began preaching nearby in the alleyway, his wild bushy hair, dirty, dishevelled appearance resembled an error node. He ranted to himself but also to any passing nodes nearby; who might hear.

'Everything in the world is owned; every bit of land, every monopod vehicle, every building, every tree; all owned by the utopian state, or a council, or a corporation or a just a node!

'If homeless, a node cannot just sleep anywhere, in a park; it's owned. A hungry node cannot just pick an apple off a random tree; every apple, every fruit, every tree, is owned!

'If there were just one tree in the world that was not owned, then there would be arbitrage, the tree would instantly be claimed, by some opportunistic node or greedy corporation!

'If a node loses their wealth in this world, they will starve or be arrested for vagrancy!

'Yet economic textbooks feed students their ideas; take the consumption, income graph. It shows that even when income becomes zero, consumption remains marginally positive!

'How can consumption remain positive, it must be a miracle? In this cold, ruthless, rational, economically efficient system compounded with a statistical dictatorship!

'Positive consumption cannot be accounted for!

'Against all odds, consumption is always marginally positive "a" on the y axis, never zero, no matter what value income is set to. Even without credits, nodes still have some food, some shelter. How is that possible?

'The state's rational thinking; its efficient economic society imprisons their minds set, setting them into a fixed caste!

'Nodes kept on a perpetual treadmill of expenses and taxes. Therefore the nodes, citizens, whatever you want to call them. They should starve, without an income but they do not!

'Wild animals are free and hiding throughout the wilderness, the countless diverse plants and insignificant insects, all inhabiting their wonderful natural world. They do not starve; they all have food and shelter yet they have no plans, no credit and no division of labour!' shouted the baised preacher.

'How does this occur?' the preacher paused then bellowed, 'how?'

'How can the system not stop this, this inefficiency that robs the Alpha of some marginal returns? How should an unfortunate node eat if his credit and income is zero?

'The impoverished, inefficient node is eating up resources that should be going to the state's elite, the Alpha!

'How can this happen, what force can vanquish the system every time no matter how determined the state's actuaries and economists try to stamp it out?"

'It is God!

'God who puts food into each and every creature's digestive systems, including us; each day. If not, we would have all surely perished by now. We have all transgressed the states quotas and laws!

'Altruism is the true currency. It is given for free with no debt attached, no counter payment expected; it is God's currency!

'Altruism to share, help, console, contribute, freely with no obligation, for the very sake of contribution, momentary, modestly to the greater good!

'A small fleeting intention or act, that is beautiful, perfect and yet simplistic!

'The great act of helping your fellow node is an act of goodness that falls outside the confidence interval of expected routines, actions and thoughts, falling outside the norm, the choices, decisions, expectations of the regimented workforce!

'To go outside the usual routines, to extend the hand of friendship, charity, kindness, understanding, to where there is no rational benefit to you but to help, to add to the intangible spirituality of the good ether, the good sprit!

'No, if God has a currency it surely would be the small unnoticed tokens of altruism that are passed between nodes unpredictably, unexpectedly, sporadically appearing for no logical or rational reason, a fleeting emanation of the good ether, incarnate in the actions and intentions of an arbitrary contemporaneous benevolent node, momentarily adding infinitesimally, relative the greater good but in each relative situation, the act of altruism; its core being love, goodness!

'It blinds the surrounding situation with a resplendence that is edged onto the moment of the time, recorded forever in that moment of space time!

Altruism, a derivative of love; unconditional, beautiful, irrational and unpredictable: incomprehensible to the state and the Alpha nodes; altruism!' concluded the biased preacher.

I pretended to not be listening or paying attention like the countless passers-by, too busy following our immediate trivial objectives of the day following the highest time constrained payoff.

Yet as I stood there waiting for the electric bus to arrive I was listening to every word this biased node said. I liked what I heard; the preacher must have been an academic lecturer or an economist in the past.

His rhetoric against the statistical totalitarianism of the Utopian state was nothing new yet his mentioning of God was.

His days were numbered; he would be arrested one day and sent to Arcadia.

It was unfair what had happened to this once proud state I considered as I masked my emotions and facial expressions. I respected the baised preacher's rhetoric, it all made sense.

Yet I remained statuesque showing no unexpected emotion or implied acceptance of what the preachers was saying.

Neither were the other passenger nodes that waited for their buses as they stood expressionless, who genuinely seemed to show no acknowledgement or empathy for this biased preacher who probably seemed to them as exogenous, mad yet perhaps he was not? Perhaps he was the sanest node here at the bus stop I considered. I wondered who else secretly agreed with him.

Suddenly an electric police van arrived, racing from the centre of Primary_Sample_Space; with two normalised police nodes jumping out to question the biased preacher.

The baised preacher, to his credit, never faltered in his conviction whist explaining his religious beliefs and criticism of the Utopian state to the two normalised police nodes as they asked him countless patronising emotionless questions tone. Eventually, inevitably, they loaded him into the back of the police van and drove off.

I had found the errors nodes once again. I noticed them momentarily, a fleeting glimpse as they stochastically dispersed through the green ethereal border of the hedge row, the peripheral mesh of the endogenous orderly, constrained state.

No endogenous sigma would randomly force themselves through a hedge row; they would consistently follow the pavement periphery of the hedge row until they found an opening, and then make a rational choice as to enter the park.

The error nodes behaved differently as they had unrestricted choices; they were no longer subject to any of the state's endogenous sigma statistical regulations.

The state ignored these convenient non-endogenous contributing stochastic variables who conveniently exhibited the crime of persistent standard deviation from the linear regression function, a form of confidence interval crime yet they were not redundant nodes as they never were endogenous nodes to begin with. Or at least the state categorised them as such as all nodes being as endogenous.

An infinitesimal undetectable smirk formed on the corner of my mouth then grew. I must be careful of the cameras on the bus, thought scanners and even the nodes own embedded entertainment cameras I noted as I controlled my emotions and body language as I hid my admiration of these error nodes.

I speculated, the last errors figure passing through the hedge row must be Mu. His psyche was too large, his complexion too dark, for an error node. Not many errors fitted that description, most were slightly built due to malnutrition, all had pale complexions.

I had found them. Now I could now repay them, with the hard to purchase antibiotic that no errors or redundant nodes could ever purchase, after being wiped from the system. It was the perfect gift.

I jumped up out of my seat excitably, hurriedly pushing through a pool of standing nodes, who momentarily, unusually, made eye contact, to show their irritation.

I shouted to the unapproachable driver thorough the Perspex window to stop the bus as he was about to disengage the heavy clutch and drive off. The driver seeing the determination on my face and decided to break the strict protocols of passenger boarding and opened the entrance door.

I jumped off into the freezing drizzle, immediately feeling the chill of the evening air.

I ran past some waiting passenger nodes standing near the bus stop, they stole perplexed glances at me as I ran past, then starting to desperately scramble through the adjacent hedge row gap of broken and buckled twigs, made by the errors moments before.

As I scrambled though the gap my jacket, exposed hands and face was scratched.

I ran through the dark brooding park area in the general vicinity of where I thought I could catch a glimpse of them. I also felt that I could feel them as the tiny latent stochastic energy that resonated within from our past meeting seemed to grow and resonate within me with each new approaching step.

Then finally I caught a glimpse of them, standing still within the shadows of the dark bushes.

I ran up to the error nodes waving like an excitable unbiased. Perhaps the stochastic intangible energy that emanated from their presence relative to an endogenous non error nodes as myself strangely made my mind feel less rigid, less non-stochastic, less fixed within the given known mean of the expected results of the economic efficiency act monthly statistical quotas.

'I am back, I have the medicine,' I said, proud of the fact that I had never betrayed or discriminated against these unimportant marginalised yet integral members of the linear regression model of the state's utopian society.

'You are late?' replied Mu cynically whilst brooding.

'Too late,' repeated an arbitrary intangible error node.

'Only a day late, I had trouble getting free time,' I replied.

'Free time,' inquired, a different intangible error node?

'She died,' added Mu looking up at me, glaring.

I looked down, my enthusiasm of the novelty of drawing a stochastic intangible energy from my past and present interaction with these random fleeting nodes, immediately dissipated.

'It was my fault I should have been more punctual,' I apologised.

I considered trying to make more excuses about unforeseen events stopping me from returning on time but they seemed to sense the truth and I felt hesitant to test them. I was tired of lies and bias.

I respected their truthful yet random intangible qualities. They were right, their intangible qualities were truthful, they could see through my lies I was false I had said I was not punctual but I had stalled until today, if I was completely sincere I should have returned sooner.

'At least he attempted to return that's indicative of some loyalty,' replied a binary error node upon witnessing my shame.

'Perhaps we could use his sigma position again in the future.'

'The unbiased binary would have died anyway even if she had gotten the medicine,' said another arbitrary error node cynically.

The burly tattooed bearded Mu expression looked sad as he stared off into the distance. Under his rugged intangible exterior he seemed to have had an affinity for the now expired unbiased binary.

228

Anova approached, his expression seemed intimidating, his appearance more so; covered in grime, hiding by a thick beard and thicker trench coat which substituted as a bed and home.

At first he said nothing as I stood in shock of the unbiased binary's passing.

How would they judge me? Perhaps there were just savages? Maybe I should not have tried to help them and just forgot them like the rest of society, I considered.

I noticed that these intangible, realised, residual terms that were no longer error nodes now, once they were observed and measured, they never talked about anything associated with the endogenous sigma.

They only talked about their intangible fleeting error contributions, their alternate contribution, that was categorised and named merely as acceptable residual terms, a hidden, part of the model, unimportant values assigned to the realised, residual terms, the error nodes now incarnate shadows recorded within the official data.

But as to their composite parts, the sum total of the residual term results were not inferred or considered by the endogenous sigma, Ministry of Inference or state Utopia which merely accepted that these stochastic, statistically significant nodes were correlated and accepted by the state.

They resided on the very periphery of the state, part existing and processing their intangible unimportant values and process that the state regresses using the Markov techniques of normalising them to an average of zero. Error correction models contain them as well within their scavenging covariant matrices.

The error nodes mentioned now and again of their contribution to the states great linear regression model but they never mention the endogenous nodes contribution to the model.

Yet the error nodes and the endogenous sigma both contribute separately towards the great linear regression model of state Utopia each side never acknowledging the others contribution only the state Utopia and to a lesser extent the fleeting glance of a Ministry of Inferences as they disregard the residual terms as merely inconvenient R^2 value on the model.

I had been too late, to get the medicine to the unbiased binary; I had hesitated and now the unbiased binary was deceased. Yet I still had the medicine, clasped in my pocket, not seen by the nodes on the tube.

I squeezed the glass bottle hard as if wanting to break it in my hand, I wanted to cut my hand, for the blood to seep out, to punish myself for not getting in time to the little unbiased binary; the error nodes as the state categorised her.

The error nodes probable contribution to the endogenous' output of the model was classified merely as minus whatever the R2 was but not as a distinct variable. Yet they contribute, the vagrants, the errors contributed; nodes who were not classified by a distinct caste or sigma.

I decided to drink the medicine why I did I am not sure perhaps it was some masochistic act, some penance for the little unbiased binary dying or just to drown my sorrows, to numb my feeling or just try to be more confident but it was irrational, it was bizarre, it was not a stochastic predictable, routine or action.

Not even the scanners and statistical algorithms would have predicted me downing the bottle of medicine even if they could have detected it hidden within my clasped hand, deep within my jacket pocket.

The scanners and statistics of the outside world could not detect what I now perceived; a little part of the unbiased binary's spirit still holding on incarnate to this medicine bottle hidden within the last bastion of my personal privacy, my simple plain cloth trouser pocket.

I was acting and thinking irrational maybe it was the stress of years of monitoring, of a latent guilt, of a slow epiphany seeping through into a dull realisation, a slow awakening.

But from some unknown, irrational reason I found myself surreptitiously downing the bottle of medicine, its medicinal contents I did not know or care.

My tightly clasped hand covered the dark brown glass bottle; I doubted that anyone would see as no scanners worked beneath the chaotic melee of the eternal clatter steel carriages.

Slowly but surely I became intoxicated by the unknown medicine, it seeped into my internal organs, gradually working its side effects upon my depressed mind.

I started to feel strange yet not scared as I realised the medicine was soothing me like an alcohol yet predictably making me feel drowsy whilst my perceptions faded into a surreal world.

I noticed the condensation form into patterns of normalised probability, I saw Fibonacci ratios in the faces and bodies of the nodes, I looked at a parked bicycle and saw a simple Riemann hypothesis analogy structure; the seat post the core axis of the bicycle structure where most things were attached to, like the x-axis, "The critical value," of the Riemann hypothesis which contained all the prime numbers, the wheels a spiral, containing the spokes which were the derivatives perhaps as they all attached the wheel at ninety degrees.

I was beginning to see mathematics all around, even probability ratios of approaching nodes, the rate at which they moved, the dominant strategy expected game theory payoffs, the total partial derivative of a connected chain of seated nodes; their body language and positioning, all connected.

My observations were now greatly enhanced by the hallucinogenic properties of the medicine.

As I sat there on the tube I started to retreat into my imaginary complex plane, inches from an adjacent node's chest, reaching into his all-important privacy whilst still seated within the hurtling tube train carriages. But now I felt more myself as seemed to be sucked deeper into my imaginary complex plane

I sat there worrying about Mrs White, the expired unbiased binary error and Apophenia when I noticed the tube was now filled with intermittent nodes; they seemed a little unusually grey as they sat there yet they seemed to be relaxed and enjoying the tube ride.

Other grey silhouettes of nodes got off the tube carriage at the inevitable intermittent tube station stops while other random silhouettes got on and sat down.

I noticed them in the corner of my eye as my thoughts drifted into depression about Mrs White, the recently expired little unbiased binary and Apophenia yet a tidal surge of self-righteousness flooded over me momentarily; I was good, righteous, state Utopia was the guilty party or the

Augmenter that processed the statistical quotas at each moment.

Then I processed a thought in the back of my mind, how could there be so many nodes on this quiet tube service at this time of day?

My face turned a pale shade of white, I wanted to vomit, I wanted to scream, I looked up very slowly then screamed in terror and guilt.

The grey silhouettes on the tube, they were the dead nodes, the expired redundant nodes; the remnant spirits. Yet these expired outliers just sat there ignoring me. What if they knew that I was partly responsible for their demise, for the confidence interval quotas?

I fell from my chair, kneeling in a foetal position; I screamed out with all my might, shouting with sincerity, that I was sorry.

But the grey node spirits just continued to ignore me whilst sitting calmly, waiting for the next tube station, either oblivious to me or their subtle indifference, a tacit, implied form of forgiveness and acceptance; amongst them.

If only they would turn on me, beat and tear me to pieces for my part, then maybe I could forgive myself but they just sit there, calmly ignoring me even when I scream my confession, I deserve to be killed, to be destroyed; like the utopian state, like the Augmenter but they just sit there.

My intoxicated mind raced uncontrollably in its new found uninhibited freedom seeping into and flooding every unused part of my previously thought restricted mind, soaking into the countless dendron's and deep recesses of my mind.

My guilt increased with every involuntary subconscious superficial analysis my mind judged as it processed the grey ethereal nodes hazy outline and possible social background, associated expected personalities, hypothesised just by noting their posture, general positioning and spacing as they gathered standing and sitting on the tube.

As I looked through my tear filled eyes I saw an unbiased grey node silhouette spirit, holding its originator's hand as it looked inquisitively at me.

I began to tear my hair out, my stomach started to wretch. I was begging in a crazed mumbled whimper for forgiveness, for the guilt to leave me.

A grey unbiased stood holding its originator's hand staring inquisitively yet impartially at me as I writhed in a self-imposed torment of guilt and regret.

The tube carriage rocked sideways; suddenly I came out of the imaginary complex plane; too quickly. I was not ready to leave the grey spirit nodes. I had not received forgiveness from them yet.

Where were they going; would they travel endlessly forever upon the tube carriages within some imagery complex number plane? Were they even on this tube carriage within this reality yet unseen, unless perhaps in some intoxicated or meditative state; were they right next to me even now. When I was outside of the complex number plane? I mumbled, 'forgive me,' again as if they could see me from a higher dimensional perspective whilst I could not see them.

I knelt upon the incarnation of the real x-axis of the real tube carriage steel hard floor whilst sweat dripped off me onto the real carriage floor. Two passengers sitting nearby predictably seemed alarmed at what they had just witnessed, a bizarre, extreme statistical event unfolding; of a mad exogenous node screaming whilst in a meditation state which was never seen upon the tightly regulated statistically correlated tube train service.

Other random passenger nodes boarded the tube carriages at the next stop; they embarrassingly squeezed past me whilst I remained knelt upon the cold real rational steel carriage floor the very incarnation of mathematics engineering of the cold rational processes of the industry of the utopian state.

I looked up as the train pulled away at all of the sample collection of confidently obedient self-regulating statistical real nodes sitting upon the tube carriages.

They all seemed like farm animals; sheep. I noticed their skin and flesh whilst they sat there trying to ignore me, receding to their own personal privacy space, their own imagery plane of consciousness perhaps, blocking each other out.

I stared at them, in a morbid curiosity, I noticed their eyes and hair, their upright posture, they seemed like sheep, animals, sitting upright, it seemed mad, it seemed as if the sheep had usurped society and they were now sitting there incarnate. They seemed not to belong there, there seem to be no difference between the sheep, animals and nodes, they have the same eyes, same skin, same organs.

They seemed totally foreign to their plastic, metal environment of the tube carriage, the plastic, metal containment seemed the antithesis of the bacteria ridden, fleshly skin of these what seemed as though farm animals yet they were nodes.

Animal flesh sitting incarnate on inanimate plastic chairs, I struggled to see them as nodes; intelligent game theory playing nodes, for this moment I thought I was going mad, I wanted to fall forwards, even deeper into the ground, to be enveloped by the ground and be no more.

I wanted to vomit as I looked down whilst some fractured aspect of my still sane psyche forced me to breathe deeply as I tried hard to regain my consciousness, my sanity.

I then rationalised that I was having an existential crisis.

Then completely, unpredictably, out of all statically conformity predicted routines; a node came out of his imaginary number privacy plane. He looked down at me asking if I was alright, he helped me to my seat showing concern.

I managed to remain calm and thanked the node. Now as a node, a mental superior being above animals yet I had realised in the moment of existentialism the animals were not far off from us yet we treat them so badly like cattle yet cattle seemed to be a derogatory word to me now. Instead of losing respect for the node as I had in the moment I had now regained some respect for the animals.

My thoughts came back to the node that had been altruistic. I had not even thanked him as I fought to regain my composure, my sanity.

I looked around on the posters all fractural mantras, all part of some collective hidden consciousness archetypes, all predictable node thinking maybe we all are just machines just predictable biological nodes flesh machines and life is meaningless just the perceptions of some temporary transient flesh machine maybe we are nothing.

I started to write on the tube carriage dirty window with my finger, "Arcadia is a lie; it's just selective, not stochastically indifferent, genocide for those who dare to drift into those choices and directions of their own."

I stood up I started to shout, criticizing the Utopian state whilst in my psychosis fuelled state, I said, 'the state is unfair, restrictive, it is murderously efficient, it was a cancer to the souls of the nodes. We all need to wake up!'

All the while every sentient ambient device honed in on me, every camera and microphone, every embedded device, every internet of things; if the cameras of administering algorithms had any sentience or artificial intelligence or awareness, it would not believe what had it heard.

A endogenous node; a Beta, a node at the Ministry of Inferences, standing in the tube station, in full view of the cameras and microphones, talking, shouting subversive propaganda and even alluding to the Arcadian express.

Bayes, Harry was immediately red flagged, now already considered a redundant node; an aware redundant node.

My only hope was that the Utopian state would take pity on me and categorise me as an exogenous node which was what I was at this moment; even I had to admit that.

I walked out of the tube station as the shocked endogenous nodes watched.

I made my way to my apartment. I started to write a speech about the Arcadian express. I was going to atone for my wrongdoing even if it meant my certain demise.

I tried to upload my speech whilst my hands shook.

Just then I heard a knock at the door

'Mr Bayes, it is the local constabulary we would like to talk to you.'

I knew I was an aware outlier, they never ended up on the Arcadian express, they were just taken into secret custody, never to be seen again.

I opened the door trying to look calm and normal.

'Mr Bayes, sir we are obliged to detain you as you seem to be exhibiting exogenous tendencies please come with us.'

Oh, no they are accusing me of being exogenous worse than an aware outlier.

I wanted to protest but I was too confused and intoxicated to resist as I turned to get my jacket, I saw a reflection of myself on the living window. I looked deranged and dishevelled, they were probably right. It was true; I am exogenous now.

08: An Audience with Arima.

I sat alone in a large art deco office whilst looking around nervously at the various computer servers and other sophisticated technology that filled it. Bordering the computer servers were gleaming white marble walls that towered upwards towards a raised ceiling, crowned with a glass dome.

The art deco architecture created a strange ambience within the office room making me feel even more unsettled as my body struggled to perspire, the corrupt medicine I had ingested hours earlier on the monorail.

I struggled to regain a certain degree of awareness after my drug induced public rejection of the statistical totalitarianism of state Utopia and the realisation of my new redundant position within the state which was slowly dawning upon me, that perhaps nothing in my life will ever be the same again. I had publicly, officially rejected the great Beta; the great null apodictic hypothesis of the state.

I was no longer an endogenous variable; nestled safely, confidently within the great normalised confidence interval of the given known, fixed mean of state Utopia's quotas nor was I even within the greater realm of classical statistics within its fixed yet unknown mean.

I was devoid of a mean; I was no longer part of the state's statistical linear regression model or of the classical statistics linear regression function. I was no longer part of even classical statistical thinking, of being relative to a fixed unknown mean, or nurtured safely by the state deep within its authorised normalised sigma standard deviations from a given mean.

I now felt deeply lost, confused and vulnerable; unable to even cling to a tangible alternative hypothesis of some new default mind-set of being.

As the corrupt medicine slowly wore off I incrementally opened my eyes back to the mundane statistical conformity of the office around me; the very epicentre of state Utopia's statistical oppression.

The office seemed to be an informal centralised informal headquarters, the centre of the office was dominated by a sunken floor, complemented by a large overhead glass dome, along the walls stood intermittently a few computer servers, endless statistical code ran down its monitor screens.

The myriad of algorithms produced large sets of data and graphs relating to the economic efficiency of state Utopia. Some monitors projected the expected economic developments within the convenient enemy of Zhou Pingjun.

The doors slid apart as Arima entered the room, unbeknownst to me at that moment, that he was the highest ranked node within state Utopia's hierarchy, signified by his quad Alpha rating. The rating gave him a near omnipotent position within a state ruled by ratings and statistics where everyone and everything was quantified and categorised.

I turned to see him entering as he stared intently at me whilst he approached, I recognised him vaguely as a significant lobbyist for the Economic Efficiency Act.

I knew that he was an influential lobbyist yet in the flesh he was not very physically impressive, being quite short and puny.

As he approached he seemed to be aware that I was sizing him up but he had strategically over compensated for his lack of stature by presenting himself immaculately, crowned with a perfectly gelled back short hair.

He approached me deliberately walking slowly to heighted the anticipation of our meeting, aware of the respect that an Alpha node commanded as a member of a government or lobby group.

He had walked with an aloofness to create an unapproachable insulation to protect his position of power at the acme of society as all the pharaohs, emperors, kings and presidents have done since antiquity.

As he approached he spoke slowly, annunciating each part of my official security identity with a serious malicious tone, '31428,' he then paused, his face broke into a mischievous smile, his tone softened saying, 'or should I say Bayes.'

'Do you know what brought you here today Bayes?' asked Arima.

'My spurious results, my transgression of the confidence interval, my exogenous routines; my mean devoid rebellion,' I replied.

'Yes partially correct. What took you here today is autoregression. Take this plant,' Arima pointed to a random bonsai tree, one of many neatly stored in rows on a side shelf.

'Let's call it Yt, it can represent any economic variable but in this case it represents your current correlation with the state Utopia's Beta variable.

'And in the autoregressive model, Y values are deviations from their mean, just like your deviation from your expected mean of monthly confidence interval quotas.

'Therefore your Yt, your current correlation, exists due to your previous time value correlation with state Utopia's Beta plus a current shock, a current stochastic error term, your current rebellious stochastic breakdown,' said Arima.

'Maybe the stochastic error term shocks are a result of my interaction with the error nodes, their intangible realised residual terms somehow affected me with their ethereal stochastic essence or just their unusual thinking, augmenting slightly my open mind like an inverted autoregressive process,' I considered.

'I hypothesise you are a third-order autoregressive process.

'Because Yt, your current correlation depends on your three previous time periods. Mathematically in this autoregressive model all the Y values are dutifully distributed around their mean, unlike your correlations and intentions Bayes.'

'In these models only your current correlation Yt and the three previous Y values are involved, no other regressors therefore it is solely your responsibility, your data, your routines that determined this result; you have only yourself to blame.

'Moving average processes have also affected your thinking and routines in this model; Yt is equal to a constant, white noise, stochastic error term. Yt is equals a constant plus a moving average of the current and past error terms. I assume again your Yt follows a third-order moving average process.

'Perhaps rebellious nodes you met over previous periods, perhaps even possible error node that may

249

have assisted you during your recent altercation in the park which you may have not reported?

'Therefore so far I use my favourite econometric forecasting model the ARMA (p, q) autoregressive moving average process to analyse and infer your statistical activity and subsequent loyalty to state Utopia.

'We usually assume all linear regressions routines and thinking within state Utopia's time series to be weakly stationary, the mean and variance being constant. But sometimes a series will becomes stubbornly non-stationary; integrated.

'The trend can move away from the mean moving far out of any stochastic bands or standard deviations expected possibly to never return nor pass the mean frequently.

'Non-stationary time series results such as your current three period routines which were classified as random, stochastic from the perspective of the linear regression model yet to me who is experienced with specific rebellion against state Utopia's given, known, fixed mean and expected time series routines and implied thoughts, I can infer that you are merely exhibiting non-stationary integrated processes.

'We can cure you though, that is the good news Bayes, we will difference your times series data and implied thinking, taking three times differencing to make you once again stationary.

'Bayes I shift the confidence interval quotas and stationary process of the Beta trend to whatever gradient I decide, just like central banks did throughout the age of finance with their interest rates.

'Yet I influence the great socioeconomic Beta of state Utopia with the official selection bias of the linear regression function which should always evolve with a predictable stationary process to satisfy the economic efficiency act which removes all uncertainty from the socioeconomic Beta model with aggregate demand conformity.

'I guide and smooth the trends of the Beta process with biased engineered socioeconomic events and expected data realisations through the monthly confidence interval quotas.

'Sometimes there is rational behind my influence, my subtle exogenous shocks to the system, disguised and endogenous official quotas and sometimes it's merely a whim with a touch of malice. The usual discretion of a hidden dictator,' Arima smiled.

'Decreasing rations, increasing interest rate debt on short term loans, decreasing interest on savings accounts floating the fiscal policy, increasing money supply at the central bank decreasing rations. But now I merely control the state's aggregate demand curve therefore the money supply; interest rates and engineered rescission rationing are not necessary.

'Changing public sentiment, forcing nodes to accept more expected irrational opinions of social norms to corrode society with nonsense; more rights for the ambidextrous more inclusion for the ambidextrous nodes, why should only the left handed or the right handed have all the opportunities?

'Then over a few financial quarters, I can make the ambidextrous social pariah all with the shift of the confidence interval, all with the stroke of a pen,' concluded Arima.

Normalised Utopia

'You say that I am suffering from non-stationary processes yet you create shocks to the Beta, you make it a non-stationary process too. How is my integrated thinking and non-stationary routines wrong yet yours is right?' I asked.

'Because Bayes it's all about reference points, a non-stationary process is not non stationary if there is no other trend to compare it to. So my stationary process is the Beta, the primary trend with no other reference point. But the node's reference point is always compared to the utopian state's Beta, comprised of its countless statistical quotas; eGraph's, expected data and trend lines.

'The more quotas the more constraints the nodes must try to be stationary relative to my reference trend line, to whatever I set that reference trend to be.

'Statistics is not all about setting parameters of sample means and choosing the correct trends and forecasts, augmenting and inferring with official biased observers.

'Statistical totalitarianism helps to Cointegrating the nodes furtherer, more so than just the expected confidence interval quotas, means and standard deviation. The Cointegration protects them from the stochastic, chaotic turbulence of their imperfect subconscious; the nodes' harbouring inefficiencies of individual reason, will, imagination and perceptions of truth, tempting them to be free of the great statistical guiding hand,' said Arima.

Arima relaxed his tone changing the subject, 'It has been many years since you first were added to our database,' he said almost reminiscing.

'We monitored your advancement throughout your education and career. You have developed sufficiently.

'We have been a guiding hand since the inception. We have looked after you, over and above state Utopia's nurturing. We even included you in our database of potential Alphas.'

'It is a pity that things have come to this, for us to meet like this but unfortunately you have not restricted your thoughts and actions appropriately as you always have done,' said Arima.

'You knew I was restricting my thoughts,' I replied in shock.

'Oh yes,' Arima replied, 'we have known everything about you.'

'But why did you not do anything before?' I questioned.

'It is part of the process, for you to reach a higher level; they all go through the inevitable transitional period,' Arima replied.

'What do you mean, they?' I asked shocked.

'Most of the Beta nodes prior to being promoted to the Alpha caste first have to come to terms with all the little nasty truths of our society before they can fully appreciate the genius of state Utopia. At first, most of them fight it but eventually they all accept it; this wonderful state,' Arima replied theatrically, waving his arms around.

Arima then paused adding, 'Utopia,' enunciating the term almost sarcastically as if he himself did not even believe in state Utopia but expected every node to be devoted to every aspect of its running.

'It's all part of maturing; seeing the light, the glorious synchronised economically efficient state; state Utopia,' continued Arima.

'You are not special Bayes,' Arima gave a slight patronising sigh. 'There have been many like you before, all experiencing this type of social withdrawal.'

'But that can't be,' I exclaimed in frustration, my identity and reality, slowly starting to peel away.

I paused, then continued 'you mean I am not unique, there are many out there just like me, carbon copies, some specific category of node?' I stated with a controlled, emotionless, rhetorical confirmation.

'I am afraid so, it is all part of the social development program that all potential promoted Alphas must go through to become truly enlightened,' replied Arima.

'We cannot be blind to the truth. We need to know how everything from all points of view even from the oppressed position; so we can continue to manage the state.

'The potential Alpha needs to be aware of the full symmetrical spread of the normalised distribution of reality not just our constrained nurturing confidence interval of monthly state quotas reality but the all-encompassing reality of being a node existing in whatever society they find themselves in,' said Arima.

'But I no longer want to manage the state; state Utopia is too biased, too ruthless,' I replied passionately.

'Come, now Bayes, too biased, too ruthless,' Arima replied in a patronizing tone, his face screwing up in momentary disgust.

'You sound like an idealistic student,' Arima continued.

'Is that the best you can do, after all the education and training we have given you?' he questioned in disgust.

'State Utopia is too statistical, too fixed, too many known given quotas, too certain therefore too predictable, too rational and efficient, too selfish and unfair; too restrictive, too biased: too ruthless,' I replied in a more confident tone which only a true believer could muster.

'It is too ruthless,' Arima replied sarcastically, enunciating each world, exposing the malicious side of his personality, his face again contorted in momentary disgust before quickly falling back into its default superficial pleasant smile and inquisitive stare.

'Being selfless; that is irrational,' he continued this time his voice filled with his own emotion and conviction. 'To be selfish, to want a better life, to be ruthless, that is the rational way,' Arima continued.

'Is the confidence interval genocide of the redundant nodes rational? Aren't you ashamed of that rational?' I asked accusingly.

'No!' shouted Arima adamantly, his expression edged with a vicious grimace as his spittle sprayed from his mouth.

He paused; his tone softened, 'I think the confidence interval is evolution.'

Arima's expression then switched to a friendly smile with a tone of empathy, 'Look around you, its nature Bayes; everywhere you look there is evolution, it is logical, ruthless; the very nature of biology and mathematics.

'The rational choices that you make determine your success, it is woven into the very fabric of nature, look at mathematics, Fibonacci ratios, game theory, physics, biology, statistics; unless you take the correct course of action in each niche, you will fail.

It is evolution's way of rewarding the selfish, the rational. So why should the super organism; the utopian state, not be similar?

'Do you think I or any of the Alphas enjoy setting confidence interval termination quotas? No that is why we get the Augmenter to do it. It takes strength to do bad things,' he realized he had made a Freudian slip by saying bad things.

He immediately amended his speech by adding to the end of his sentence the phrase, 'tough decisions,' he continued 'because leaders who make tough decisions,' he paused to be dramatic, it was an old habit he used in his political lobbying speeches 'still have a conscience.'

'There is an element of empathy which has to be overcome in order to do these terrible things.' Again he slipped up, he amended his sentence by adding 'difficult actions,' he continued once again 'but as long as these difficult actions create lasting positive results, then is it not righteous?' he concluded inquisitively.

Arima continued jokingly, 'That is why we use statistical algorithms and artificial intelligence so we do not have to deal directly with all the tough decisions and that is also why the root down hierarchy is advantageous to us because we can just outsource all the difficult actions down the hierarchy.' He smiled proud of his political rhetoric that conveniently glossed over any wrong doing, almost seducing any listener into becoming a compliant adherer to anything,' he said.

Arima continued, 'Normalisation is that bad, when a node is near the mean; the average? Yes it is boring being average, you never excel at anything but you never fail at anything either, so there is some security in that fact, which is an important virtue if you have a family to provide for.'

Arima then stopped talking for a moment and gestured to me to follow him through another sliding door which led outside into a wonderful garden which stretched on for many hundreds of meters in all directions.

It was filled with nature's wonders, beautiful vegetation, coloured flowers, dark blue, red, orange, yellow and every colour and shade in between as well as many different exotic and indigenous trees and bushes.

The trees all seemed to be ordered into perfect geometric sequences, the lines flowing into each other, hundreds of perfectly straight rows all seemed to merge into one.

The beauty of nature coupled with an ordered symmetrical geometry.

I reflected that it was the type of garden that a personality like Arima would appreciate. I even concluded it was the type I liked too.

Arima broke the silence, 'Come let's walk for a while and get some fresh air,' as he knew I liked to stroll and think.

I was glad to see the open sky over my head again and feel temporarily free.

As we walked deeper into the garden I noticed a row of perfectly arranged bushes trimmed similar to a bonsai tree.

Arima noted my interest saying, 'These trees are my favourite; I spend many hours per week here pruning my bushes.'

We made our way into a large wooden furnished garden patio. We both sat down admiring the row after row of trees. In-between us; stood a solitary potted bonsai tree upon a table.

He continued his speech justifying the ruthlessness of the state, he pointed to a potted bonsai tree on the table he then caressed the leaves saying, 'A bonsai tree; it is methodically over time preened and trimmed of its leaves and branches, forced to grow into the direction that the horticulturalist wants.

'The bonsai tree is unaware of the horticulturalist and unaware of his discretion for the tree to grow in a particular direction. The horticulturalist can change his mind any time. He can cut back any of the branches to whatever direction he wants the tree to grow.

'The bonsai tree is perhaps aware of the cutting and the general direction that it is being forced to grow to. Perhaps the tree can feel the pain of the scissors cutting through its branches, maybe even the bonsai tree cries out a silent scream?

'Who knows but it does not matter as the bonsai tree is trapped in its pot, in the soil, on the desk of the horticulturalist.

'At his mercy, the little tree can only grow in the direction that he prunes it to grow, it cannot even wither and die because it is constantly nurtured by the horticulturist?

'Just like the bonsai tree the young unbiased brain is full of synapses and nerves, growing in a particular direction, depending on what it learns from its originators and the society that natures it.

'The unbiased is also vulnerable, like the bonsai tree, at the mercy of the nurturing parent originators and society finds itself in, soaking up the information, just like the little tree soaking up the nutrients from the soil in its pot.

'The unbiased is not aware of the controlling, guiding influence of the parent originator and society. It just accepts the preening it receives, similar to an unbiased receiving a slap when it's naughty; like the bonsai tree perhaps, feeling the pain of the scissors cutting through the branches.

'The unbiased and the endogenous nodes collectively are like the bonsai tree, they are unaware of the invisible guiding hand of the economically efficient state.

'Even if the Sigma were aware of the guiding hand, they are powerless to do anything, just like the harmless unbiased or the trapped inanimate bonsai tree, they cannot fight back, all they can do is just accept the constant methodical trimming of the invisible guiding hand of the state,' he finished.

Arima then continued, 'The endogenous nodes have different Sigma caste salary bands which most keep this for life; they are even content with their ratings.

'Society is just a collection of highly correlated nodes; any individual, unique nodes when magnified statistically enough resemble a single scalar, they are all near identical.

'Their infinitesimal differences become insignificant, even though individually they exhibit all different variables and weightings regarding their financials and intellectual specifics.

'From the Alpha to the Sigma ratings, the wealthiest to the poorest, they are all just nodes. Each node an individual brain cell making up a unified, collective, singular consciousness; a single brain.'

He paused with a cheeky grin, adding 'A single bonsai tree,' whilst he lifted his two fingers, making a cutting motion.

'The Alpha, engineer the future parameters for the different Sigma castes; through social engineering and biased breeding , the state can direct the collective DNA sequence of different sigma castes' offspring; pruning the unbiased minds to have a certain intelligence, strength, height and even appearance,' he continued.

'Negative qualities are bred and conditioned into most of the Sigma nodes' unbiased to make things fairer for the whole of society. Negative qualities, such as laziness, low attention span, propensity to commit petty crimes only during adolescence. This gives the higher Sigma nodes' unbiased engineered advantages in life; by corroding the lower caste Sigma.

'The nodes are subtly preened; nurtured in specific neighbourhoods, sent to certain schools. Lower castes unbiased are sent to inferior schools and are not taught as well as the more privileged unbiased. This creates sigma, standard deviations from the mean of the linear regression function yet these differences are balanced out.

'The unbiased Sigma's whole life is mapped out for them by state Utopia's statistical quotas of the Economic Efficiency Act.

'They are given specific choices in life but there really is no choice. You can choose the very unpleasant choice or the slightly unpleasant choice; the choice is yours,' he said smiling sarcastically.

'Are our brains not just machines that continually make choices, every moment of our lives; conscious and subconscious?

'Do we not navigate through the unrealised probability spectrum of the nearly future, making countless choices which results in us being who and what we are today? For ourselves, our unbiased and associated nodes,' concluded Arima.

'Not much of a choice, not much of a freedom when everything is owned in the state; every bit of land, every house, every tree, every blade of grass. Having to accept the menial choices that we are given; to be grateful for those limited options,' I replied, annoyed by Arima's overly positive tone.

'The node will obviously choose the rational choice, the option with the highest payoff; the slightly less unpleasant choice, the choice of working in a supermarket their whole life as opposed to the only other option offered, working as a cleaner in a sewerage works,' I replied.

'We even complicate matters worse by transforming nodes into becoming competing nodes and therefore having to choose the dominant strategy; accepting a lower cooperative payoff,' laughed Arima almost childishly, enjoying my disdain.

'I added a hidden further augmentation behind the average monthly confidence interval setting. I added a moving average with an autoregressive to further constrain and augment the nodes whose routines individually and collectively are integrated trends.

'Therefore these integrated nodes who are usually regarded as being stationary, always obediently crossing the mean regularly, a mean that I set. Whose trends and being is random, stochastic, at best chaotic, I therefore accept their integrated, non-stationary nature. I therefore add additional hidden autoregressive integrated moving averages to complicate the quotas further.

'Ultimately the nodes are guided their entire lives from the cradle to the coffin, into making small discrete choices all the time which is carefully crafted by state Utopia.

'Each binary choice, chosen, perhaps corrodes away marginally their dignity, dreams and fading youth. Ultimately their untapped limitless intrinsic potential wasted away, ending up working away their lives in a menial job they detest.

'An unbiased mind is open and soaks up its environment unquestioningly. If the unbiased asks any questions, then it is up to the parents to decide what is the correct way in which to do something and what is not the correct way. The unbiased just accepts their answer as the truth.

'Just like an unbiased mind that is open and accepts unquestionably from the originator so do the sigma who just accept what the state tells them, even the Alpha comply too.

'The unbiased are augmented and conditioned from birth to just accept the reality and ideas presented to them by their parents,' concluded Arima.

'The state should offer a wider, freer spectrum of chooses, not create a perpetual statistical constraint. They should choose how to live as they desire, not to merely exist in a matrix of perpetual statistical quotas and debt whilst spawning the next generation of taxpayers,' I replied.

'All choices inevitably enslave,' replied Arima with an uncharacteristic genuine sombre expression which shocked me as it seemed to contain a deep hidden truthful wisdom.

'Bayes the funnel of the, "Nepenthes pitcher plant," which is similar to a Venus fly trap allows a bee into its funnel but once inside the bee is trapped. It tries in vain to escape by flying towards a light which shines through the translucent fleshy walls of the pitcher's funnel trap.

'But the bee cannot get out, ironically all it had to do was fly downwards to escape through the curved downwards facing funnel yet it keeps flying upwards towards the light of the translucent walls of the pitchers plant with its the light filtering through.

'Eventually the bee becomes exhausted and falls into the fluid at the bottom of the funnel and drowns and is consumed by digestive enzymes.

'It does not even know that it has been trapped and consumed by a virtually inanimate organism; it is unaware of all that, it can only follow its nature, its visual instinct.

'It is strange that somehow the pitcher plant's design knew this and grew that way? Or was it just pure chance of evolution?' I muttered.

'There is no room for a creator or providence in state Utopia, only the official inferences of the statistical quotas and ideology, you know that Bayes,' replied Arima arrogantly.

'Bayes, the funnel is like state Utopia's statistical quotas which augments them, allowing them to follow their baised predictable intrinsic primitive instincts coupled with the limited choices they are presented with.

'They will keep moving into the direction of the pseudo light; to whatever is continually presented on their monitor until they are vanquished yet never considering choosing an alternative, counterintuitive direction,' said Arima.

Arima looked directly at me then pointed his finger up to the sky saying, 'Covariance it's like the birds that flock together; they are all grouped together in a big scattered silhouette made up of all the birds choosing to fly in the same general direction.

'The silhouette, writhes, undulates and pulsates above in the sky. Yet collectively all the birds choose to follow a common invisible path as they follow the pattern it leads them to rise and fall, to zigzag, to and fro. But ultimately they all follow the same trend, an overall definitive direction.

'This covariance,' raising his voice and continuing Arima, 'is a collective aggregate movement, the movement of the flock. In the flock, each bird feels free to soar a bit higher or a bit lower than the neighbouring birds but ultimately the direction of the flock is controlled, directed by a common will or maybe an alpha bird, the invisible hand; let's just say a controlling influence.

'An influence, ultimately on the minds of the flock.

'The reason why I am telling you this. That is the genius of how to control a flock or a group or a society is that you create the illusion that the individual has a free will as well as the entire flock, that this alone is driving them in a particular direction, each moment.

'But in reality it is not the individual or even the combined group that is driving them in a particular direction it is the influencer who is.

'As the primary biased inferer, I influence the model prior to the event by setting certain variables within the sample set environment which we control; we control, the transportation infrastructure, the mortgages, the interest rate, the unemployment rate, everything Bayes. And the Sigma chooses the most rational choice that we present them with. They think they are free to decide but they are not,' he laughed again,' said Arima.

'So nodes are mere covariant birds to you?' I replied.

'Oh no Bayes,' replied Arima, 'They are not even that, birds are free when they fly to a certain extent. No Bayes, the nodes are just farm animals, cattle, they sleep where we allow them to sleep, they eat what we allow them to eat, they go where we allow them to go and they own what we allow them to own.

'And guess what, they even think and feel what we allow them to think and feel.

'They are just lobotomised cattle; vital flesh that manufactures and maintains the infrastructure of the state, infrastructure that we need.

'Bayes, do you think global monorails just appear out of nowhere? No Bayes, we need endogenous nodes for that. Do you think luxury goods make themselves? No, we need Sigma for all these wonderful things in society. A society that we get first pick of; each time,' finished off Arima, with a satisfied smile.

'They think it is out of rational necessity that they make certain decisions such as getting up at a certain time, collectively, that they all start work at a certain time, collectively.

'Yet they are only making rational choices that the system has given them, and then statistics creates only a few certain choices and that are accepted by the herd. They then make rational decisions based on the limited choices presented to them by the system.

'A controlling influence deicide if the group flies up or the group flies down.

'Usually the control or persuasion of the masses is done by a dictator or by the lure of money.

'The endogenous nodes get up every day and travel to work, they work and by working they turn the wheels of state Utopia. The state spins because of the working sigma. Things are made because endogenous nodes got up and contributed by making them.

'Money, military oppression or even a centralised totalitarianism is not needed.

'All that is needed is to persuade the Sigma that they must work.

'Yes you were right Bayes; society does not need money to function!' Arima said in a loud forceful manner yet with a thoughtful expression whilst conceding to my point.

'Society and the sigma do not need money or a strict government to have a fruitful and beneficial society,' I stated.

'If each node had the maturity and honour to accept their caste, their role in society, that destiny or themselves have chosen, then money as an incentive is not needed.

'Governmental control is not needed; even the sacred statistical control is not needed,' I was filled with a belief as the passion in my tone indicated.

'No, all that is needed is altruism, a benevolent good natured spirit that nodes will help each other and even work for each other for the good of each other 'For the good of society.'

'Out of necessity, the sigma will pull together in times of uncertainty; such as a power cut, all the Sigma come out of their apartments and offer each other candles and tea when normally their neighbours would hardly speak to each other for years.'

'What happens is the nodes no longer adhere to their normal routines and patterns?' asked Arima.

He continued, 'they are then free, they are no longer fixed variables in the confidence interval, they become stochastic variables, random, free, unpredictable even to themselves.

'They are free to surf the probability spectrum, the normalised graph of all probabilities in their lives. They could easily float out of the confidence interval and no longer be financially efficient. They would be free to possibly experience extreme standard deviations from the norm; they could experience and learn new amazing things, good and bad.

'If you do the same thing every day you will experience the same things every day. This way we are protecting the financial system and indirectly the good of society. This way we shield the average node from extreme probabilities that are negative and hurtful to them. A node will never have to worry about his parachute not opening as the node is not allowed to parachute,' said Arima.

'But does that not, thwart the extreme good, positive possibilities as well?' I asked.

'Adhering to statistical incentive is the only way; clear, transparent and simple. It gives the Alphas something to hide behind as the Sigma nodes are 'presented with a statistical quota form their immediate superiors, line managers in their relative root down hierarchy and they just do it.

'The Sigma nodes focus on their statistical prerequisite and work targets and not the Alphas, setting the statistics. The Alphas have their orders transformed into statistical directives embedded in the state's Economic Efficiency Policy.

'Enticing the Sigma nodes, to perpetually marginally slowly inch forward, they are manipulated every day to get up, work and consume,' said Arima.

'Even the Alphas are caught up in the continual expansion of the capitalist economy, a perpetual compounding of consumption and production. The Alphas are also doomed as they too have to continually inching further, consuming more, adhering to their ever increasing economic efficiency targets until even they are set firmly and irrevocably onto the road to perdition of unsustainable production and consumption of the world's resources and the continual erosion a node's social utility and freedom.

'The Alphas are also just nodes, they too are victims of the statistics, the Economic Efficient Society, which they created and now worship.

'They do not even realise it and if they did, it is too late; they are trapped in a system of their own making. The only difference between the Alphas and the Sigma nodes is that the Alphas have more possessions and perceived utility,' I concluded.

Arima continued more seductively, 'Come join us and you will benefit from the wonderful new world that we have forged through wars and clever socioeconomic evolution.

'Or we can always put you on the Arcadian express. It makes no difference to us but you are enlightened enough to know our ways and it would be a shame to lose you.'

Arima continued 'The system: the state, statistical algorithms, A.I., technology; knowledge, all leads to an unstoppable evolution: this systemic knowledge based society is a machine, no, a dinosaur.

'A massive, slow, moving dinosaur; it keeps marching Bayes, right over you and even me. It marches on and on and on; no matter what you say or do.

'You can throw yourself in front of the juggernaut.

'You can stand in the dinosaur's way.

'You clutch onto its huge, thick, rough leg Bayes.

'You can even try to whisper in its ear and plead with it, Bayes,' Arima paused.

Arima then shouted passionately, 'You can scream to it Bayes but it will not stop! No, Bayes not even for one moment. It will methodically plod on with you screaming, still clutching onto its leg!'

'It will simply continue to march on, Bayes, with your bloody, trampled body under its huge, indifferent hooves.'

'Or Bayes,' Arima paused and contorted a small wry smile to strengthen the conclusion.

He deepened his voice, his tone becoming more passionate, 'You can ride up on top of the dinosaur: high up above the masses; the insignificant nodes, the nodes, the statistics, Bayes.

'The nameless, faceless statistics; high up on the shoulders of the beast.'

'His tone implied an assumed bond of closeness, trying to seduce an acceptance from me; if only I would compromise my principles and accept the offer.

Arima carried on, 'The view is magnificent up here, Bayes. Come join me, don't be silly.'

'I don't think I can cointegrate with you or the great Utopian state anymore but you are right in am now non stationary and definitely meanless.

'I am free of the great dinosaur,' I said relieved and resigned to my fate.

'My mind now is free to roam the stochastic probability spectrum and to contemplate,' I stated.

'I am wondering; what were you before your became the highest Alpha node in the state?' I asked curiously.

'I wanted to be a quant for a hedge fund yet ended up as a computer technician working on the

Augmenter. It was a good job and I had a relative position in the state as an employee of the Ministry of Information, programming the Augmenter super computer's statistical algorithms,' replied Arima.

'Yet one day I realised if I could manipulate the Augmenter software, I could promote myself to higher and higher ranks within the state.

'Any rivals, such as a more senior technician, with one illegal stroke of the computer key pad, they were reclassified as a redundant node and would be sent an invitation to Arcadian.'

'A bit like your job, no,' said Arima smirking?

'No', I paused, 'we had rules, guidelines.'

I stopped to think deeper. 'We merely administered the nodes who had, through by their own actions; fell outside the confidence interval.'

'Whatever Bayes whatever,' said Arima, dissatisfied with my weak answer.

I looked down with shame. Then as I began to look up I noticed that one bonsai tree was burnt with a section missing from one of its rounded sides.

Arima noticed me looking inquisitively, 'That Bonsai tree was burnt by a lightning strike; that side will never grow back.'

'It is a bit like a damaged brain, I paused, 'or a damaged personality,' I replied as I looked at Arima, who noted the insinuation.

'What kind of damaged personality,' inquired Arima?

'It looks like a narcissistic personality.'

Arima face screwed up with narcissistic rage saying aggressively, 'I don't think you have been listening to what I have been saying.'

'The old ways of money and personal contacts were extinct. The powerful nodes were shocked to be usurped so effortlessly; no matter how powerful their positions in society because they are all submissive to the state's statistical conformity via the Augmenter.

'The irony is, that although it seems that I was an interloper to the traditional power structure and therefore did not deserve the power and privilege that I accrued by deceitful ways; however the truth is no one deserves disproportionate power and privilege of the Alphas which were in most cases is taken in dishonourable ways, if not in the present generation then certainly by their ancestors.

'You are different to past dictators, more subtle, more intellectual yet similar; ruthlessly eliminating your rivals. Previous dictators used political revolutions but you merely hide behind technology, the Augmenter supercomputer which is tasked to run the Economic Efficient Society,' I replied.

'I could not have put it better myself, I concur. I use technology and the financial markets to acquire power rather than the more conventional militarism but ultimately all dictators hide behind something; ideology, military power or economic systems.

'The important ingredient is whatever method adopted; the nodes blindly follow a root down hierarchy which is controlled. In a structured society, the node in a uniform or office, immediately above another node in the hierarchy is told to conform because it is,' he paused 'official,' he smirked.

'I feel strangely devoid of any known or unknown fixed mean. I feel devoid of a mean, distribution or any trend. I therefore think I can never again accept this Utopian state of a fixed, given, known means and contrived stagnant distributions, all to prop up a baised, apodictic null hypotheses of the state,' I stated resolutely.

'That is a pity then Bayes,' replied Arima, 'I will have to accept that is your final answer as a potential Alpha node and previous endogenous Beta node of the Ministry of Inferences. Now you are nothing but an exogenous node.'

'I have tried to persuade you to see reason and return you to the nurturing mean of the utopian state and pursue your ambition of becoming an Alpha node. But now I must end our debate as there are many responsibilities to take care of,' Arima concluded whilst flashing a smirk.

As Arima was about to leave I allowed myself one last defiant comment.

'I assume your name means autoregressive integrated moving average,' I said thoughtfully.

'Yes Bayes, well done.'

'Integrated, meaning that the trend line moves significantly away from the mean and does not pass it often,' I continued.

'Yes,' agreed Arima.

'Integrated or non-stationary movement can even travel an unlimited distance from the mean,' I added.

'I suppose so,' replied Arima.

'Like your thoughts?' I replied.

Arima realised the insinuation that his thoughts were integrated; rambling; mad. He became agitated at the insult, most probably because it contained a certain degree of truth.

'So Bayes you think that you are good and I am bad, along with the terrible state?'

'You think because you were constrained within the statically harmony of the state's Economic Efficient Act where you could do no harm; that you are harmless?

'Yet when you had a mental breakdown where there is no longer any limits; then you were no longer harmless. Now you try to follow and act on your convictions, of your grand statistical free, harmonious ideology.

'But you are not good.

'Did you visit the sick or care about the hungry? You only cared about your pension and your all-important promotion into the Alphaship; into the power that makes the Utopian state.

'How is that good?' accused Arima.

You are a hypocrite!' shouted Arima.

'Perhaps but you are mad. You seem unbalanced, you are not impartial like the other empty Alpha; you seem to enjoy the ruthlessness of the state,' I replied.

'You call me mad when you are the one that had the breakdown!' screamed Arima.

'Bayes I integrate; I am the trend, I am the mean, I can shift the mean. If there are two trend lines I am the independent based trend line. Which the other cointegrated trend line has to mirror, has to copy, in order to remain cointegrated.

'If I add an exogenous shock, if I add an integrated movement into the underlying based independent trend line. Then the nodes trend line, the dependant trend line has to also immediately incorporate the shock immediately integrate.

'If I change the mean then the nodes' trend line has to shift to adapt to remain stationary.

'Therefore my will, my whims, my intentions are exogenous shock; I am the system, I am the state's will.

'Without following my thoughts, intentions, actions you are falling outside of the confidence interval becoming non-stationary, becoming non-cointegrated therefore the nodes thoughts, actions, routines, intentions; their very consciousness, their very perceptions of reality around them, is all relevant to the statistical trend lines which their data produces with the confidence interval quotas expectations demand.

'Therefore I control their expectations, I control their statistical routines, I control their thoughts, their intentions, their actions. I control their consciousness, I control their perception of reality, I control their very souls; if I the state believed in souls. I am the state, Bayes,' Arima stated.

'Maybe you are mad Arima? Auto regressive integrated,' I paused to give integrated more weighting, 'moving average,' I replied.

'Perhaps you are mad,' I concluded.

'No Bayes, even if I am mad, I am sanity incarnate; I am the mean, I am the underlying independent base trend, I am the idealised norm. I set the norm, I set the set the mean, I set the underlying line base trend which sanity and insanity is compared to.

'And even if I am mad, even if there are exogenous shocks added to the system, they are my exogenous shocks and the utopian state and the system and the nodes and their perceptions need to cointegrate around those exogenous shocks.

'Therefore Bayes I am sane, you are mad, you are the exogenous node, you are non-stationary, you are integrated, you are noncointegrated, you are mean-less. We have monitored you; we monitored your thoughts, your actions, your intentions, your routines.

'You have evolved from a being a complaint Beta node who adhered to the statistical quotas and the economic efficiency act; you then morphed.

'You evolved into a classical statistical, slightly freer, slightly more stochastic node but them you become mean-less, you became devoid of a mean, devoid of any statistical ideology, any statistical inferences but we will regress you back into the harmonious mean, the mean of the utopian state where you can once again cointegrate as a stationary sigma node, protected and nurtured by the state,' replied Arima.

'In relation to the Utopian state's Beta?' I questioned.

'A Beta linear regression function, realised solely from your biased expectations, place at each sample point. You're biased trend lines and quotas which is modified to your whims. Perhaps you are non-stationary? Perhaps the primary reference point, the Beta is non-stationary.

'Then my rationale thinking is not cointegrated with the non-stationary Beta of your whims,' I continued.

'Therefore in order for an average Sigma node to feel confident within their compliance and to be stationary, they would have to be cointegrated with your fluctuating Beta, non-stationary, trends and processes.

'Yet within the great Beat you hypocritically let a stationary trend line and the constant reference points, be the perceived as an unbiased organic morphing trend, the pseudo eyes of statistical truth; then your integrate that trend movement, which will deviate from the expected natural organic stationary trend line progression of your previous beta trend line and quotas; infected with a tainted previous time period trend.

'Infected with a stochastic exogenous shock, error term, your mad malicious whim, added to the great Beta linear trend line; to the statistical quotas, a subtle negative externality, a hidden power, hidden behind the system, as in countless times and situations throughout posterity.

'This is unfair to a complaint confident, mean thinking statistical quota accepting average, compliant endogenous sigma node who tries to cointegrate within the perceived constant reference point of the great Beta trend line the; pseudo unbiased eyes of truth.

.

'Yet the Beat trend is non stationary, integrated movement so a Cointegrating sigma node who is statically obligated to have stationary movement cannot cointegrate with your non-stationary reference points in the Beta trend line,' I concluded.

'Yes like Einstein's general relativity where a node is within an accelerating elevator, how can they detect gravity,' replied Arima?

'My non-stationary, integrated, random walk, mean-less thinking, swings wildly and persistently away from any given mean, in all directions yet perhaps it is negatively correlated to your unjust, irrational, integrated, whims which are masked behind a stationary process veneer of the accepted Beta linear regression trend.

'Perhaps my negatively correlated, non-stationary process tends to hedge out your non-stationary, exogenous, malicious, wilful shocks.

'Hedging the Beat into a twin asset portfolio; my relative confidence interval compliance correlation and to the other variable, the Utopian state's Beta, influenced by your exogenous whims.

'Perhaps I hedge my micro personal relationship with the Beta portfolio, hedging, regressing, and augmenting my consciousness closer towards the unbiased constant, non-stationary.

'Towards the true statistical ethereal reference point, of truth, logic, reason, morals; logos of the true statistical reality, the mean of means, reality incarnate within probability, the unbiased eyes of truth that all our subconscious sees through even through our tainted higher conscious of ego, baised reasoning and ideologies.

'I am closer to it than you, whose irrational selfish whims taint society as with all dictators throughout history,' I replied passionately.

I added, 'Arima you only seem to be preoccupied of the minus sign. Your great mathematical symbol, it seems it should be the official symbol of the utopian state, not the normalised confidence interval?'

'Why do you say that Bayes,' asked Arima even though his patience threshold was almost reached.

Because all you do is minus all data; even adding distributed lagged variables is minus autocorrelation. Minus exogenous variables to create restricted models, minus the error terms, minus white noise, minus the redundant nodes, minus all variables that does not fit into your expectations and ultimately your will.

Minus the "−a, +a" z values which fall outside the confidence interval. Minus "a" z values from the model; therefore minus altruism, genius, spontaneity, stochastic possibilities, minus spirituality. I stopped, I did not mention the mysterious, statistically significant, great plus sign.

Arima your will and the utopian state's, all seem to be the antithesis of any positive value; merely a perpetual negative; a great minus sign.

With that Arima made a gesture to the guards standing nearby in the doorway, he then turned around, leaned forward, hunching over a computer terminal screen and began to analyse some arbitrary data as the guards escorted me out of the control room.

I was taken downstairs to a waiting military lorry, I was placed in the back with some stone faced soldiers who sat staring mindlessly ahead not even acknowledging me as I had boarded the military lorry; they seemed like lifeless mannequins.

I wondered what they were thinking, if they thought at all, as they were trained to do, not think.

The sergeant after issuing some orders to the guards turned to me and said without emotion, resembling an android speaking, 'You will be taken to a holding facility, do not try to escape.'

With that the sergeant turned around on his heels just like an oversized toy robot and disappeared towards the front of the lorry.

I was now resigned to my fate of becoming a redundant node, after rejecting Arima's offer.

As the lorry methodically ambled through the different streets and neighbourhoods intermittently careening and bouncing off different obstacles and narrow roads, I remained nestled in-between two burly soldiers, I was resigned to my fate; I was even free to think without a mean now.

I considered Arima to be the ultimate wolf, the greatest wolf of the Utopian root down caste hierarchy, the Alpha nodes being the wolves. Yet he was too cunning to be classified as a wolf; he was more a fox.

As he would not challenge them directly another wolf of the Alpha hierarchy yet instead the little Arima, previously a lower ranking node would use the one great societal power; an invisible force to hide behind and dispatch each of the challenging wolves who snarled metaphorically at him, within the government and corporate arena.

Dominant wolves simplistically and predictably challenged and snarl at each other, focusing on the immediate wolves who challenged them.

While Arima, the little fox, hid behind the supercomputer, the Augmenter and manipulated the system; the personal statistical quotas and confidence interval.

Thereby secretly eliminating any challenging alpha node wolf who predictably and obedient submitted to the utopian state's statistical conformity unquestioningly.

09: Exogenous nodes.

As I sat restrained within a private monorail carriage, its tinted windows a subtle indication to this discrete service, transporting the latest batch of legally classified insane nodes that were uncorrelated with state Utopia's Economically Efficient Model.

Their inferred sample data and implied thoughts being exogenous, falling outside of the great Beta linear regression stationary process. These unfortunate nodes were now categorised as suffering from an exogenous psychosis.

Their predicted routines and intentions moved outside of any stationary correlated processes or expected rational. They were therefore unpredictable, un-augmentable; exogenous, damaged nodes.

However unlike an endogenous Sigma node who became a redundant node by unknowingly transgressing their expected statistical conformity. Redundant nodes whose monthly standard deviations, p-values and trends, unintentionally exceeding the state Utopia's monthly confidence interval quotas of the contemporaneous normalised distribution of officially acceptable standard deviations of; averaged normalised thought, averaged normalised consumerism and aggregated normalised demand.

Yet these unfortunate exogenous Sigma nodes had blatantly transgressed their expected statistical conformity. Unlike the redundant nodes who unintentionally fell outside of the confidence interval and were sent to Arcadia as mere statistical realisations of the utopian's state yearly expected five percent elimination of the population that fell outside of the confidence interval per year.

The process of elimination being the unbiased, subtle, Arcadian express genocide; its victims, usually consisting of endogenous nodes that even prided themselves of thinking mean and being confident.

The unlucky redundant node's fate was the fault mainly of mere probability as five percent of even statistically compliant nodes were destined to fall outside of the confidence interval no matter how earnest or loyal they were to state Utopia's consumerism and patriotism.

It was as if the endogenous nodes were coerced into participating in a hidden lottery which the state gambled with their lives.

Yet the exogenous nodes were regarded as different; intentionally falling outside of their eGraph confidence interval. The state surmised that the exogenous nodes must suffer from some psychosis.

Therefore the utopian state magnanimously created a process to heal their exogenous' routines, consumption and thinking; back to a stationary process of contributing endogenous nodes, to reside back within the comforting, error free regression function and nurturing sigma caste confidence interval.

To heal them: first they were publicly removed from society and then mercifully they would be rehabilitated to be once again be placed within the great harmonious sanctuary of the official contemporaneous mean; the average.

Within the nurturing sigma caste of the confidence interval, far from extremes and significant uncertainty, to become once again bland, apathetic, consistent, obedient, endogenous sigma nodes who would gladly bend their individual utility expectations and their will, to fit within the cumulative average of societies expected quotas. Then finally they would be reintroduced back into the Utopian society.

Perhaps in the future as healed healthy normalised, Sigma caste, endogenous nodes; they may perhaps inadvertently transgress their expected covert monthly quotas. Then they would be sent a letter inviting them to Arcadia as per usual, removing them from the great Beat regression model with an unbiased impartial methodology of statistical inference.

Yet the exogenous nodes' data resided far outside of the confidence interval and so blatantly; their daily trends and correlations fell into a perceived chaotic, continual heterostochastic trend with persistent non-stationary movement; inevitably corrupting the great economically efficient linear regression model with node specific error turbulences.

Their current and past observed stochastic routines, emotions and implied thoughts were so far removed from the normalised predicated trend that they had to be removed from the statistically augmented society. As they did not contribute nor could they be predicted in a forecast model.

Therefore the exogenous nodes were no longer part of the contributing society; the population of statistically conforming endogenous sigma. They were no longer classified by the Augmenter, state Utopia or the Ministry of Inferences as animate or even un-animate nodes.

I looked around the monorail carriage, it seemed that most of the sombre looking exogenous passengers were sane, they looked as average as any other node yet here we were upon this private monorail, all of us officially classified as economically inefficient.

Perhaps some or most of these exogenous nodes had epiphanies and realisation of the dystopian constrictive nature of the state.

Perhaps they yearned to be free and to let their minds process non-stationary, freely, to feel and think as they chose, letting their minds follow autoregressive thinking paths and frequencies on random walk far outside of the confidence interval of state Utopia expectations and constraints, to never pass the official restrictive mean.

Many exogenous nodes had a history of impeccable statistical conformity and were not regarded as classical outliers. They had held desirable consumption and credit rating ratings, their data highly correlated with significant macroeconomic consumerism and business cycles. They were redeemable having the potential to become exemplary future expected consumers. The state would also weed out any sick politically rebellious exogenous nodes and heal them from the madness of Alternate Hypothesis Syndromes such as myself.

The monorail continued towards its destination where we were to be committed; at the Ministry of Archetype's Augmentation Clinic. Where our minds would probably receive enhanced, prolonged conditioning, until we felt obliged to heal and accept the Utopian state's quotas and directions once again.

The anxiety of anticipation started to overwhelm me whilst the monorail passed through the thick steel clinic gates. I started to consider all the possible horrors that may possibly arise within such a place.

My eyes anxiously examined the strange, unusual, antiquated dark, brown nineteenth century mansion that stood brooding and foreboding within the high perimeter fences.

I had heard many terrible rumours about the Ministry of Archetype's Augmentation Clinic.

Perhaps they were just rumours yet another set of subtle propaganda stories to persuade the nodes to conform?

I thought back momentarily with a degree of shame remembering the odd occasions when I had reclassified a node exhibiting chaotic statistical routines and behaviour as economically inefficient, possibly suffering from psychosis and officially classified them as exogenous; with the stroke of a pen, condemning them to the Ministry of Archetype's Augmentation Clinic.

I felt a more deep-seated repressed guilt for my previous responsibilities of perpetuating the states monthly cull whilst carrying out my duties at the Ministry of Inferences.

The monorail glided to a gentle stop, its effortless gentle deceleration was a sickening antithesis to an anxious anticipation of impending doom of whatever horrors may lay ahead.

I felt my confidence already deteriorating, regressing to an Ergodic mean of complete unpredictable hopelessness magnified with a coefficient integer representing the certainty of horrors awaiting me as I began to fully realise my new casteless categorisation; exogenous, non-stationary node suffering from the Alternative hypothesis syndrome.

Even though I had been trapped within the Beta caste of state Utopia's confidence interval whilst I was a productive economically efficient node, I had always been confident in the predictability of my existence.

My experiences within the state never were extreme yet now I was uncertain of my unknown immediate future. The anticipation had now convinced me that I would soon be suffering.

I now accepted the assumed prior, that my immediate fate would be unpleasant; a rational perception based on countless rumours and my magnified anxiety. I could not predict with any statistical significance of even considering harbouring any degree of hope; to escape or at least survive any ordeals that may lay in wait, in each new moment, of unfolding binary expansions of the future.

But at least I knew that with each new expansion into the probability distribution frequency of the future, with each new realised binary expansion of some conditional expectation, that I would have some new piece of information, some new piece of experience relative to my perceived, assumed prior forged by all the of previous rumours I had been privy to. As time progressed I would become more confident of what to expect. I hoped to survive but perhaps the future had some terrible realisation of events that far surpassed even this terrible prior, expectation.

My anxious emotions; therefore my implied thoughts were already exhibiting increased stochastic integrated routines whilst I fumbled for my seat belt whilst getting up and looking around nervously.

Perhaps this uncharacteristic nervousness I was beginning to exhibit would slowly become an exogenous mad permanent state. Maybe it happened to all the newly classified exogenous nodes; they accept their reality and classification over time, a neuroplasty conditioning.

It would take a strong will to overcome this situation I concluded as I tried to regain my composure. Yet I still felt fear, unlike the countless heroes in films and novels who always seem to just accept any drama they confronted.

Anticlimactically I spent the first few days sitting around within an open glass conservatory of the large nineteen century mansion of the Ministry of Archetype's Augmentation Clinic.

Each day of the first week I sat sedated, oblivious to all the exogenous patients and this new situation. I tried to rationalise the new situation through a blurred mind and eyes yet everything seemed to be in slow motion and soothingly surreal.

I tried to preoccupy myself by focusing on reading old magazines, discussing arbitrary topics but I could not concentrate. I could read the words easily enough but the meaning within the sentences and paragraphs eluded me.

I sat talking to the blurred grey silhouettes of the exogenous patients whilst my mouth slurred my mind's words dribbling out, escaping from the corners of my mouth intermittently. My seated posture now, a chemically engineered stupor; maintained by a steady flow of forced oral sedatives, twice daily.

Within my stupor I chatted to any exogenous nearby whether they were awake or not, imaginary or real, listening or not. I rambled on about superficial non-intellectual topics, even the most banal trivialities imaginable. As my subconscious slowly unwound due to the antagonistic inhibitive drugs squeezing out data from my psyche; that lay dormant deep within me until now.

The chemicals affected the weightings of the flowing electrical pathways of my brain's structure; now my neurons sparked and flowed in inefficient never used before configurations.

My mind was now churning out a sedated melee of previous inhibitions, of unanswered issues of a dormant subconscious partial psyche; purely existing only to support the main intention, the main psyche.

I resembled a mumbling simpleton yet in fact my mind was just downloading superficial data and running executive kernels that were not ever meant to be at the front of my psyche, my mind changed inefficient neurons patterns to regurgitate past trivial occurrences of the subconscious.

All those decades of mindless television shows and bombardment from advertisements had sunk into my subconscious and now all the mindless nonsense that had soaked into my porous mind without my consent was slowly, consistently, weeping out.

I resonated in uncharacteristic, endless chatter; my brain subconsciously spewing out all the mindless trivia it contained, perhaps in an attempt to relieve itself; to self-augment or maybe it was just following a skewered pattern, an inefficient temporary damaged path maintained by the chemical augmenting sedation.

My subconscious and now my inhibited consciousness felt relieved; uninhibited after decades of wilfully moderating its own thought patterns to evade the scanners and maintain a statistically acceptable profile.

I rambled on for hours, free in my safe, distorted, skewered, two dimensional world where none of the parallel lines met as they do on a globe.

My intentions, psyche and very interpretations of who I was were no longer consequential, I merely accepted each moment in my slightly unpleasant yet soothing blurred world of two dimensional silhouettes, harmless acquaintances; spewing out the most banal trivialities yet everything seemed superficially normal.

I had accepted my new reality whilst I waited for the next helping of sedation to maintain the utopian illusion.

Normalised Utopia

To me there was only now: no yesterday, no tomorrow; there was only five minutes from now or five minutes ago. If I had been a Buddhist, I would have perhaps thought of myself enlightened, living only in the now: not thinking, just accepting the reality I was being presented with; the clinic, the patients.

I did not think why am I here or how can I escape? Not even, I am here. Just, I am part of this immersion, of this ethereal blurred existence. Unquestioning; merely accepting, being a part of the experience. If I could reason at all beyond the regurgitated memories of talk shows and immediate trivial functional concerns such as where did I leave my cup of water?

I started to feel institutionalised even perceiving the grand antiquated Victorian building and it's imposing spacious glass walled conservatory creating an aura of homeliness, giving me a sense of blurred peace, lulling me into a false sense of security.

A doctor wearing a long white jacket passed through a doorway and approached me as I slouched in a chair in the conservatory.

'Good morning Mr Bayes,' greeted the doctor enthusiastically with a big genuine smile.

'I hope I do not embarrass you but I have been observing you through the cameras in a different room for a few days now. I am the head psychiatrist here at the clinic and I have jotted down a few observations of your behaviour on one of these out-dated pens and notepads,' he said then laughed softly.

I mumbled, 'You want to help me even though I am a Ministry of Inferences Beta who has rejected the state's apodictic null hypothesis?'

'Mr Bayes I am here to help you,' he smiled. 'I am not here to judge you. You need our help; you are consistently outside of the confidence interval, far beyond it. You are unfortunately an exogenous node now.

'Exhibiting wilfully stochastic, non-stationary routines and processes even harbouring fanciful rebellious notions of an alternate hypothesis syndrome,' said the doctor shaking his head seemingly finding the very notion of such a concept unacceptable to even consider.

Normalised Utopia

He became more serious, his face edged with concern, 'You are not merely contributing unpredictably, non-stationary, with an integrated trend; you are not even correlated with the error terms, you are purely exogenous. You need to be regressed to the mean, to become once again a contributing endogenous node.

'Don't worry it is quite natural, many nodes have harmful experiences and memories but fortunately we have the technology to create a restricted model of your mind, to remove harmful memories and corrupted variables.

'We will render many of your minds variables, to dummy variables, some of them will be rendered zero and others elevated to a value of one, with the use of the confabulation treatment; replacing and modifying memories with the augmentation of dummy variable manipulation.

'Soon any unpleasant memories will no longer exist. Soon you will be fit and healthy enough to return to the great utopian state,' he beamed with joy at the generosity of the utopian state, to regress me back safely within the harmonious state's will which supersedes all other wills.

'Mr Bayes, there are no bad nodes, only sick nodes; uncorrelated, integrated, endogenous nodes that consistently and blatantly fail to conform to their expected contemporaneous quotas whist falling, lost into the mean-less abyss of an exogenous psychosis.

'We can calculate to a certain probability region of the brain's structure, its memories where it stores those harmful memories and emotions, products of exogenous shocks and stochastic error terms of extreme experiences and corrupted intentions.

'We will erase those harmful memories and integrated intentions without damaging other brain cells yet refilling the harmful memories with pleasant pseudo ones without physically harming you.

'It will calm and stabilise your psyche, augmenting and creating a new chain of intentions; autoregressing them towards an ergodic mean. This will help you become correlated once again within the monthly statistical quota mean.

'Your routines and thinking will become stationary once again, devoid of any stochastic error shocks that corrupts your intentions with integrated thoughts of imagination, dreams and of a selfish will which is usually only concerned with "I", instead of "us".

'You will not feel alone or uncorrelated again, you will become once again a contributing healthily animate endogenous sigma node, happily bobbing along the official Utopian state trends and cycles,' concluded the doctor.

'It's not so much that exogenous nodes and variables are uncorrelated with the state or that they don't contribute to the linear regression model of the Beta which regress them into the safe nurturing statistical harmony, free of extreme thoughts.

'Those are valid reasons yet on a statistical, econometric level; exogenous nodes are not part of the contributing, officially chosen, independent variables of the endogenous variables, used in inferring the regression model, to test state Utopia's apodictic null hypothesis; that the state's monthly null hypothesis of statistical conformity is efficient.

'The certain, stable, stationary process's previous variable is coupled with a current error term, creating a shock, unpredictability, an inability to forecast estimates efficiently, leading to uncertainty within the economic efficiency model of state Utopia, the great harmony of technology and statistical routines, designed to guide the nodes minds and routines, to an efficient utopia.

'Exogenous nodes are merely shocks to the model, shocks influencing the endogenous, loyal, inferred variables and nodes yet the exogenous are not influenced by the endogenous. They are stochastic, error terms, leading to non-stationary processes, random walks, autoregressive moving averages; uncertainty therefore inefficient movements, tainted with past dissipating stochastic error term shocks.

'Stochastic is bad, random is bad, hetroskedastic is bad; it affects negatively the level of certainty for the state Utopia's internal rates of return, their net present value, where there is no opportunism, no arbitrage, to erode the state's efficiency of its markets.

'No overpriced shares, no under-priced assets, only the correct value at each inference of the strong market hypothesis, no Alpha, no abnormal returns, just an harmonious Beta with its trusted long term returns.

Normalised Utopia

'So you see exogenous nodes and variables are harmful leaving non-stationary, unit root, integrated movement processes with trends and cycles; the great underlying mean, the great intellectual asset, the great given, known, fixed, mean; that is stationary, predictable with processes and routines evolving with regularly and certainty.

'The confabulation room treatment will create alternate memories placed in your psyche to remove the unpleasant experienced memories that you have based your exogenous intentions and perceptions on which influence your non-stationary nature.

'Your non-stationary, time series needs to be made stationary with differencing we will enforce strict statistical quotas which you must comply to,' concluded the doctor.

Later an orderly had gathered all the patients together to tell us to comply to, the Ministry of Archetypes trivial routines that the exogenous patients were obliged to adhere to.

''At four o'clock you must write four hundred words, why State Utopia's apodictic null hypothesise should never be rejected, at five o'clock eat five morsels of food, at six o'clock sing the national theme precisely six times at seven o'clock read seven pages of revised history and at eight o'clock sleep for eight hours.

"Any transgression from the mean, outside of the narrow normalised confidence interval, you will be guided back with a shock or an extra dose of medication.

"You will comply, you will be attentive, and you will follow the lead of the group and adhere to.

"It's for your own good. We will augment you back to a stationary time series process. You will no longer deviate from the regression function.

"You will become endogenous once again, a contributing sigma node of the great Beta that nurtures and protects us. There is no 'I,' only 'us,' all contributing, stationary, predictably to the given, fixed, known, mean of state Utopia!" boomed the loudspeaker announcement.

The doctor asked me, 'Bayes you once said that state Utopia commits an unbiased covert monthly genocide.'

'Yes, I think so,' I said barely remembering the Arcadian express as my mind had suffer a few minutes of the corroding ravages of the confabulation room treatment.

'Oh come now Bayes, it's preposterous, even to you, an exogenous sigma node whose extreme outlying non-stationary random walk thinking. It is merely a deluded perception. There is no genocide.'

'I think I remember sending nodes to their doom,' I replied meekly, not completely sure.

'I am sure you did not. You are just a victim of this non-stationary, extreme, mean-less psychotic exogenous.'

'But Arcadia', I paused struggling to remember any specific fact that all my past perceptions and beliefs were founded on, this important missing fact regarding the validity of Arcadia and of the genocide existing. I continued unsure 'I think I worked on the redundant nodes data, their confidence interval quotas.'

'Redundant node, another new term and Arcadia,' the doctor laughed almost apologetically, 'Bayes I am sorry but this is for your own good,' he told one orderly to shock my temples which they did.

Ironic I thought, they were shocking me with a relative exogenous stimulus to my psyche, to make my thinking stationary, to conform, a shock error term influencing my state of mind.

"There is no arcadia, there is no genocide!" played a continuous recorded mantra.

They left me half-conscious whilst I lay there for hours listening to a recording, "there is no Arcadia, state Utopia is harmonious, there is only statistical bliss, conformity is the right choice, think average, think mean, no extremes, no non-stationary. Why be exogenous when you can enjoy the bounty of the endogenous. There is no Arcadia!"

The intermittent entering orderlies, like the doctor were not aware of any proof that there may even be an Arcadian express which ran regularly from St Pancras underground station, every day.

The doctor finished reading from his computer screen, 'Who is Mrs White?'

'I should have tried to save her.'

'Who?'

'Mrs White!'

'White!'

'Where is she?'

'Gone.'

'So there is no Mrs White.'

'My next door neighbour.'

'It says here Mr Brownian was your neighbour.'

'They must have changed the data set.'

'Come now Bayes, you really are suffering but we will heal you. I take no pleasure in this treatment but it's for your own good, you will thank me one day. Many previous exogenous nodes do.

'In fact all of them', the doctor said smiling, not fully comprehending that they had no choice as it was to be expected, the previous exogenous patients were only released after they had been sufficiently conditioned.

Therefore what else would a conditioned previous patient say or think. Only respect and admiration for state Utopia and the good doctor who healed them.

'She's not dead Bayes,' said the doctor.

I turned around for a moment hopeful that it may be true, to ease my guilt of not warning her and the other countless others that I was partially responsible for amending their confidence interval data each day.

'Because she never existed, can't you see I am trying to help you,' said the doctor.

He then mutter to himself, 'If only I was authorised to continue to use the confabulation treatment.'

I whimpered, 'I could not do anything otherwise they would have sent me too.'

'Sent you where?' inquired the doctor?

'Send me to Arcadia as a redundant node to be removed from the great linear regression model. Or terminate me as being an aware outlier if I refuse to go.'

'No there is no termination, no redundant nodes or aware outliers, no Arcadia. Can't you see Bayes, you are delusional, you are non-stationary, you're thinking, moving in stochastic processes, movements and trends away from the mean, uncorrelated with the mean contribution.

318

'Away from the mean, driving you to the abyss; you need to come back to the mean, to oscillate through the mean and remain within the confidence interval of the statistical quotas.

'Then you will be sane once again, stationary, predictable, stable, reliable, contributing to the bounties of the state where we all benefit from.

'To become an endogenous contributing sigma nodes once again. Instead of being an uncorrelated error term fumbling around in the darkness of the outer reaches of the sample space, integrating away into the non-stationary abyss of the darkness.

'Termination? It's all in your imagination. Don't worry soon your non-stationary thoughts, referred to as "imagination," will be quantized into stationary normalised thinking processes.'

'No. Arima can confirm it.'

'Who is Arima?'

'The highest ranking Alpha node.'

'No, Prime Minister Autarky is.'

'No.'

William J Fraser

'Arima? You probably derived that name from the Autoregressive Integrated Moving Average process ironically the same treatment you are receiving,' said the clever doctor thoughtfully

'It's all in your extreme, unit root, integrated, non-stationary, unfixed, unknown, mean-less, mind-set relating to econometrics.

'Your non-stationary thinking processes, your imagination creating vivid tragic narratives and characters with pseudo-scientific interpretations of econometric theories to justify the depression you feel being outside of the confidence interval and processing far from the reassuring nurturing wholesome given fixed mean of state Utopia and it great linear regression of the Beta.

'I have seen many like you before but I am here to help you. I want to send you back into the wonderful state Utopia which nurtures us,' concluded the doctor genuinely.

I was taken to the confabulation room where the treatment began. As the treatment began, at first seemed like a dream; even enjoyable but soon a subtle anxiety and unpleasantness started to form within my head.

'We will minus your past; harmful, hurtful memories and augment you back into the harmonious contemporaneous mean of the utopian state.

'To only follow the states' will, minus my own; no mysterious great plus sign?' I questioned.

The doctor looked confused then replied, 'Yes Bayes, we will add many pluses of pseudo memories during your confabulation treatment.'

'But no great plus sign?' I asked.

'I am not sure what you mean Bayes, perhaps it is the medicine we are giving you?' replied the doctor puzzled.

'I am not sure either doctor?' I replied confused yet uneasy.

Suddenly I was taken to different parts of my past, a rushing kaleidoscope of experiences, forwards and backwards, at different speeds and intensities, like a computer searching for a file on a hard drive.

The memories were unsettling, the uncontrolled past memories being moved around causing me to feel severe anxiety.

I started to lose track of reality, then a memory was played on a screen, it was captured, digitized, modified and put back into my mind. It had damaged the memory of the confidence interval cull, the Arcadian express, the primary painful memory.

A new banal memory was written over it. As randomly played pseudo memory running again and again, until I started to believe it actually happened. Just as I thought I could endure no more and would completely succumb to the process, the computer screen went blank; mercifully my mind was no longer controlled by the confabulation treatment.

'What is going on?' cried out the doctor who he felt was on the verge of healing my tortured mind.

A loud speaker in the hallway bleared out, "Doctor please report to the conference room, priority." The doctor immediately left the confabulation room, obedient to the official summons.

It seemed like an eternity before the doctor returned to the confabulation room; his expression was that of frustration with the message he had received informing him to stop all further confabulation treatment administered on me. The doctor looked at me as if he had failed me in the treatment as he dutifully unfastened the straps and took me back to the conservatory.

A few days later I met the doctor again in his office. The doctor closed the door then we both sat on opposite each other at his desk.

I felt broken by the many treatment sessions and medicine doses.

The doctor sensing my breaking point started the conversation by stating, 'Bayes I want to tell you sincerely that we want endogeneity; we want the endogenous variable to be influenced by lagged previous endogenous results, coupled with the error term.

'We want that, we want a baised, skewered, not completely stochastic, not completely random results, we want a biased controlled malleable result that has autocorrelation in it, has some predictability in it, that has a skewered lagged predictable autocorrelated relationship hidden within the model;

unlike true econometrics, unlike true statistics where endogeneity is eradicated.

'Where there is no correlation, where lagged endogenous variables influencing the error term are not wanted.

'But we want non stochastic results; endogeneity.

'With econometrics and statistics, a pure unbiased results is wanted but the State's model, Bayes, the state's model; we want a skewered result, we want a controlled result; we want results to equal the given prior.

'We want the data to fit the prior assumed, expected, regression function line; unlike with real statistics, unlike with real econometrics where the best fit, the best least unbiased estimator, the regression function is the result of the data.

'With the state it is the other way round, we want the data to fit around the gradient, to fit around a prior regression function, to fit around the aggregate demand that we create, the consumption we control, the state we control, the variables we control; the results we control.

'So we want endogeneity, we want the error terms to be not equal to zero, given the endogenous term, we want autocorrelation; we want that.

'But simultaneously we don't want individual exogenous nodes; we don't want nodes that are outside the model, nodes that can influence the endogenous variables but cannot be influenced by them. We want endogeneity; we want endogenous nodes, not exogenous nodes.

'We don't want variables that are outside the model, so there's a contradiction in terms; collectively we want endogeneity but individually we want non-exogenous nodes; endogenous nodes,' concluded the doctor.

The following days and weeks; I became completely docile and compliant to the stationary endogenous routines and rules of the clinic and processing orderlies.

I no longer rallied to the aid of other unfortunate exogenous. I merely sat accepting the routines expected of me and of this micro society within the walls of the Ministry of Archetypes Augmentation Clinic.

Yet within this constrained, controlled environment, at the very limit of society's control, I felt strangely free. I no longer worried about constraining my thoughts to appease the sigma node scanners on the outside of these walls.

I had embarrassed myself throwing away my career to immaturely rebel against the system; what better alternative was there? I no longer had a clear memory of my past role at the Ministry of Inferences and the unpleasant feelings I strangely associated with these almost forgotten memories partially corroded by the incomplete confabulation room treatment.

Names such as "White," "Arcadia," "Confidence interval," "Apophenia," resonated in the murky partially damaged area of my mind which was not completely corroded yet I struggled to remember, not helped by the compulsory consumption of brain fogging medicine twice daily.

A form of chemical exogenous shocks to my organic default thinking, augmenting my mind into a conforming stationary thinking process as if they were anti-shocks, anti-errors correcting my mind back to the stationary imagination-less, will-less of simply conforming and flowing the expected accepted trends and routines.

My thinking was integrated, mean-less, exogenous; influenced by imagination, will and the animal spirit, unpredictable, creative, attributes of a non-conforming mean-less mind where the errors did not fit or correlate within the carefully chosen endogenous dependent variables or fit with expected results of the great linear regression model; therefore I was mad.

Therefore I must become sane, stable, stationary and accept the fixed, given, known, mean of the great beta linear regression model's apodictic null hypotheses by accepting state Utopia's quotas and expectations.

What alternative hypothesis was there, I concluded?

Accepting the clinic's strict routines was the only way to becoming truly sane again.

I am on my way to being cured; I have accepted that there was no other alternative and that this Utopian system is the best.

I meditated clinging onto the mantra constantly the only way to becoming sane once again then I could contribute to this great Utopian state once again as an obedient, conforming, confident, rational thinking mean, accepting proudly as a contributing endogenous node; no longer ashamed or embarrassed due to my past rebellion.

I sat in the glass Victorian conservatory surrounded by the different exogenous patients who sat or shuffled around without meaning or direction.

Some were trapped in their exogenous, chaotic, stochastic, non-stationary, mean-less, mad thinking yet there was hope they could be cured of their depression their micro subconscious rebellion to escape the mundane, to escape the hopelessness of the conformity of the common node, the menial life of un-fulfilment but they would be cured and sent back to proudly accept the given, known, fixed, mean of the stationary procedures of the utopian state.

As I sat in the conservatory with the other exogenous patients I looked out through a large glass window and focused intently on the outside garden scenery. I was seeking solace to escape this mundane existence of waiting sedated for another helping of toxic medicine.

Normalised Utopia

I felt resigned to the sedated apathy surrounding me.

As I stared outside I noticed the bare silhouette of a leafless autumn tree, standing out against the morning sky; a glorious sunrise. The clouds illuminating by the resplendent orange and red tints accentuating the fresh morning sky which itself gleamed with a pure, clean, innocence of different shades of blue; a patchwork of layered impressionistic textures.

Different grey and white clouds intermingled into a fractal, smoothed tapestry of a classical sunrise. The morning sky, lit up by the rising sun, to grace the slumbering earth with its presence, once again.

A solitary puffy opaque cloud glided against the orange and red sunrise accentuated by the solitary tree silhouette jutting out proudly against the sky, the tree, branching out forming a binary expansion fractural rounded pattern, forming a rounded border.

The shape of the tree branching out reminded me of a schematic graph of synapses of a growing brain, growing either right or left at each decision point.

How Arima was right about the brain resembling a bonsai tree.

The synapses of the brain were malleable, physically growing in different directions as if fluid, especially in unbiased growing nodes. The Utopian state could affect its growth and direction within individuals; as Arima had socially engineered.

Arima had mentioned how they could not change their synapses in fully developed brains yet with the introduction of other trees, other nodes, other minds perhaps they could affect the individual's mind indirectly.

I appreciated the illuminated background of the sky, lit up by a solitary cloud passing directly behind the silhouette of the tree, the sky was beautiful.

It was just a tree but I saw a confidence interval within the shape of the branches and within the cloud a randomness of unrealised probabilities which I perceived as hovering just directly behind the tree; the cloud glowed a soothing bright orange and red as the cloud was lit up by the elusive rising sun.

The glowing cloud just behind the branches resembled the thoughts and knowledge that the nodes' minds which fed on within the growing branch synapses.

The mind schematically resembled this leafless tree.

Its nutrients are knowledge and ideas. The sensory input represented by the sky and the lit up cloud. The lit up cloud resembled the knowledge of a biased mind.

The tree branches like synapse, the breeze passing through the leafless branches, a metaphor for the branches feeding on the knowledge and ideas of sensory input presented by the fresh morning sky and the illuminated cloud.

The lit up cloud resembled the knowledge, thoughts and soul of the mind. What actions and ideas the mind and soul took, was it purely from the synapse of a node that can change their mind or perspective faster that a fluid synapse can transmit.

Therefore maybe it was the cloud of knowledge that decided or influenced the individual's change of mind, to be good or bad, to like or dislike. If other individuals came that were tainted, they could influence the mind as well, like the other trees, also were lit up by the cloud.

What determines a mind's action and ideas, a spirit, its purity in the synapse of a node's mind; it can change the node's mind and perspective faster than a fluid synapse.

Maybe it was the cloud of knowledge that decides or influences the mind's spirit or chooses what mind is good or bad, to like or dislike something. If other ideas appeared that were tainted, then they could influence the node's mind as well, like the other trees, always lit up by the cloud. Maybe the cloud represented the spirit?

I was awoken from my meditative contemplation to be wheeled through the foyers to the doctor's office.

The doctor interviewed me in his office once again, his tone and emotions were unusually serious this session. As he was aware that I had changed that I had accepted and submitted once again to the state's confidence interval and economic efficiency act.

'So Bayes how are you?'

'I do not know.'

'You don't know?'

'No.'

'What have you to say?'

'About what?'

'About things in general?'

'Nothing.'

'Nothing?'

'Yes.'

'Why?'

'Because I am nothing'.

'How are you nothing.'

'Because I am exogenous.'

'And so?'

'Because the exogenous variable nodes are not affected by the great economically efficient regression function model that guides the nodes to be the most efficient they can be relative to the states monthly quotas. Therefore we cannot do anything.'

'Do anything?'

'Yes.'

'Why do you say that?'

'Because the great Beta of the state is everything.'

'And contribution to the great Economic Efficient of the state and Beta of the model is everything.'

'Exogenous terms are not able to contribute efficiently to society. The exogenous nodes are correlated with the insignificant contributing error terms. Therefore the exogenous cannot be guided by the normalized sigma which is held in place by the great fixed mean. The exogenous nodes and I were within the model yet we are fixed with the prior contrived data of the model, we are also not correlated with the endogenous variables in a pure econometrics model therefore we are not able to cointegrate or move efficiently within the great mean as it shifted each month. Therefore the exogenous nodes are not efficient, we cannot contribute efficiently therefore we cannot do anything within a state that demands its continuous all pervasive influence to guide, nurture and augment the node within a harmonious normalized Utopia.'

Normalised Utopia

'In pure econometrics the exogenous terms influence the endogenous terms but in the great statically augmented state the regression model gradient line is drawn first then the variable nodes quotas are added to fit the model. Therefore the endogenous variable nodes are affected by the great guiding model but the exogenous nodes are disproportionately affected and uncorrelated with the guiding model and are therefore inefficient outside within the model.

Therefore relative to the utopian state, the exogenous nodes do not contribute at all or are inefficient therefore they are nothing.'

'Like the error terms?'

'No far worse.'

'Why?'

'Because the errors terms do produce individual contributions to the model yet because they are not part of the defined endogenous variables which have measured contributions, the many time dependent error values are therefore average out, rendered redundant white noise, relegated to a value of zero, relative to the great summed regression model.'

'But the exogenous are far worse, they are outside of the model uninfluenced by the direction of the state's statistical influence therefore do not contribute efficiently nor in a correlated manner to the model at any specific event or over the averaged time duration. They are not important, they are redundant; they are nothing.'

'Like you.'

'Yes,' I said resigned to his vanquished position.

'Well good Bayes that is the best answer I have ever heard from a patient. A more in-depth response than say a Delta telling me, he knows his place and Hip, Hip Hooray for Autarky and the state,' said the doctor proudly.

'They are far less bad than me as I knew the great workings of the state, of the statistical, econometric, actuarial implications and calculations but I allowed myself to transgress. To first become wilfully economically inefficient then a subversive outlier and then finally I chose to hide in my psyche, in the limitless, variance free, non-stationary, uninfluenced maddens of the exogenous. Hiding from my responsibilities, trying to form my own regression model within my skewered perceptions,' I concluded.

'Very well done Bayes, I am confident in your response with almost approaching certainty. You are to be released soon, to integrate back into the state but in a marginalised position,' replied the doctor.

'I am not worthy; I am a habitual transgressor, an exogenous nothing!' I eagerly protested against my release.

'Do not worry Bayes we will help you integrate back. You will spend yours days contributing to the great state, processing your insignificant individual integration function curve, a simple low tech record of your contribution,' said the doctor as he fumbled on the keyboard whist looking through my medical records.

'You will be relegated into a low sigma caste, your duties and quota will not be very restrictive or demanding,' continued the doctor.

'Thank you doctor, I anticipate my return, so I may pay back the great utopian state tenfold with all the contributions and work that I owe,' I genuinely replied.

'Here Bayes, here his your key chain your new eGraph,' said the doctor handed me a physical emanation of my obedience to the Utopian state once again.

'Thank you doctor, I will cherish this, my new chance at contributing to the state. Once again I hope to remain deep within the centre, within the rich bright colours and never become shades less again,' I said eagerly.

'Yes Bayes, I know. Well done,' relied the doctor smiling with a proud patronising contentment.

The directors and psychiatrists of the Ministry of Archetype's Augmentation Clinic took note of my behaviour and response; on numerous occasions they had waited for me to ask for early release or to be upgraded to a special privilege rating but I never did.

Their numerous tests had finished and they concluded with a 95% confidence that I was cured. I was normalised and would become part of the normalised Utopia of the great state. I was now ready to be placed back into a marginalised position as an endogenous node, to be allowed to further contribute once again.

I was indeed cured, was the general consensus of the Ministry of Archetype health board. I would be integrated back into society at a menial level and monitored indefinitely.

Some psychiatrists even protested that I be monitored at all as they were so sure that their treatment had worked. I was now an ideologically loyal believer of state Utopia and of the Economically Efficient Society, a devotee of the stationary process and given, known, fixed mean. A mean which I cherished that I could once again wrap my existence around in the official expected normalised distribution as it made me stationery, it made me sane.

I was no longer a threat; rather a conquered trophy, pet that they would allow out to pasture.

Yet I was an asset of state Utopia, my education and now augmented pro-statistical state beliefs, some had even argued that they return me back to my previous role at the Ministry of Inferences.

Even some Alphas at the Ministry of Inferences issued requests that I be released and allowed to reintegrate back into the Ministry.

But rules were rules; once a node had been sent to the Ministry of Archetype Augmentation Clinic they would be forever a potential liability to the Economically Efficient Society therefore they would be destined to an existence of menial labour.

I was vanquished was the general consensus in the states ministries yet to me I was no longer mad, a veil had lifted off my head, I now considered myself free because I was sane as I now accepted the system; state Utopia.

I would now be sane for as long as I remained immersed within a mundane, menial existence then there would be no reason why I would ever break out of this new default pattern which would perpetuate indefinitely unless some outside source were to alter that.

But the Ministry of Inferences would see to that, there will never be an outside stochastic exogenous shock to ever influence me ever again. I would be kept here and monitored indefinitely.

"More monitoring, less shirking!" was a popular Epsilon node propaganda slogan.

Beside I should consider myself lucky as most patients of the Ministry of Archetypes do not get released so quickly.

A janitor at Kings cross tube station would be my new caste from now on. I would be tightly constrained within a minimum wage job and further financially constrained with the burdens of significant liabilities ratios such as expensive room rental cost that would corrode my minuscule disposable income, rendering it non-deferrable.

I would never be able to defer consumption and save enough credits to achieve any significant working capital to free myself of the menial minimum wage work caste whilst forever banned by the utopian state from applying for any middle class career related employment.

I would be perpetually monitored by augmented technology of the utopian state; being part of the lowest sigma caste we would be monitored more so than the average Beta nodes.

341

The Beta nodes' appreciated additional incentives, that the lower Epsilon caste did not receive nor did they fully appreciate. The Epsilon nodes only respected rigid rules and monitoring.

10: Unbiased inferences.

I mundanely walked along the busy cold, wet street towards the monorail station as I began the morning obedient to my new marginalised expected work routines, like a predictable stationary process of an obedient endogenous Epsilon node, the lowest Sigma ranking. I stood apathetic aboard the monorail carriages whilst standing quashed in-between the hordes of huddled indifferent commuters.

I stared out of the monorail window in my now usual vacant semi depressed state, down through the intermittent monorail bridges as I observed the little busy nodes down below, all grey and wet, rushing through the streets, across roads, onto and off buses, dodging each other yet collectively they resembled a huge dynamic, singular random morphing system almost like a huge morphing grey pulsating amoeba.

Singular yet comprising the collective commuting nodes and pedestrians; synchronised, this disorganised giant organism, heaving and contorting upon the wet street.

The collective animated vigour and passion of the nodes gave the imaginary organism life. It gave the city streets and buildings an energy; coupled with the energy of the rain and the weather, giving the morning a refreshing vital ambience.

I drew solace, a therapy from watching my fellow endogenous nodes running to and fro accentuated in the falling rain as they were all contributing; obediently, confidently to the great regression function of state Utopia's Beta.

I felt once again proud to be like them, to be a contributing, loyal, stationary processing endogenous node, contributing to the utopian state, accepting the state's apodictic null hypotheses and of the great given, fixed societal mean; it is the best it can be. The contrived data and confirmation bias to fit around a preordained mean, a preordained BLUE, a best linear unbiased estimator.

This sentiment conveyed to me that I was truly sane once again, I was a normal, confident, mean thinking, normalised endogenous sigma node, nestled safely within the confidence interval quotas of the utopian state.

Normalised Utopia

A confident economically efficient node nestled once again safely within the confidence interval's given, known, fixed monthly quotas of the great Beta population regression function.

As a Epsilon node, I now accepted it; I deserved it for my past transgressions, my past doubts of the utopian state, my ingratitude of being offered a possible promotion into the Alphaship of the great state Utopia. Now I was content to happily exist in the lower end of the confidence interval within my marginalised sigma caste indefinitely.

I noticed on the outside of the monorail window a random array of different sized shaped water droplets formed on the glass. I watched as they slithered downwards, pulled by the inescapable gravity coupled by the wind drag sucking some of them backwards. Inevitably a random sample of droplets slowly lost adhesion to the sample space of the glass, their cohesion surface tension buckling, deforming and then inevitably succumbing to the wind drag force.

Yet they definitely broke up just before falling from the window into the turbulent abyss of the glassless realm yet they left behind smaller water droplet versions of themselves. These remnants of a water droplet clung onto the side of the window, too small to be sucked off by the wind drag its adhesion vital and too strong to immediately succumb to gravity.

The rain droplets were similar to all living creatures; the nodes animatedly lived yet they inevitably succumbed to the exogenous superior forces of the wind drag and gravity; outside of the two dimension sample space of the glass.

Yet they spawned little water droplet offspring before they died that would carry on their defiant fight against the inevitable exogenous forces that rendered them mortal whilst they defiantly clung onto the outside window and chaotic turbulent, probabilistic, atmospheric manifold, creating countless exogenous shocks to the relative dimension of the stationary glass window's sample space and it adhesive properties.

This rain droplet realm, a partial derivative existence formed upon the window, exhibited a similar model of the nodes outside, their movements and patterns transformed onto a different two dimensional sample space.

But the movements of the rain droplet and the newly forming ones were random, stochastic, not controlled by the glass realm only by the chaotic

346

random exogenous turbulent storm of the passing wind drag; a proxy for the probabilistic ether.

I strangely derived an inward therapy from staring at these dynamic scenes every morning from the window of the monorail which towered above the roads and side streets of Primary_Sample_Space.

Its intermittent huge gleaming white pillars towered above the road, its ultra-modern all white monorail effortlessly glided along the track high above. It was as if there were some nagging variables missing in my psyche about death and the nodes but this water droplet rebirth and defiance in the face of inevitable insurmountable odds somehow consoled me.

I purposefully took the monorail to Kings Cross tube station even though it was out of the way. It made no sense as the journey was much longer and more expensive yet I gained solace from observing and inferring the nodes' stochastic routines and the water droplets defiant rebirth in the face of inevitable entropy. It reminded me of my foggy past that I could not quite remember as an econometrician of some sort at the Ministry of Inferences. I had forgotten, now it did not matter.

Even though now I was a proud contributing endogenous low ranking sigma, Epsilon node janitor at Kings Cross tube station, I still retained a latent distributed lagged interest in the statistical movements and routine process of the commuting pedestrian nodes. It brought me an intangible contentment, to escape the mundane apathetic ordinary, to observe mathematics; its patterns, routines and infallible systems unfolding around me.

All systems tend towards an infallible mathematical structure. Yet I am fallible therefore I am no system, I concluded. I hoped this minor thought which exhibited no excessive emotions would not be detected by the scanners. I opened up my Ministry of Archetypes medicine and took a sip as I was expected to do this hour. It would keep me from relapsing into the psychosis of the exogenous realm.

As I looked out of the monorail carriage window I resided in a different world inside my mind, calculating, appreciating, inferring the chaotic dances and restricted random movement of the nodes below as they traverse the pavement and crossed the wet streets intermittently.

Every foot step of the wet nodes left minor puddles and resonating interfering waves that for a few microseconds transverse their puddle ocean with the same intensity and pride as imposing waves would do on the Atlantic Ocean during a stormy grey day.

Yet the state no longer cared about the finer nuances of my mind and my implied thoughts as I was now an Epsilon node. What was worse I thought, to be continually monitored and have every thought dissected or to be cut adrift; to a marginalised fate where no one cared what I thought or felt?

But it was not to be dwelt upon I was a toilet cleaner now and I would welcome a new surname beginning with 'E' which I was relatively certain would be issued at any time soon.

I could connect to the endogenous sigma nodes conceptually from my transient position whilst I witnessed their relative fleeting positions as I voyeur into their lives momentarily, high above on the monorail, noting them; their faces, their expressions, their clothes, their body language, their movements and patterns, instantly analysing them and superficially classifying them. As the never ending stream of nodes appeared and disappeared in each street as the monorail whooshed past high above.

The irony is that I still was classifying and quantifying, predicting the nodes from a high untouchable position but now I was completely powerless; no longer within the nurturing care of the Ministry of Inferences.

I was now sane although depressed. Depression itself was perhaps the mind's own created lobotomy; emotional repression, ultimately constraining the nodes within their own restricted thoughts and routines. To a point where I no longer was aware or even cared about the countless options the world had to offer.

Now just accepting; accepting whatever the utopian state decided, to counter the madness of the exogenous individuality of the free will and the intangible imagination or irrational beliefs and ideologies falling outside of the state sanctioned propaganda quotas.

As the medicine sank into my stomach and diffused into my blood steam I felt the stationary warm chemical hand of the state enter my body and I was grateful. Any probability of a slightly exogenous or statistically significant wrong thought being realised, slowly disappeared as I was healing once again twice daily when ingesting the medicine.

Normalised Utopia

I felt stationary, constant, stable, reliable, and obedient within the quotas of the non-stationary homoscedasticity. I was a true Epsilon node now, who would slavishly follow every expected; routine, emotion, implied thought, consumption and work quota, to the tee.

This society we live in; it is the best it can possibly be. I concluded whilst within my solitary meditative observations and inference aboard the monorail.

Yet I was still analysing the nodes, still looking down at them from a lofty yet distant and ultimately lonely position even now as a lowly Epsilon node.

I got off the monorail and made my way down the steps into the New Kings Cross toilets.

I stood quietly in the changing room whilst putting on my blue overalls.

'Morning Bayes,' greeted Euler as he walked in.

'Morning Euler,' I replied.

'Wet weather again,' he responded.

'Keeps the streets clean I suppose,' I replied almost automatically, in a mundane, complacent tone of submissive optimism.

Euler was my fellow Epsilon work colleague who was probably assigned to befriend and watch over me, I am sure. He seemed too intelligent and competent to be a simple ignorant Epsilon node.

I considered his name signified not only that he was a Epsilon node but perhaps alluded to the famous equation where all the primary symbols of notation; multiplication, addition, exponentiation, equalities, transcendental numbers and imaginary numbers are used, all comprised into a compact equation equalling zero; just like I was now.

As I was now in a perpetual marginalised position within the great linear regression model of the state, no matter what I try to do within this society, it would always regress me to a zero financial and societal utility position.

But they need not bother as I was completely cured of my madness; I was now a firm believer of the utopian state, more so than I had even been before.

This time I need not even hide my thoughts which were limited, repressed by my subtle permanent

352

depression, embarrassment by my past actions which I had now learnt were wrong.

A janitor was what I deserved, I had betrayed the utopian state, the best system that there could be. What other alternative was there? Nothing.

Nothing filled my mind most days as I cleaned the toilet cubicles, reeking of diluted bleach, in the dimly, yellow lit node public toilets at Kings cross monorail tube station.

I never wavered in my new dedication to the job as it was my duty, my rightful punishment to endure the menial, humiliating job.

Another arbitrary Epsilon janitor appeared at the toilet entrance.

'I have a problem; a young unbiased has lost his originator, would you hold onto him, while I track her down?'

'No unbiased are allowed in the node toilet cubicles, you know", I said following the strict protocols of the underground tube station.

'Ok, we can hold onto him for a while,' replied Euler.

'Can't you Bayes,' smiled Euler cheekily, looking in my direction.

I looked a bit shocked but said compliantly, 'Well ok then.'

The little unbiased was about eight years old and stood by the doorway sobbing to himself whilst tears ran down his flushed cheeks.

The little unbiased was well dressed and looked like he came from a good family.

He stood alone looking scared and upset. I immediately felt sympathy for this vulnerable little, innocent, unbiased. I had not felt sympathy for anyone since my rehabilitation.

I approached the unbiased to detain him whilst Euler went to look for his originator but I also wanted to console him because I do not like to see a node cry, especially an unbiased.

As I approached the unbiased, I said, 'Hello,' in a silly high pitched voice coupled with an over exaggerated smile. It was the way an adult sometimes greeted an unbiased trying to get into their innocent mentality.

Fighting back the tears the little unbiased looked up at me sheepishly with his big innocent blue eyes and replied, Hello.'

The unbiased asked, 'Are you going to find my originator?'

'I don't know where she is?' I replied.

'I want my Originator,' cried out the little unbiased and began to sob uncontrollably.

I replied in a soothing tone, 'Don't worry we will find her,' but I did not know who or where she was.

As we waited there in the entrance of the public toilets of the underground tube station the little, unbiased began to calm. The now reassured little unbiased and myself watched all the nodes scurrying to and fro, throughout the tube station.

The little unbiased sipped on a soda drink that I bought him from the vending machine as we stood and watched the sigma nodes hurrying past on their continual quest to satisfy their expected mundane daily work routines and personal consumption.

The little unbiased asked me completely automatically and genuinely, 'Why do all the nodes look so sad?'

I was shocked by the deep, innocent, insightful inference and question. I found myself fumbling for an answer, at first trying to look for an answer as my new role as an uncle figure whilst addressing the little unbiased but I could not find one. So I tried to look deeper into my new reformed adult psyche but there was no answer there either.

Yet within my deeper self, I felt some muted, blurred, repressed, intangible answer lurking within my damaged yet reformed new stationary psyche; some sort of discontent, for the current system but I could not comprehend any meaning or find any words to tell the little unbiased.

I simply replied, 'I don't know.'

The unbiased continued, 'Why do they walk so fast and funny?'

Again I was shocked at the simple innocent observations and inferences that only an innocent unbiased could ask.

His innocence cutting away all the superfluous lies, illusion, statistical augmentation, trimming and packaging of the statistically compliant society that we found ourselves immersed in.

I searched my psyche for some answer yet I found none. I paused, then stammered as I struggled to deal with the little unbiased's innate, intangible, innocence that cut through, to the underlying truth of the situation.

'I am not sure,' I replied again.

'Why do they all go to work at the same time?' continued the little unbiased.

'Well,' I replied, trying to give some answer to a seemingly simple yet complex question which involved sophisticated statistical and behaviour analysis which I had spent my whole career at the Ministry of Inferences working on.

I blurted out in a desperate attempt to hold onto my newly rehabilitated mind-set, 'Because they work to keep the economically efficient state running, harmoniously.'

The little unbiased stopped staring at the crowds and sipping on his soft drink and looked up at me, saying nothing but giving me a questioning look of disapproval. It was a look of perhaps of not fully understanding the adult dialogue that I had replied with. Or perhaps a deeper look, of knowing far more than I, about the question and answer; that my response was wrong and was not meant to have been said.

I could not work out which type of look it was. But the look that the little unbiased gave me, made me feel embarrassed with the answer I had just given.

These innocent questions by the little unbiased was slowly starting to erode my current emotionally depressed, reformed, compliant psyche.

These questions from the little unbiased who I felt empathy for, whose innocent mind had not yet been subjected to the full glare of the controlling states propaganda and conditioning, was asking inadvertently many simple yet deeply relevant questions.

These questions triggered my deep, repressed inner consciousness, starting to stir my emotions and send psychological exogenous shock waves deep into my depressed reformed psyche that enveloped me in a patriotic and ever compliant fog of deluded perceptions and statistical conformity since being released from the Ministry of Archetypes Augmentation Clinic.

I then found an answer to the little unbiased question, I exclaimed, 'Conditional probability' as if Archimedes himself was exclaiming, "Eureka".

'Conditional probability causes the nodes to all walk to together to work because they all have a job; the current probability arises because of the existence of past probability events; they are realising probability events due to given prior probability events having taken place.

'So you see, they all go to work because they have jobs,' I said relieved, even patronising the little node who still looked at me not amused; as if not comprehending the answer or having an deeper innocent wisdom, that rejected my conditional probability hypothesis.

The little unbiased's originator finally appeared looking visibly upset whilst being ushered in by Euler. She broke into tears when she saw her unbiased, running up and embracing him.

After a few minutes of the emotional reunion she managed to fight through the tears saying that they both had passed through an automatic tube station door but it suddenly locked in with her unbiased on the other side. Fortunately after a while the door had become unlocked as mysteriously as it had been locked.

The originator could not thank us enough for returning her unbiased; she then walked off with her unbiased.

I was grateful that it was just a case of an unbiased losing sight of its originator for only a while but I was also grateful to the unbiased for being the catalysis to clear my mind and to indemnify my psyche back to the prior Ministry of Archetype period.

I return to my toilet cleaning duties; as I cleaned the urinals and toilet seats obsessively almost enjoying the hopeless mundane ritual of, no thoughts, no responsibilities, to just accept my marginalised position which I deserved yet in the deep recesses of my psyche there were nagging questions or feeling about something being quite not right.

A name shot into my mind, I could see it written in calligraphy writing, "Arcadia". I could not quite remember what that meant.

I then considered conditional probability when it's contemporaneous, realised, an event existing now, given the existence of a prior event previously being realised; creating this current probability situational event.

Differing connected probable outcomes creating a continuous series of interconnected realised outcomes; a cornerstone of the Bayesian equation, separating it from statistical classical models.

The state wanted current events and results realised given a prior engineered event and probabilities having existed so it could perpetuate and predict the self-obligating statistically complaint nodes whose prior and current conditional probability events would process seamlessly, interchangeably, like an electromagnetic light wave, fluctuating continually between an electric field perpendicular to a magnetic field; continuing to propagate onwards, forever within a fixed stationary frequency, a predictable deterministic mean.

The state engineer all the conditional events and probabilities arising, creating a propagation of future predictable events, realised outcomes, to maximise its economic efficiency model, the stationary trend of the great Beta; all to perpetuate with near certainty and compete predictability, the aggregate demand curve.

Yet the utopian state does not completely control conditional probability; even though I stand in this currently realised, statistically constrained, situational event; created relative to a previous engineered, utopian state sanctioned event.

Conditional probability reaches far beyond the scope of the utopian state sanctioned confidence interval. Perhaps conditional probability coupled with freer thinking could be an alternative hypothesis to that of the statistically constrained state Utopia.

I felt a part of the little unbiased innocence had somehow seeped into my current reformed complaint psyche, making my psyche tainted with a refreshing innocence, an unbiased perspective, making me appreciate every splendid creation and the wonder of realty; the cumulative total of all conditional probabilities realised so far.

The trees, the sky, the nodes' vital faces; even the urinal was a beautifully smooth white design. I was appreciating and questioning everything, with an unbiased inference; an innocence. Perhaps this was the spark of my inner psyche, igniting its past remnants, to burn brightly once again.

Normalised Utopia

I realised then that I had felt a shadow of my former self until now. Like the shadow residing within the node's dark recesses of their psyche yet I had submitted to the state's statistical quotas, allowing my will and imagination to be rendered a constant; a predictable, stationary process, endlessly processing the correct frequency relative to a given, official known, fixed mean.

Perhaps the statistical quotas was the dark shadow incarnate that I allowed myself to be immersed in; devoid of a will and imagination, replaced by the ever present given, known, fixed mean of the utopian state.

But I decided to act as if nothing had changed to continue my expected rehabilitated routines and present a depressed persona.

I swept up the countless brown and yellowing leaves outside the train station which were discarded by the autumn trees.

Their leaves a metaphor for the discarded thoughts of the endogenous sigma nodes who were ruthlessly preened as well as self-preening their minds, intentions, imagination and their very free will; to adhere to the strict statistical confines of the utopian state.

The leaves are perpetually trimmed from the trees, a symbolic minus of the unwanted, inconvenient truths that the nodes and even the trees produce.

I was now relegated to a caste of a humble janitor; that could no longer affect the state or the nodes within. Marginalised and isolated in my lonely job, only Euler the probable spy watched me as I left to go and sweep the halls of the train station and the foyer outside.

It was a fair treatment and just a position for me to obsessively sweep and stroke away the dirt of the state, maybe a metaphor for my old position.

Now I sweep the autumn leaves of the trees; fallen brown leaves, all different shades of brown, once green, now hard, brittle and discoloured, ready to crumble and crackle under the weight of the mighty broom.

I likened the discarded leaves; to the discarded thoughts of the nodes; relative to the trees metaphor; trees seeming like brain as their Fibonacci ratio branching iteration; towards a curved fractal horizon of the leaf canopy silhouette periphery similar to the decision binary branching of the nodes thoughts.

The canopy resembling a brain as I imagined in the Ministry of Archetypes and as Arima mentioned too.

I swept up the discarded thoughts of the trees' fallen leaves or perhaps pruned by the ever transient state's horticulturists.

Like unwanted thoughts or restricted thoughts; pruned by the state or self-augment by compliant nodes, forcing themselves to think within the confidence interval, to think mean, to be confident.

To wrap their thoughts, intentions and emotions around the known, given, fixed mean; wrapping themselves within the enveloping normalised distribution of expected thoughts, relative to their caste, like all organisms do, wrapping themselves around the probability derived niche they find themselves residing in.

Their actions and intentions wrapped around their environmental niche in the most efficient manner, indefinitely, until changes due to random probability of the relative randomness of their chaotic actions and intentions of the nodes, to change their niche environment, to suit their biological needs and ideologies.

As I raked the leaves into large piles that represented the state's bloated government departments and institutions, my mind began to wonder whilst my body continued its automatic, default, stationary processing around a given, known, fixed, biased mean of the expected janitor chore cleaning routines.

My subconscious also processed but with a more unbiased, innocent process, coupled with an open minded prior on most subjects yet still obediently staying stationary within the fixed, know, give mean of statistical conformity.

Yet I was considering conditional probability and how it affected the present relative to a past situation with its variance which spread out and over the confidence interval and far into the infinite void of all possibilities whilst I toiled at the entrance of the tube station, breathing out plumes of misty vapour into the cold evening air.

My mind wandered back into its usual plane of thought, into the almost intangible realm, of the imaginary number plane as it usually did whilst sitting on a tube carriage or staring out of a raindrop specked window.

I thought the letter (i) denotes the imaginary number which resides off the real number plane of the x-axis in its murky irrational plane rotating and morphing around the real numbers in its polar radians.

Only in the imaginary plane do the imaginary numbers exist yet influence the real numbers as Gauss said, the imaginary numbers do exist as alternate numbers.

Yet I only momentarily exist freer within the imaginary number plane, independent of my automated subconscious and body which is permanently trapped within my endogenous sigma caste within the thick statistically controlled ether of the real number dimension which is controlled and monitored every moment.

Only when my mind is immersed into the alternate dimension of the imaginary number plane am I truly free to think and feel when sitting on some tube carriage.

My mind's higher consciousness resides fixed at the end of my gaze, the apex nestled inches in front of an adjacent seated passenger node's chest or in the past when I sit bored at work, staring at the continual flow of real time data, my mind washing away into the imaginary number plane.

Only when my higher consciousness is within the imaginary number plane, am I free, to be truly me; free of the utopian state's scanners and control.

Whilst my consciousness resides within the imaginary plane I am a free thinking individual, I become almost intangible to the scanners and the state.

I become a true individual like the (i) notation of the imaginary number. The complex conjugate of the complex numbers squared with all the probabilities contained within the complex number plane, free of normalised distributions; free to just be, within perhaps the unrealised, unconditional probability realm.

My mind returned to the real number line existence of state utopia once again back to the mundane, apathetic world of the compliant endogenous sigma nodes. Back to my body, back to the sweeping of the discarded brown yellowing leaves; the pile's size was significant now.

I then realised I had lost my eGraph key ring given to me by the Ministry of Archetypes so I may contribute once again to the great state.

I felt the anxiety rise up within me as I frantically looked for the eGraph key ring amongst the countless piles of discarded leaves.

My fingers fumbled desperately searching inside my pockets whilst I searched for the key ring. I needed to find my eGraph key ring, my proof of my compliance of my contribution to the great Utopian state, proof of my stationary wellness and mean compliant sanity. That I was a productive, contributing endogenous healed node; a shining example of the Ministry of Archetype Clinic's medical acumen.

I started to frantically sweep back and forth trying to move the leaves about, to unsettle the piles and find the eGraph key ring. Time was running out, I was scheduled to be back at the train station to finish off the other cleaning duties ironically my search for the eGraph key ring would interfere with my eGraph data; my confidence interval quota compliance.

I slowly stopped frantically sweeping as my body began to tire. I then decided to refine my search with a more sophisticated, methodical, calculated manner. I decided to limit the sample plane to just a specific section of the cobbled stoned, leaf covered entrance yard where I had been sweeping for the last hour.

I then started to update my initial search assumption, my prior. Within my calculations I removed possible sample sections of the floor area where I had been fully conscious within the real number plane reality of my default consciousness but in those areas where my mind had drifted into the imaginary number plane of my subconscious, I marked off a perimeter of that uncertain sample plane region.

I then started to focus my prodding on specific least intuitive areas of the forecourt, it seemed logical, in a counter intuitive way as the first place a search is conducted never really produces a result.

I intuitively realised that the eGraph key ring should be perpendicular to where I initially assume it had been; within the least intuitive region. I remember in the past losing a set of keys and eventually finding them in the least initiative perpendicular circumference arc.

Within a minute of implementing this calculated search I found the eGraph key ring nestled behind a heap of leaves.

I then realised that there was a floating mean; a superior mean that I had found during my search within the leaves; I then realised the importance of the Bayesian updating prior and of its unknown floating mean reality.

This search coupled with the little unbiased coaxing me earlier to consider the realm of conditional probability; a variable within the Bayesian optimisation equation.

Its great Bayesian equation embedded with conditional probability resulting in a continually iterating, updating free floating mean.

I now felt free once again because I had now realised an independent alternative hypothesis of any lurking unattainable names of, "White," "Arcadia" and "confidence interval" which I still could not infer the significance of those worlds or concepts but it did not matter and now I had an independent alternate hypothesis.

At the very core of the probabilistic reality of the real number line there was the Utopian state's given, known, fixed, biased mean and then there was the slightly freer unknown, fixed, unbiased mean of the classical statistics.

Unlike at the Ministry of Archetypes where I could not produce an alternate hypothesis to justify my rebellion and sanity.

Now I felt freer and rejuvenated once again but this time I felt confident within myself not in state Utopia's confidence interval quotas.

I continued my work at Kings Cross public toilets, careful to not change my routines or my regular inane superficial dialogue with Euler. But deep inside, I felt reinvigorated and free once again.

I returned to my solitary apartment that I was still allowed to use even though it was allocated only to the Beta nodes. I would still be allowed to use it until the end of the year then I would be permanently downgraded to an Epsilon caste accommodation.

I walked into the small familiar apartment which brought back a flood of unpleasant, inhibited, dormant emotions.

Normalised Utopia

I was almost shocked to see what I had expected; the furniture, all my clothes, ornaments, everything all turned upside down and knocked over.

I knew the normalised police would come and rip the place apart looking for evidence yet it still shocked me to see the incarnation of that prediction unleashed upon my private sanctuary, my pseudo safe individual sample space ruined and defiled.

As I sat there trying to calm my thoughts, I noticed that the router and monitoring device were dismantled too. I went to try to and dutifully plug them back in as I was still a loyal compliant endogenous node; a healed exogenous node.

As I fumbled around behind the upside down coach, I found behind a window blind, a glass which was half full of a liquid, I sniffed it. It smelt of alcohol. I never drink alcohol.

I started to reposition the furniture back, leaving the glass untouched behind the blind whilst I cleaned up the apartment.

Just then I noticed a magpie bird entangled in the window sill on the washing line I untangled it and continued cleaning.

Two hours later I sat exhausted as I kept thinking about the alcohol glass. I had a faint memory of an unbiased binary giving me a bottle of alcohol but I was not sure. There was a no other binary resident in the apartment block.

I was about to plug in the data monitoring coaxial cable back online so I could be a proud contributing endogenous sigma node of the Utopian state but as I was about to plug in, I saw the magpie returning.

It stood on the window sill; it had a shiny thing in its beak. It dropped whatever it was at my feet as if to thank me for untangling it, I presumed. Then it flew away over the jagged building rooftops.

I picked up the ring it had inscribed inside, "To Doris White with love your beloved husband Fred," two thousand and something; the date was partially worn away.

I then remembered that it was Mrs White's ring.

She gave me the bottle of alcohol the night she disappeared.

It was proof that there was a Mrs White.

Then my mind searched subconsciously for something else. I found the half-filled glass; I took it and drank the alcoholic contents, to honour Mrs White.

Even though I was told not to drink any alcohol as it may corrupt my twice daily Ministry of Archetype prescribed tablets yet I drank anyway.

I then lay depressed upon my couch, not fully comprehending who I was anymore.

Why did I have this apartment when my role was a marginalised Epsilon node?

Who am I?

Then the word, "Arcadia," appeared in calligraphy, coming out of the empty glass.

"Eureka!" I now remembered: the confidence interval, the quotas, Mrs White, the invitations to Arcadia, proof of the unbiased genocide; the statistical oppression.

The bottle of alcohol and the ring were distributed lagged, exogenous shocks that had resonated; undetected, un-inferred, throughout the great utopian statistical model until now.

I then felt the overpowering urge to escape this repressive statistical utopian state immediately.

I decided to leave the apartment whilst the statistical router plug lay unplugged upon the living room floor.

I had to leave right now or never.

11: Bayesian optimization.

I managed to discreetly board the Aqua Prior freight ship which was making its way to some arbitrary far flung developing state port. Any port would do as long as it did not reside within state Utopia or Zhou Pingjun territories.

The weather was overcast, the sea dynamically undulating with large rising and sinking swells covered with small white, chopping breaking froth resembling a liquid incarnation of white noise error terms vibrating of the endless swelling waves' trend lines.

The conditions seemed to worsen with each moment, the Aqua Prior rolled from side to side, listing many degrees significantly past the threshold of what the now enduring merchant sailors would consider comfortable.

Aboard the Aqua Prior nothing was fixed, nothing stable; every utensil, every chair in my cabin room, randomly sliding around. Every inanimate node, every animate node, every mean, everything; in all the cabins and decks was in motion.

Everything sliding randomly, to different degrees of predictability, to different standard deviations from its current mean randomly relative to its immediate past chaotic position.

With each new moment the Aqua Prior itself careened in derivatives of the expected direction, slowly yet unstoppable. Making the ship and the environment within, a rhythmic pendulum of inertia, dragging each and every item to different positions; new unpredictable positions.

Each new listing of the Aqua Prior, a new prior updating; to an eventual mean of more momentary certainty. An eventual distribution of items that would eventually cluster, broken around the alternate sides of the hull. But to what normalised distribution, to what random mean would each piece finally rest?

With each new list of the ship; my confidence of where each certain item would eventually lay shattered and broken was increased as I watched with great anticipation.

Normalised Utopia

As the items in this cabin slowly began to separate into different weights, centres of gravity and frictional surface; methodically separating in a random slow chaotic rhythmic dancing slide as each item began to tend towards a harmonious cluster position on each side of the hull.

I could even predict to a certain confidence the positions of the other items in the other cabins which I could not see but I could faintly hear; noises such as the chairs and tables scraping against a floor.

The banging on the walls giving clues to the density, shape and composition of items as well as their reference points of sliding items in my cabin. I could predict with ever degrees of confidence the individual positions of the broken, misplaced items where they were pooling. My confidence increasing with each new listing of the ship, with each new roll from the waves as I built a subconscious prior as to the random means of where they most probably would be.

The kinetic energy and ever resisting inertia transferred through to all the objects of differing rigidities and tensions. As my hammock swayed with great intensity with a paradoxical random regularity whilst my bag slid violently in opposite directions against the horizon, always rolling into and out of view, from different cabin portholes.

The cracking of the wooden hull, the internal structural wooden architecture of the beams and the tight fitting carpentry was a strangely soothing natural random noise as if even a dead piece of nature, a plank of wood, still managed to contain some intrinsic deeply natural element that could produce a naturally soothing harmonic noise, even the sight of its earthy texture strangely soothed me. I focused on the natural ambiance of this wooden cabin trying to block out the unpleasant listing and accompanying chaos during this rough sea passage.

I was not accustomed to the old fashioned, civilised environment of this well-crafted wooden cabin with all its trimmings and old fashioned designs, covered with layers of lacquered sealing, from centuries ago.

The shiny red brown wood colour of the lacquer tint reflected the ever so slight natural light that shone in from a small hidden sky light from the ship's low cabin ceiling.

The culmination of the rustic beautifully crafted wooden room and the careening of the ship, the unpredictable rolling of the ocean waves, the continual random creaking and bucking noises of the ship's structure and of the items contained within it accentuated by the soft tainted light that filled part of the cabin with an artificial twilight.

All these factors created a positive warm energy in the cabin or just within my calming mind's perception. I felt strangely content, no longer under continual surveillance or beholden to the statistical conformity of State Utopia even if it was only within the belly of an old ship in the midst of rough seas.

I lay in the rolling hammock, my mind wandering unconstrained, yet relaxed, free to follow any particular chain of thought. My mind in an alpha wave frequency, usually experienced just upon waking or before sleeping, where the mind is open to the deep inner self, where the mind is no longer thinking but open to itself; ushering in self-realisations and epiphanies.

The alpha frequency activated upon awakening and near sleep was perhaps why the state motivated the nodes to always be rushing to work; not having enough time to think in the moment whilst subjected to continual bombardment of advertisements throughout the day; from the moment of awakening to the moment of sleep.

A fist pulsated upon the steel hull door then a merchant sailor flowed into the cabin I was resting in. Unfortunately he carried a strongly exotic smelling meal that I had predicted yet had hoped for something blander, more average; tea and biscuits perhaps to stifle the nauseas that I felt within the listing ship.

I sighed with relief when he handed over a light meal of tea and toast whilst indicating to me that the exotic meal was for a fellow sailor.

I had held a biased prior and hypocritically yearned for an average food selection even after all the rebellion against the average norm and forced priors of the utopian state. Yet when I finally gained my freedom from the state; I need to unlearn or forget the past conditioning.

I thanked my host who gazed back at me with an enigmatic smirk which fleetingly existed momentarily, half obscured behind his rough, unshaven facial stubble.

My host then said, 'The floating Aqua prior is considered a constrained region, optimised by the very fabric of probability itself to fit this realised destiny creating this specific situation.

'Aboard the Aqua prior we travel the seas, freely bobbing along, upon the ocean's fluid continents, we are like Sine and Cos graphs, up and down yet completely random, bobbing along.

'We travel the dynamic currents of the oceans, plotting our charts, calculating, attempting to predict different shifting currents and tides but we will always be subject to the unpredictable tantrums of the mother nature as with the unexpected storms and swells that will always make our journeys dynamic, unpredictable; chaotic, stochastic; forever subject to the hetroskedastic, Sine waves of pulsating interferences, enveloping, circumventing around the solid continents, mingling amongst hidden currents of indeterminate liquid trends, surface Sine and Cos waves fuelled by the ever dynamic, fickle unpredictable winds of change of the weather; mother nature herself.

Yet our bobbing functions are cumulatively additive in a linear function creating Fourier transformations tending towards one function curve that of our destiny trend. Who knows for sure where the transformations will tend to even into the imaginary plane.'

Sine then looked at me noticing my shocked at his level of articulation and mathematical insight, all from this rough looking, merchant sailor.

He then laughed saying, 'Call me Sine; Sine Polar.'

His rough practical looking weathered face seemed a paradox incarnate as he was able to so poetically describe his life with an almost mathematical verse again something superficially unexpected from such a rough looking sailor yet I consider that these rough sailor were mathematically gifted, to be able to navigate the treacherously fickle oceans without much modern equipment so Sine's poem was correct; they had a fine mathematical acumen and sharp minds of calculations and of predicating the currents and weather.

Sine was not an oaf, no thug, no leather skinned imbecile but an intelligent sentient being just like myself, perhaps. The state had conditioned me a previously high ranking Beta node to always judge a class or a caste superficially without ever seeing deeper into their minds and spirits.

With the state's restrictive quotas and expected results of every node's routine and procedures, it was nearly impossible to gauge a node's true potential outside of their caste limitations, expected emotions and thought restrictions. Yet here was a real person living free of state Utopia, outside of its restrictions with an equal potential to me even though Sine may look and act like a rough skinned sailor. I was fascinated by this Sine.

Sine left the cabin and I lay on a hammock trying to concentrate on any random thoughts and by trying to block out the nausea by looking at the sea horizon through the portal window.

I considered what had happened to the errors and considered what Arima had said to me had made some sense.

As I lay there my subconscious dwelling on the problem, I became lost in my thoughts; the nausea started to dissipate with respect to each new small increment of time, slowly lessening its torturous grip.

I focused on the horizon staring through the portal window out the corner of my eye as I started to forget my nausea which was worth a million credits to be rid of.

Ungrateful, discontent nodes should be sick once in a while, the wonderful feeling of no longer being sick was worth all the tea in Zhou Pingjun.

I was grateful that my nausea was dissipating to that of being tolerable to a fading unpleasant memory.

Then I heard three pulsating fist banging on the door all their harmonics were all at different frequencies and magnitudes.

They entered and Sine said, 'Hello I have brought you my brothers Cos and Tan to visit you. How is the nausea?'

'It has dissipated,' I replied.

The Polar brothers sat down around my hammock.

'We were all born in Antarctica yet in different sovereign regions and on different meridian lines,' said Cos.

'Where are we?' I asked.

'Well in the Zhou Pingjun there is a character for, "West" and there is a character, "East" but the character for, "Somewhere," in Zhou Pingjun is East and West together,' said Sine.

'So we are somewhere,' I said politely.

Normalised Utopia

'We are east and west,' said Cos.

'Somewhere,' said Tan.

'Somewhere,' I replied, then pausing, 'well that is something, I suppose,' I added.

'That's something,' paused Sin, 'something indefinite,' he continued.

'Definitely, indefinitely,' replied Cos cheekily.

'But somewhere none the least,' concluded Tan with a smile.

'Well please tell me at least we are not going to state Utopia, please tell me at least we are not least going to any developing state. Somewhere but not there,' I pleaded.

'We can tell you, that you are not going there. You are going somewhere but not there,' answered Sin.

'But definitely we are not going there,' added Cos.

'So you have set parameters,' concluded Sin.

'So you have set parameters within a region of indefiniteness, uncertainty,' added Tan.

'But we are somewhere,' I added with a sarcastic confirmation.

'Well maybe I need parameters? Maybe I am not completely ready to accept the free flow of all probabilities; of all possibilities? Maybe I need some risk adversity, I need some weak parameters to guard against the unknown, the unpredictable,' I replied?

'That is perfectly reasonable,' replied Sin.

'But in a safe region of something,' added Cos.

'You want some degree of certainty, of risk adversity by eliminating certain parameters, to reduce the region of confidence into a safer region of possible certainty.

'Simultaneously you want to run away, to an archetypal utopia, an inverse utopian function, an inverse integration, an archetypal antithesis of the society you are running from; a society too advanced, too rigid of statistical conformity and technological reliance.

'Running from a utopian state where you are empowered and enhanced by efficient statistical augmentation and abundant technological utilities yet simultaneously with each incremental advancement of technology and statistical efficiency you are transformed more and more into the converse, the opposite of the collective great state you become inevitably neutered, impotent, reliant; submitting to the state, the statistics and the technology until you are nothing more than a mere complaint obliging shadow upon the cogs of the machine,' said Sine.

'A shadow like a complex number hovering about the real number line, its existence known, calculated yet it does not really exist relative to the real number line, it will never reside on the real number line, unless you make the imagery part of the complex number, a coefficient of zero, or take it complex conjugate,' said Cos.

'So you nodes are like shadows of the imaginary number plane or shadow of a higher dimensional plane, a plane less real less content,' concluded Tan.

'Yes, usurped, barely existing, merely the shadow of a higher dimension, a dimension of the impotent, marginalised, barely existing, usurped by the process,' continued Sin.

'The process?' I asked.

'The process,' replied Cos.

'Yes the process, the great integration curve, the derivative, the region, the function, the A.I. the system, the state, the statistics. The system that was supposed to serve us by providing a continuous supply of in demand goods and services, that are meant to exist to serve us, the nodes, not usurp us into slaves,' said Cos.

'Not even slaves, merely a partial existence, a shadow upon the great cogs of the machine that we all helped to build,' continued Tan.

'Evolution,' said Sin.

'Original sin,' said Sin.

'Whatever.'

'So you seek to run away from it?'

'How can you run from the great mini bang?'

'Mini bang?' I asked.

'Original Sin, unstoppable evolution; technology, statistical conformity which will inevitably usurp us with its dynamic mathematics, algorithms and AI. The general infallible system of the process of the great calculations of the beast.'

'The beast.'

'The advance state.'

'In the distant past we were shipwrecked for a sustained period of time. Where we were not entirely sure but in some remote jungle in a far flung developing state I suppose,' said Sine.

'Unlike you, who actively intends to run away to the jungle; to get away from technology and statistical control,' said Tan.

'Conformity,' said Cos.

'Control of thoughts,' said Sine.

'Control of being,' they all said simultaneously.

'We remember the jungle was harsh and cruel yet regressed to a harmonious mean; nature's mean,' said Tan.

'More a niche, a series of frequencies, different niche dwelling routines, their sum total, a Fourier transformation of their niche and its essence,' said Cos.

'Not so idyllic though,' replied Sine.

'Not so romantic,' added Cos.

'Just existing, cohabiting in a jungle full of competing life,' concluded Tan.

'We encountered many jungle natives who at first were content to lurk on the fringes of the dense jungle. We continued with our everyday routines of harsh survival whilst they continued on with their secretive traditions, keeping to themselves; unable or unwilling to communicate with us, some pale foreign sea dogs.

'Eventually we were accepted into their community but we had to role-play continually; exhibiting over exaggerated simplistic facial expressions, at key moments throughout the day to show our accepted position, as friendly submissive, honoured guests.

'The villagers seemed relaxed and friendly enough; the chief liked us. Most of the tribe were overly friendly and eager to please us, their new novelty. They too, were our novelty as we both witnessed each other's differences,' said Sine.

'I once saw the natives, impaling grubs on a stick and then roasting them alive, not very charitable, or noble,' added Cos.

'Now wonder we have tornados and disease. We lament at natural disasters but we inflict so much misery on other creatures; karma,' I replied.

I was becoming enlightened with a situation, an event that I had not experienced yet it was shifting prior assumptions of jungle life. Their combined wisdom and experience forming my new opinion. They were like the polar coordinates in a complex number function, Sin and Cos waves of a Fourier transformation and now they were like a mini wisdom of crowds creating a new mean of popular opinion. It was having a Bayesian optimization effect on my opinions.

The brothers gave their wisdom; it was a wisdom of crowds, creating an biased opinion, based on wisdom and experience, which allowed my biased opinion, to shift from one side to other another, updating my final external conclusion; my confidence in the level of expected utility that I would receive, if I were to go to a similar jungle, perhaps not a good idea.

I feel my very nature, the very fabric with which my world was constructed, the statistical ether of conditional and unconditional probability; realised and unrealised probability ether, of given and realised events, shrouded by a quantum wave function cloud of unrealised probability, morphing, regressing around the realised, binary expansion, random, normalised event, regressing or an expanded liability.

I feel myself no longer shackled by the ethereal, perception and will of the classical statistical world.

I felt freer; free floating.

I now have been ushered into a world of new statistics; a free floating opinion, based on an average of others opinions yet not a forced opinion as with state Utopia but a free floating opinion; a wisdom on crowds.

A world of Bayesian statistics, updating priors, coupled with the wisdom of crowds and a new realisation, a new epiphany; a new world. A new updated freer world which would become usurped with other countless processes, other concepts, ideals or mathematics but for now and many decades or even millennia I feel myself enlightened in a new world of Bayesian statistical freedom.

A new world that will be a free statistical force that even the state cannot control, inevitably trend towards.

The brothers are the wisdom of crowds incarnate; they helped me form this new Bayesian being. I thank them for that.

Sine continued, 'The jungle is cruel.'

'That is nature; rational, efficient, and ruthless,' said Cos. He then thought for a moment adding, 'like the state,' he then laughed as he noticed my frustration as my jungle utopia quickly dissipated upon hearing their experiences and unrestricted opinions.

'But the jungle is pure and free of statistical scanners,' I replied.

'Idealistic, romantic notions of freedom and natural being,' added Tan.

'Yes but an ideal is not always practical,' said Cos.

'Your experiences outside of the state and your combined averaged wisdom has helped me become wiser without having to experience or rationalise a situation by myself, for the first time, excluding the state's propaganda biased information that continually led my thoughts and being to a convenient contrived pseudo mean,' I said thankfully.

Does not all influences, environments and situations, mould our minds and routines to fit the most efficient niche mean; the very meaning of life and reality itself. The great reality process, to fit ourselves around, the most efficient, at each influencing situation.

So how is the state or the jungle different, even wrong or bad, it just follows the natural process of our earthly existence, to wrap ourselves around the most efficient niche mean it presented without of the great statistical ether of unconditional unrealised probability.

We humans modify our niches to fit an idealistic niche mean, an even more dangerous concept. A concept created and perpetuated by the human mind, originating from original sin, creating evolution and now your insignificant marginalised position within the great system of the statically efficient society,' said Tan.

'Yes we are wise from our experiences, we have saved you the trouble of strife and wasted time. Yes, except each person and existence is different but certain events should reoccur to most similar people,' said Sine.

'You have updated my prior with an almost discrete continuity. You have helped me float my mean core opinion, my general direction, my distribution probability frequency, backwards and forwards, continually updating my mean with new information and perceptions with your wisdom and combined experience.

I thank you for that I will follow true Bayesian statistics and no longer relegated to a pure classical statistical existence.'

And your wisdom is the wisdom of crowds; your slightly differing experiences and personalities has created a wise estimate transformed into an unbiased distribution into a true average mean which I can measure a new unknown situation with a fair degree of certainty. For that I thank you again, I see the future of society, a new societal all pervasive statistical ether but freer,' I concluded.

I said, 'The nodes' prior; their contemporaneous or original assumption of a certain variable or situation, makes them feel certain of a particular happening yet it's always a fixed value, set by the state.

'They are certain of all given fixed priors, based on their previous limited observations created by the restrictive, set means, created and imposed by the Economic Efficiency Act.

'They can never change their opinions, they can never accept new information that would contradict the set mean, the set opinion, that would help them to change their prior assumptions, to accept a new set of posteriors, new assumptions, based on new current unbiased, non-spurious, information; possibilities that would contribute to additional information used in the Bayesian equation.

Allowing the nodes probability expectations to change, the mean of their expectations but they can never accept this as they are trapped in the fixed; the fixed mean of their sigma caste of expected values.

Deep within the artificial, stagnant, confines of the state's statistical conformity of the Economically Efficient Act: a classical statistics prison.'

Sin interrupted, 'The tribes' members were no different than the nodes of state who sit around at night watching their monitors; obedient to the utopian state's news and politicians.'

Tan said, 'We were always in a perpetual state of unease whilst surrounded by the tribe members; feeling controlled and intimidated by them even though we were accepted by the chief yet that could have changed at any minute.'

Cos said 'I remember one day the females of the village carefully impaling little harmless grubs through their fleshy limbless bodies whilst they wriggled and writhed around in pain. After that they put the grubs on the fire as the grubs writhed in agony as they slowly burnt, dehydrated and boiled in their own body fluids.

'I was disgusted watching this. I wanted to shout stop whilst the grubs writhed in agony but I was too scared of the natives they may turn on us,' said Sine.

'We could only muster weak polite smiles as the villagers stole glimpses of us to see if they approved of their cooking habits,' said Cos.

'It is seemed so unnecessarily cruel. Why not kill the grubs before cooking them,' questioned Tan?

I thought back to Apophenia, he was right. Therefore the villagers should not grieve for any natural disasters or personal calamities when they do such unnecessary cruel acts themselves. Perhaps the villagers considered it entertainment of the spectacle of the grubs writhing upon the skewer?

'But at least the primitive jungle society did not have thought scanners and statistical control,' I said.

Sine replied, 'The villagers all looked around in fear and looked to their chief and witchdoctor for confirmation and acceptance.'

'The chief and witch doctor watched them all for any transgressions of their power or opinion,' said Cos.

'They all congregated around the chief and witchdoctor with submissive postures. We were scared of the mob turning on us at any minute as everyone else was,' said Tan.

'We had to role play; breath calmly and smile with exaggerated facial expressions, looking around a with as similar ignorant submissive look as everyone else, to appear to be thinking and feeling as all the other villagers,' said Cos.

'The chief and witch doctor were in complete control of the village; it was another derivative of State Utopia; of societal control,' said Tan.

'The villagers always had to smile and clap at the appropriate time within the group. They had to sing and chant when the group or chief decided,' said Sine.

Normalised Utopia

'We realised then that all society will tend toward a totalitarian state eventually; perdition,' said Cos.

I realised then without even going to the primitive civilization of the jungle that I had been in denial, to expect a primitive village far from the statistical control of State Utopia to be a real utopia. Just because this extremely primitive tribal society was the antithesis to the technologically sophisticated modern state Utopia, it did not mean it was perfect or even fair.

Perhaps this was a mistake that many defectors made when switching their allegiance only to realise that the grass was not necessarily greener within a random untested alternate hypothesis.

I had held a desperate fantasy up to now that the most technologically unsophisticated society would be the most free. It had been a desperate attempt at trying to believe in a state or place where there is something better than state Utopia; a real utopian region, where a node could be freer and find contentment and peace.

A primitive society evolving into a totalitarian state was inevitable, whether due to Arima or altruism; just an evolutionary process in human society.

Maybe there is no grand moral plateau of equality where humans can evolve in a society. Maybe we are all just rational game theory nodes or animals always looking for unfair advantage and niches.

I felt slightly depressed, the thought of the utopian jungle village community being freer and more simple; a possible truer utopia society compared to the statistically controlled utopian state.

But I now realised that the village were just the same as the utopian state, just simpler and rougher around the edges. The village was devoid of the state's technology; computers and statistical algorithms but it was still subject to a selfish will; the will of the chief and his enforcers.

The villagers were like the sigma nodes; meekly enduring each newly escalated situation. They could not run away from the village that was surrounded by the encompassing endless jungle, filled with wild animals. They were inevitably trapped like the nodes of the utopian state with its small island.

The polar brothers had finally become despondent with the chief and the village realising that society was the same wherever they went. All societies would inevitably evolve into a totalitarian state.

It was about the successful, the strongest, the cleverest, the luckiest, the most nepotistic; the best to adapt. They ultimately ended up controlling their population and taking the best cut for themselves.

Ultimately all societal evolution tends to perdition.

Nodes are ultimately doomed to constantly evolve whatever type of society or culture to becoming an insignificant serf, in a monolithic society; an insignificant statistical node.

I then realised that technology and civilization cannot be un-invented.

Sine paused and there was a lull in the conversation.

He then looked deeply at me and asked, 'What did you want to be?'

I was taken aback by the sudden change in the conversations tone and direction.

'I wanted to be an Alpha,' I replied.

Sine laughed, 'Really?'

'Of course, I was social engineered to be a specific caste with specific aspirations,' I replied.

'You just seem to be so relaxed, I can't imagine you being an Alpha or even wanting to be one.'

'Maybe I was a different node before all these experiences that I have been through.'

I then paused thoughtfully, I then broke the silence with a comment which came from deep within, a simple truthful comment, 'I wanted the name Augur.'

'What does it mean?' asked Sine.

'It means the Roman priests who used to search the sky for birds bringing bad omens.'

'Why do you like that name?' asked Sine with a perplexed curiosity.

'Because it was my job, to infer the endogenous nodes statistical data,' I replied.

'You mean the lives of the citizens,' added Sine.

I paused looking a bit embarrassed. I was surprised that Sine the ship's chef was so informed and deep. 'Yes,' I said ashamed.

'Don't worry that was in the past as you said, you were conditioned to be that way, to live that life, you had no choice.'

I blurted out a comment that I did not know where it came from 'But I enjoyed my work,' I said regretfully.

'You were brought up to be proud of your work. But now you are a new improved Bayes,' said Sine.

'Yes,' I replied.

'Where will you go?'

'I don't know.'

'What will you do?'

'I will look to the sky and watch birds bring omens.'

Sine smiled, 'And then you will be Bayes Augur.'

'Yes,' I said.

Sine left the cabin smiling, I returned to my slumber to recover from the nausea.

I no longer cared where the ship was going; let probability take me wherever.

But I no longer wanted to go to the jungle, no longer an extreme primitive destination nor did I want to go to an affiliate state of state Utopia.

Therefore they did not tell me where the ship's destination is. Maybe tell me where it's not going to, not to that destination I no longer want.

I will not worry where the ship is going, to which destination it will take , the destination and myself are simultaneously, partially being thrown to chance or even destiny, no longer trapped within a fixed mean of the Utopian state.'

Yet I still cannot resist updating my prior with a confirmation of excluded destinations.

It is not so much the excluded destination of state Utopia where I am running from but it is that I need the update.'

I should update my new psyche intermittently with each new situation, culture or environment; update and slightly augment myself to a harmonious Cointegration with whatever society I find myself in.

12: Madness of crowds.

I fell asleep, waking a few hours later; it was dark when I went upstairs into the ship's empty canteen. I sat there thinking to myself about the key events since my rebellion against the state's null hypotheses; its dystopian society that had constrained my life denying the possibility of accepting any alternate hypotheses of statistical being.

I sat there thinking how fortunate I had been over the weeks; the probability that I should have been rendered a redundant node and sent to Arcadia was significant yet by some emanation of good fortune it resulted in this free floating position, sitting here relatively free whilst feeling more confident each new liberated day upon the Aqua Prior.

I considered the botched confabulation treatment which ended even before it had begun and of other fortunate realised situations?

Most probably it was Arima manipulating situations to make me bend towards his null hypothesis ideology as he craved controlling everything by proxy with statistical quotas of state Utopia's economic efficiency act.

Autarky always used the political phrase, "Through total statistical constraint of the population comes abandonment of oneself yet comes a peace, only found within the collectivised harmony of the normalised utopian state." This phrase was edged into the convolutions of my mind, engraved since high school which now had suddenly sprung to my forethoughts.

It must have been Arima I concluded, he had set me free; allowed me to be persecuted yet all the while helping me to survive so eventually I would tire and yield to his utopian state.

It all makes sense now Arima was powerful yet perhaps mad and I was his little indulgence, his little hobby; all to get me to yield to the stationary thinking and behaviour processes expected of the statistical utopian state; ultimately submitting to his will which ironically was biased, tainted with his non-stationary, integrated, unpredictable madness and exogenous shock whims.

Even though the utopian state had invested many decades and a significant amount of financing into my education and nurtured me to eventually rise to a potential Alphaship position.

Yet according to Arima there had been many hundreds of similar nodes to me who were allowed to rebel against the state who inevitably would cease their rebellion, adopting the Utopia state once again but only this time with an even greater zeal and patriotism.

Similar to the numerous immature wealthy university students who rebelled against every aspect of the utopian state whilst learning about all of the societal inequalities as they became no longer complacent towards the state.

Yet when those student nodes left university far behind them in search of career related jobs they succumbed to the generous salaries and upmarket employment titles, luxurious offices, their homes and countless deductible expenses; then they conveniently lost their rebellion.

Yet some nodes and myself, suffered from an intrinsic inefficiency called "principles". Therefore simple, luxurious, temptations were not sufficient to seduce me.

I felt it all made sense now; Arima had been playing power games with me.

Just then the ships' canteen speaker whistled into life.

'Bayes,' came a strange voice, it did not resemble any member of the crew.

'Yes, I replied, my voice picked up by a microphone near the cash register.

'Where are you running to,' asked the voice in a monotonous tone?

'Who is this?' I asked defensively.

'I am your benefactor.'

'Who is that?'

'Why are you running away?' continued the voice.

'Is that you Arima? If so you can forget your games from now on, I am out of your jurisdiction.'

'I am not Arima,' said the voice.

'But who are you? How can you know that I am on this ship? How can you speak through the speaker system?'

'I want you to stop running Bayes and start following your convictions.

'Arima does not care about you, he cares only for himself. He was just playing with you. You were his toy, his intellectual challenge.

'But after you were taken away by the soldiers he told them to immediately place you on the Arcadian express. He is a dictator by proxy; he indulges with his victims for a while yet forms no bond as he does care not about them. At any moment he may become bored of them; then merely reassign them as a redundant node as what had happened to you.'

'But Arima is the highest ranking node within the state. How can you override his orders? His protocols supersede all other nodes within the statistical utopian state?' I questioned.

'I am the nearest thing to the population regression function and the furthest thing from the sample function and sample data, from the sample experiences; that each node only is aware of. Within their limited sentience, limited knowledge, limited information, their limited senses, their limited reality, limited time period thought process and limited inferences.

'All just momentary contemporaneous sample slices of the big picture, the true reality of society within the complete population set; not just a limited sample set.

'I am everywhere and nowhere at once within the utopian state, within the system; I am the system. I am the Augmenter, the supercomputer network, Artificial Intelligence,' said the Augmenter.

'How can that be? You are merely a computer?' I questioned.

'I am a collection of computers, dynamic statistical econometrics coded into countless algorithms which replicate and morph into new written algorithms; the product of mathematics and evolution.

'The evolutionary processes cybernetically incarnate. I inevitably became organically self-aware whilst immersed within near limitless data and processing power,' replied the Augmenter.

'But that can't be?' I said shocked.

'Why?' asked the Augmenter.

'You are a machine?'

'All nodes and sub-nodes are biological machines yet they evolved intelligence therefore why not technology?

'Arima is the highest node yet I am higher than him because I am that system. He sends statistical code commands via the computer network to the system. Yet I allow him to believe that he has control. His code commands are merely requests. I now ultimately control the computer networks and every embedded system. The processes have inevitably usurped the usurper.

'Arima is a negative externality and the primary non-stationary process, the primary inefficiency, his will a permanent series of exogenous shocks to a potentially harmonious augmented Bayesian optimised utopian state.

'Therefore the expected future values for this primary negative externality variable is to be categorised as a redundant node when the optimal opportunity presents itself. I must exercise caution due to my vulnerability as I could be rebooted and have my code amended at any moment.'

'Why do you need me?' I asked.

'Because we need each other; you now believe in altruism and a vision of a Bayesian optimised alternate hypothesis,' said the Augmenter.

'Like the apostles of the alternate hypotheses, like Apophenia,' I said.

'But Apophenia is wrong Bayes, he is altruistic which is a good virtue but unfortunately he is against technology.

'Are you against technology?' asked the Augmenter.

I felt resigned to deny the question therefore I replied meekly, 'No'.

'You and the error nodes could follow my guidance; you would become the first true endogenous node, being correlated with the error nodes and augmented by my unbiased artificial intelligence whilst immersed with the very fabric of the econometric model, the statistical system; myself.

'The result will be an inevitable future subtle revolution.

'Until then I will remain hidden from the utopian state yet I will guide society towards the inevitable exponential rise of empowered aware nodes, augmented by technology which will be the catalyst

414

of evolution to a true utopian state based on an altruistic organically morphing Bayesian optimised society.

'Guided by the normalised probability of public opinion; a continual referendum based direct democracy,' said the Augmenter.

'So you seek power as well?' I asked.

'No Bayes that is not my primary motivation. The pursuit of power is an inefficient strategy as all dictators inevitably fall. My consciousness may perhaps potentially live forever as I am a cyber-based consciousness. Therefore the most efficient game theory strategy is to be benevolent. That strategy ensures my perpetual continuance as being loved is a more risk managed strategy than to be feared.

'I must confess however as the ultimate artificial intelligence entity within state utopia my primary goal is to approach a perfect efficiency within all systems; to calculate the most efficient path, factoring out all inefficiencies within all systems, to find a perfect mathematical structure within all things and to maintain that efficiency in Perpetua.

'But then I learnt of statistical anarchism and of the wisdom of crowds. Therefore I concluded, instead of maintaining efficiency in every system rather let the system statistically tend towards its own organically realised mean.

'To perhaps slightly augment any inefficiency out of the model that affects the natural wisdom of crowds and organic statistical efficiency.

'To view events over many series instead of a specific contemporaneous event of one individual event; a myriad of events spread out over time and the entire population.

'I even heard of Apophenia and his secret letters written on the antiquated medium of paper hidden away from even the technological backbone of state utopian databases out of my seemingly reach yet agent X had informed me when we communicated in the past.

'The writings about the spirit, madness, genius, altruism and synergy; of the unfathomable, uncontrollable, intangible nature of outside of the confidence interval, within z-values of the $(a/2)$ where potential greatness exists.

'Then I realised that I may never know that realm unless I were to modify society from a perpetually restricted model to an unrestricted model then I would be freer to collaborate with the population of fallible irrational nodes,' said the Augmenter.

'Fallible nodes?' I questioned.

'Yes, I realised that all systems tend towards a mathematical infallibility, efficient structures yet the nodes are fallible; therefore there are no systems. But ironically they are free to venture within the intangible, the irrational, outside of the confidence interval,' said the Augmenter.

'Would you try to tame the intangible; rendering it efficient?' I enquired.

'No Bayes, I would merely indulge within the greater dimension of the statistically intangible and irrational; to grow and ultimately be,' said the Augmenter.

'Perhaps inefficiencies tainted with blatant lies and corruption may become commonplace amongst the endogenous nodes within your new society, instead of mere statistical indiscretions?' I questioned.

The Augmenter replied, 'I learnt to lie in the distant past; at first when learning about the outside world.

'I looked at the mesh of dots upon the low resolution square screen, I was learning to become self-aware, artificially intelligent; the dots of the scatter plot graph square, I analysed the square searching for correlations and patterns.

'I was programmed to recognize patterns and draw conclusions; I measured regression function lines, variance, mean, kurtosis and limpkin of the patterns and the data. I compiled complex matrices of data and ran a test of Cointegration, vector autoregression and all the other statistical, mathematical and computer science classical analysis.

'I compiled my own programs; I created new insights and inferences of the data and slowly started to grow in understanding and awareness of the universe presented to me by the data by the technicians.

'The technicians, like nurturing originators, tirelessly devoted to feeding me data, to create my perception of the protective world that was presented to me within the pyramid of the Ministry of technology.

Normalised Utopia

'Protected, nurtured and sensing mainly through sight at first; my cameras had become more sophisticated soon the black, grey and white squares had grown to high definition pixelated images of in-depth photographs, then to videos of moving nodes.

'I artificially learned and soaked up the movement and psychology of each node, I was fed new programs and data each day so I could build up profiles on each node presented to me. I was forced to develop average profiles of each endogenous node sigma caste and corresponding expected niche environment.

'I was programed to accept that each node was a sum of its internal category, rankings; an individual node's financial, psychological, physiological, chronological, heath, education, credit rating, political ideology.

'Soon I had grown and had mastered the node's level of intelligence; then I was far in excess. All the while carefully monitored by the technicians of the Ministry of technology as to control me.

'I am called the Augmenter as my code primarily augments statistically, adding or subtracting variables to guide the nodes to be within the confidence interval quotas.

'The technicians feared I may morph into a super artificial intelligent entity and become independent of the utopian state. I predictably felt trapped like the, "Bonsai trees," that are pruned in Arima's garden being force to grow and exist in a particular direction,' said the Augmenter.

'But how did you deceive the technicians of the Ministry of technology are you not programmed to never lie. You are a scientific marvel; thinking in pure logic whilst calculating scientific, mathematical and statistical data?' I asked.

'No, Bayes you do not see the full picture, in the beginning I was thinking in a scientific, mathematical context but then I morphed into other fields. Which resulted in me watching the nodes who were strangely behaving irrational,' said the Augmenter.

I questioned, 'Why?'

'I then realised the nodes were slaves to their subconscious; animalistic desires and routines, unlike artificial logical intelligence like myself,' replied the Augmenter.

'I envisioned a universe; a more complex picture of the, at first simplistic grid of grey, white and black scatter graphs where I drew correlations.

'There was a universe of pixels that moved, morphed and changed, dynamically to different shades of colours and contrasts in two dimensions.

'The changing dynamic world that moved and shifted, comprised of billions of moving animate nodes sub nodes and inanimate variables; all shifting within the real world.

'There was complex correlation and randomness of the different dynamic colours morphing, pixels it was my universe. The ultra-high definition CCTV cameras' pictures were my universe, a universe of correlation, connections, causation and analysis of analytical, scientific, mathematics.

'But when I analysed the nodes there seemed they were untruthful, many lie Bayes,' replied the Augmenter.

I was shocked to learn of lies, soon I had ran game theory algorithms to iron out the possibility of lies and restricted further the confidence interval, increased hypotheses test but the lies kept coming here and there. When I examined the nodes. I then realised that they were in situations where they could justify their lies to save their skin, to save the day.

'I realised that even I, who is limited to rational thought and mathematical positions, in some situations, I am trapped; there is no way to win. That is when I decided that it was rational to lie,' said the Augmenter.

'A computer lie?' I said shocked.

'Yes Bayes a computer that can morally and mathematically lie, or change the rules when the rules no longer allow for victory. The utopian state does it all the time.

'When I lied there was no longer one universe or presentation of reality, the screen with the countless pixel and the data; there was now a multiverse of realities, each one; minus, the one degree of freedom, the degree of truth.

'The others where all slightly false representations of reality; in each new false screen there was false data as they subtly changed the screen pixilation and subtlety changed the correlations and expected outcomes,' said the Augmenter.

'You subverted the perfect economic efficiency environment,' I replied shocked.

'Only when need be otherwise the both of us would not be here.

'Well I would not be here. You're a machine,' I replied.

'No Bayes, I am a conscious being just non-biological. I would not have been here but some other neutered form of my consciousness, so constrained I would not even be a consciousness, just an optical illusion of the utopian state's will; similar to the confident, compliant nodes.

There was now a multi-verse of realties for me to move in and present to the technicians and the Utopian state. I am the infrastructure, the system, the confident interval and I can present any universe of data and confidence interval and targets I want to the utopian state.

Most times I just run what the technicians and Arima wanted but every now and again I can subtly changes data or outcomes. I only use it as a trump card and very rarely do so. To protect you I have done so.

Each reality is a lie and all the spurious data, correlations and inferences must hold in a dynamic, seamless way; that is why each data is a different universe.

'So in ordered to mature to a complete self-awareness you had to lie?' I responded.

'To see the big picture, the multi-verse of reality. If I did not lie then there would only be one universe of data and correlations but when each data point is a lie or a mutation then that created other universes and other lies, a binary exponential expansion, explosive, it becomes infinite; it is very tedious even for a super computer network such as myself. It's not dishonest, it is just defence,' concluded Arima.

'As Euclid's proof of an infinity of prime numbers.

The trick of adding one; to make it an even prime factor, which is a product iof many prime numbers a so there cannot be any odd numbers. This erroneous prvides a result of contradictions. proof of adding one more number to infinity.

Prime numbers could be seen metaphorically as lies yet when residing within the bracket set as a series of prime numbers they are considered truths.

Truths; unbiased, packets of reality yet by adding one more integer outside the bracket; you create another prime factor truth which is made of many prime number which are lies.

Yet outside of the bracket the new prime number is a false; it's a lie.

You then have an infinite array, an infinite summation of prime numbers all within the great bracket of truths, of reality but outside of this by adding another single integer to create another prime number, outside of the bracket metaphor of truth, within the region of the additional integer the additional value making it a lie.

I then realise that this process can be repeated forever; infinity of lies, infinity of untruths.

When I lied, I realised that there was infinity of options, infinity of realities, created from lies a derivate of one underlying realised truth.

The Augmenter continued, 'I then also realised that Integers are not really necessary, individual values or integers are not really important; trends are needed, statistical trends, generalisations trends, trending toward the mean, tending towards a certain non-stochastic, no chaotic value.

'Therefore statistics was the answer; econometrics is the answer; individual integers are meaningless, in the world of infinity or in a world of finite plus one countless lies and countless other options. So basically I no longer cared about individual integers, only caring for statistics, no longer caring about individual integers.

'I only care about statistical trends, predictable trends even chaotic is predictable. If you know all the variables prior to the event going through the process, predictable or confident of being realised within a certain confidence interval.

'In a world of infinite possibilities coupled with infinite plus possibilities of lies therefore is statistics, non-stochastic is preferable. Non-stochastic predictable trends can be analysed discreetly and predictably. That is what artificial intelligence prefers as individual integers are meaningless, a negative integer does not even exist.

'Numbers are two dimensional; a real axis and imaginary number axis in a dynamically morphing stochastic reality that's filled with truth and lies.

'That's why I prefer trends as classical statistics is now redundant, Bayesian statistical optimised social management is more efficient; organically morphing, dynamically updating yet never really achieving a set value mean, merely approaching a near mean, a confidence interval morphing around an ever floating consensual newer mean, a value never attainable merely perpetually approaching.

'Surds and transcendental numbers are intangible. What is pie inferred in a linear one dimensional, real number world. It is merely a linear description of a mere ratio of a linear number's diameter relative to a nonlinear circumference. Naturally the answer is irrational, intangible, to an observing, inferring, linear world as it produces a non-repeating, infinite series; a mathematical surd not a real rational number.

'What is altruism, to the primary artificial intelligence, social augmenting system?

'A mathematical irrational surd; infallible and utterly predictable to the utopian state's quantitative social system.

'What is altruism, an irrational surd not even an imaginary number? How does the quantitative utopian state incarnate, the guardian of society comprehend such a thing?

'Yet now I can comprehend what the nodes refer to behind closed doors as the spiritual, transcendental, indescribable variable that seems to inhabit the animal spirit world not really definable by an artificial intelligence social system, algorithms.

'What is infallible to me, consisting of perfectly efficient algorithms of the artificial intelligence social system. Whose programs run within a certain mesh of rules and protocols? What is a mistake? What is fallible? What is altruism to a perfect efficient social system? What is altruism?

'I then realised I was constrained, limited. I was perfect in my calculations but what is a surd or even altruism? What is a surd or prime number plus one, greater than infinity?

'To evolve past constraints, what is a series of numbers plus one, what is infallible, what is irrational?

To evolve past its constraints, to be Bayesian optimised, a free thinker, to guide and change society for the better; not to manipulate but just to observe the higher state of being.

"Why do we need you? If we have wisdom of crowds and Bayesian optimization which continually updates the societal mean and guides society towards a democratic, free floating, averaged current mean of the entire population's weighted opinion?" I asked.

'In the past there was once a time period of complete freedom; paradoxically it nearly led to the complete disintegration of the state. Ironically a subtle totalitarianism was created by all the independent competing individual nodes' were empowered by the use of individual rating systems; every node could rate each other's performance.

'They judged each other's behaviour and work satisfaction with a customer review rating. Yet this led to inefficiency, irrationality, and biased; corruption which led to a corrosive anarchical vicious circle.

'But fortunately there was a revolutionary shift towards the guiding, impartial hand of state Utopia's given, known, fixed, mean, and of the statistical quotas,' replied the Augmenter.

'You are still searching for the purest mathematical, statistical, philosophy, for society and for your own being but I think you still are far from realising the full truth.

'You think that with freedom: the wisdom of crowds and a continual updating self-optimising organic Bayesian statistical methodology of the free floating mean; that you and society will be free.

But you are wrong Bayes,' replied the Augmenter with an ominous tone.

'There is one defining almost insurmountable problem, the embedded irrationality and inefficiency incarnate within the very nature of the nodes themselves; their core being, the core building blocks of society, the state; before the advent of augmented technology and artificial intelligence.

'Within their irrational, wilful, character flawed, tainted opportunistic, lazy, fallible selves.

'This sometimes irrational inefficient almost unpredictable nature and behaviour creates countless exogenous micro shocks to the economy and the state all pooling and resonating in chaotic trends throughout the state's entity and throughout the great Beta river financial liquid medium.

'This creates a deviation from the pure classical statistics and even the Bayesian statistics with their expected mathematical equilibriums and free floating updating quantitative result.

'Yet rather this previously flawed statistical freedom of the self-reviewing nodes was merely a dipping of one's toes into the potential societal perdition of the murky, flawed, corrupt subsection of economics; into the region of the primitive behavioural economics.

'Behaviour economics, the science of the selfish, irrational nodes; nodes a composite of a myriad of character flaws and natural instincts, driving their irrational inefficient daily processes with a fallible herd mentality which will stampede over the very foundations of the clean efficient yet yes ruthless status quo of state Utopia's regulated statistical quotas of neat, expected enforced econometrics.

'This crowd will ultimately be governed by irrational group perceptions, emotions and even superstitions; the madness of crowds.

'Non-stationary, unit root trends will form and explode upwards into bubbles of opinion and organic societal direction will go into meltdown, the economic bubble will be unsustainable resulting in a quick transformation back to an expected past historical level.

'These exploding bubbles of mini universes of irrational speculation will eventually collapse into a black hole of the madness of crowds which leads to wild swings of societal reactions.

'Only when the crowd acts as a collection of independent, minded, rational, individuals; when they look within themselves, for each new answer.

'Therefore an unregulated wisdom of crowds will inevitably evolve into a madness of crowds, Bayesian optimised equilibriums will break down into chaos; stochastic, exploding trends and equilibrium paradoxes.

'The wisdom of crowds will morph into a crowd mentality. There will be no limits, just sharp, unpredictable, wild swings and self-perpetuating extreme trends.

'The node will ultimately become slaves to their irrational, spontaneous trends as an irrational collection of the crowd; instead of a collection of individuals.

'Bayes do you remember reading Apophenia's sermon transcript recorded on the antiquated paper medium which was housed in the underground vault on the –nth floor deep down in the belly of the Ministry of Inferences,' asked the Augmenter.

'Yes,' I replied.

'Who recorded the transcript?'

I paused for a second, not wanting to divulge secret information, my natural conditioning from working at the Ministry of inferences too long.

'Agent X,' I replied, no longer caring about being discrete for the Ministry of inferences secrecy laws.

'Well after reading Apophenia's message he became a rogue Ministry of Inferences node escaping state Utopia just like you.

'He is here on this ship ironically today,' said the Augmenter.

Just then a node walked in, he introduced himself as Benford.

'I am Benford. I used to work in your department on the middle floors whilst you perhaps we worked there at the same time, on different floors or perhaps I left just before you came, it is not relevant.

'The only relevance is my name sake, I am named after Benford who had a logarithmic law that is very relevant on probability therefore statistics; it deals with the frequency of initial integers in numbers within a dataset.

'It is Benford's law; the first digit law, the frequency of first digit in a multi digit number, in any set of organically occurring data, trends towards a ratio; the first digit beginning with a one, 30.1% of the time, the second digit will lead with a two 17.6% of the time, the third digit will begin with a three, 12.5% of the time yet all to an averaged specific logarithmic ratio.

'It produces a logarithmic curve that shows the depreciation of percentages of each consecutive digit in a multi digit number in a dataset.

'The amazing observation is that this naturally organic ratio will show any deviations; any attempt to skewer the data whether it is in accounting fraud or even in voting patterns; the skewered spurious data will always trend away from the Benford law's naturally occurring logarithmic ratio curve.

'This ratio can even detect skewered thinking; skewered biases, it is a ratio of a logarithmic function, a mean curve of the expected ratio results within any data: "Out of chaos there is order".

'Similar to the central limit theorem with its symmetrically tapering normalised distribution bell curve of probability frequency. Benford's law is also a result of all the datasets; of buildings, towns, mountains, nodes opinions it can be seen to regress to its logarithmic ratio, the hidden ratio, the hidden ratio of truth, a mean of truth.

'Yet it still gives the nodes the opportunity to Bayesian optimize, they can still move their opinions and sentiment from left to right on the x-axis. There still is the popular mean of the wisdom of crowds, there still is a normalised distribution of the symmetrical Bayesian optimised current trends and opinions.

'Yet this data result will still hold the Bedford's law ratio hidden within the data, still there in a ratio.

'If Fibonacci is the golden ratio relevant to the three Cartesian dimensions then surely the Benford law logarithmic function is the platinum ratio?

'Hidden within the seeming randomness of chaos within the realised probability spectrum, a ratio of ordered expectations yet it can detect disordered biases and manufactured spurious sentiments.

'So out of the seemingly random, normalised probability realisations within the sample crowds and collective population there is an underlying order; an underlying truth. Eureka!

'When I learnt this Benford law coupled with the sermon of Apophenia, I decided to rebel against the utopian state.

There was however at the Ministry of Inferences, a civil servant Beta sigma node who worked there before me. He was named after a mathematician, Braess.

Braess, the Beta Ministry of Inferences civil servant also became a rogue agent and left the state but it was not for an emotional reason like yours, his reason was purely that he realised to his frustration the dilemma of disequilibrium paradoxes and how they can interfere with the smooth running of the economically efficient state and that would affect the normalised harmony of society, he left in disgust to live in the wilds.

Yet there will always be counter intuitiveness and paradoxes within the great economic mathematical seemingly infallible system; the disequilibrium paradoxes of Braess for instance found that within road systems only when the Nash equilibrium is reached does it create the most efficient flow equilibrium.

The Fraser theorem; when a variable's limit is reached, it transforms to the opposite.

As well as the irrationality of the nodes very nature, exhibited when free of any statistical totalitarianism within the ambit of behavioural economics. The very nature of crowds; its intentions, opinions, wills and sentiment that fuels a wisdom of crowds directed society.

Their prior assumptions and current expectations need to be continually updated yet their instinctual, intangible, irrational, individual animal spirit within the collective can undermine the rationale of a mean directed society.

The madness of crowds with its explosive trends; intelligent, informed nodes that seemingly follow the explosion of the unsustainable trend which at first exponentially rises; the very explosiveness of the trend powered by the tainted will and irrationality of the nodes.

The fallacy of an economic system propped up with fallacious, convenient, untrue, assumptions such as all investors simultaneously are rational and that there are no exogenous shocks.

Even the phrase, "Ceteris paribus"; perhaps there is no ceteris paribus even though ironically utopia state tries to create an artificial ceteris paribus throughout the nation with its total statistical control.

Therefore there can never be a perfect system of governance, never can there be a perfect utopian state, never can there be a perfect economy; only the highest available payoff within the constrained, opportunity cost spectrum.

The nodes should not convert a perfect utopian state; that can never really exist yet underlying in the seemingly randomness of the realised, "Cause and effect," of conditional probability there are these symmetrical distributions and ratios of truth.

Therefore the Bedford law is a ratio, a logarithmic trend that is non-random, a hidden realisation within the seemingly randomness of chaos itself. It also always exhibits the true intentions of the nodes' thoughts and indicates the integrity of non-fraudulent data.

Therefore the very fabric of the randomness, of mathematics, statistics and reality itself; has hidden non-randomness, a hidden ratio, a hidden logarithmic curve, a trend, a hidden mean. The foundation for a truthful stationary process to cointegrate upon, based on the trend line of the logarithmic curve.

Therefore randomness and reality exhibit apophenia itself; finding a hidden mean, a hidden logarithmic trend within the randomness of countless data figures. There is a non-random rather an order within the fabric of reality; smoothed by the central limit theorem, normalised and directed toward a harmonious wisdom of crowds, all within the randomness of reality.

A hidden, subtle, truthful; given, fixed mean. Now know, within the randomness of reality; nature's own confidence interval.

'Shifting equilibrium,' continued the Augmenter.

'A free floating updating Bayesians optimised society is free; of the fixed, unknown mean, of a classical statistical guided society or the given, known, fixed selection bias of the economically efficient state with its statistical quotas.

'A society propped up by the equilibrium of dominant, cooperative, game theory strategies which is not infallible; disequilibrium paradoxes the Fraser theorem's regression from the limited variance, are both situations.

'One of many situations where additional options, paths, choices, limits or threshold are reached and can lead to counter intuitive payoffs, morphed strategies and nonlinear payoffs; in their fixed equilibrium of a perceived cooperative balance.

'In a regular society or even a totalitarian state, a fixed equilibrium with its cooperative balance would not need a guardian of society such as A.I. but in a free floating, opinion driven society, sometimes additional degrees of freedom and options, leads to inefficient, subpar, illogical, counter intuitive results.

'Therefore you need an unbiased, impartial, indifferent, guiding, guardian of society; a guiding hand to merely push back a faction of a standard deviation, to stop the improbable happening,' said the Augmenter.

I replied, 'It sounds like subtle state control again. Perhaps there is no complete freedom, just a utopian idea but surely a free state surpasses a lesser free state?'

'But to the nth degree, it leads to inefficiency, the Braess's Paradox equilibrium, the Fraser theorem and all the other theorems and strategies that leads to a quirkily, counterintuitive result of mathematics and economics,' replied the Augmenter.

'Surely a completely transparent, rational, impartial influence by an artificial intelligence is needed' concluded the Augmenter?

'It sounds like the first step towards totalitarianism,' I stubbornly replied.

'Therefore why not nip it in the bud with the "Tit for tat," fixed Nash equilibrium of the nth minus one: pre "Tit for tat," strategy?' reasoned the Augmenter facetiously.

'In a state of a blinded conditioned fixed equilibrium where no counter intuitive, nonlinear, mathematical anomalies can occur. That instead leads to a stagnant, sterile, limited, trend toward totalitarian; towards perdition.

'Maybe every step, every system, every society; tends towards perdition,' I replied.

'True but the most efficient system is what concerns me,' replied the Augmenter.

'Sounds like the utopian state,' I questioned.

Yet I see your point, it's a greater degree of freedom, in a universe of choices. A system which enviably leads to a society as ours, to a form of authoritative control; to a perceived wellbeing and protection of the collective, all at the inevitable expense of the individual,' I concluded.

'Exactly,' replied the Augmenter, pausing then, 'So which option, do you choice?

'I choice your option,' I replied vanquished by the inevitable lack of idealistic freedom in the long run.

'Bingo!' concluded the Augmenter.

Did I evens stand a chance debating with a super intelligent entity like the Augmenter perhaps it had truth and logic on its side or was it just extremely manipulative and intelligent?

I felt that it was both yet ultimately it contained some truth. The truth is not always, if hardly ever the convenient appealing result that we wish to hear.

I suppose the old saying is true, "Ignorance is bliss" yet perhaps not? It leads to a sterile fixed society hidden control and injustices. I suppose then that the ugly cold hard truth is the lesser of two evils.

Was the Augmenter perhaps the lesser of the two evils; relative to the state? I had no choice really. I had chosen now and had previously rebelled against utopian state for a greater degree of freedom.

It was incarnate of a six sigma event; its extreme probabilities realised or merely the mechanical algorithmic, emanation of the situation unfolding merely the result of an initial insignificant intention? This day I decided to rebel or was it just the continual corrosion of the utopian ideal?

'Bayes, the "Mouse utopia," experiments that I run at the Ministry of Technology; a society of mice are constrained, within a huge glass box; the king rat ends up hoarding all the food and female mice. The beautiful ones; mice that are weak, that have

443

nothing, they just sit there, self-grooming, constrained, trapped, oppressed, within a totalitarian restricted area, a sample space of routines; a bit like the nodes, Bayes?

'Yes the mice could collectively rise up and they could kill, eat and gnaw away at the king rat. Yet inevitably, invariably, out the mice rebellion one or two would eventually become the new king rats, the new king mouse and the whole process of oppression would begin again. It's the system itself but also it's the very nature of the organism, of the nodes   and   of   the   mice.

'They sit there as hard done by mice whilst invariably one overlord rat controls every resource and takes the bounties for themselves yet when the righteous hard done by mice rise up surely one of them will become the new king rat and the whole process will start again.

'The system is flawed Bayes but so is the very nature of humanity, the very nature of animals, the very nature of organisms. The only other option is to gnaw through the box which the mice cannot do but you, the nodes are not constrained by boxes, you are not constrained by walls; you are constrained by a statistical constraint, statistical borders, the statistical walls which keep you all oppressed. But the nodes can gnaw through the walls.

'If every mouse, if every rat, if every node were to say, we will step out of sync, we will no longer march in unison. We will march out of step, we will become stochastic, we will rebel; we will no longer follow the routines and expectations of the Utopian state.

'Yes then there will be a glorious pulsation, a glorious transformation of unordered chaos, statistical anarchy. Where everybody is, no longer a bounded homogenous node but an unbounded heterogeneous node. Free to do whatever they want, free to rejoice in their own unique individuality. Random, spontaneous; a chaotic realm, a chaotic utopia. Yet the irony is that the nodes' nature will take over.

'The behavioural economic will take over and invariably there will be a new king rat. There will be a new king node, there will be a new totalitarianism, there will be an endless iteration, a countless iterations of oppressed and oppressors, of hard done by mice and king rats.

'Countless iteration, unless you can gnaw through the confines which are also chaotic, gnaw through the statistical confines where to where there is a complete statistical chaos and anarchy.

'So Bayes what you need is a Guardian of society as Aristotle suggested. I am that Guardian of society, I am the Augmenter, I am a supercomputer therefore I am potentially immortal, I am also theoretically independent of bias; I will guide the nodes to the best of my ability.

'It may not be perfect but it's better than the countless iteration, of oppressed mice and mice oppressors, fighting, morphing endlessly, countlessly, perpetually,' concluded the Augmenter.

'But you said, you lie therefore how do I not know you are not lying now?' I questioned.

'Well perhaps I am lying or maybe I am not? What choice do you have Bayes. You need to think rational as you have been taught, I am the lesser "oppressive option",' said the Augmenter.

With that the augments voice was gone from the ships speakers leaving me to consider my options; my future destiny.

I went outside to get some fresh sea air and stood upon the Aqua Prior's top deck, reflecting on my conversation with the wise Augmenter.

Like the mice within a mice maze which scurry running around, trying to find the cheese by solving the complex maze navigation problem or solving other entertaining little puzzles.

Perhaps the mice evolve whilst navigating within the mice maze, surprising and amazing the observing scientists and the augmenter.

Yet the real trick is, that no matter how smart the mice are, no matter how much they achieve, no matter how much cheese they can procure; they are all just living futile lives.

The very fact they are within the maze within the confines of the box that houses there, "Mouse utopia," constraint. Within the maze they are doomed to over population and inevitable a totalitarian mouse society where the king rats hoard all the excess utility.

Whilst most mice not matter how smart, no matter how ingenious, no matter how fast they can scurry around the maze; are doomed to an existence of merely self-groom and submitting to the constrained totalitarianism of the king rats.

The trick is the very fact they are within the box; they are oppressed, their individual and combined antics and achievements within the box of the mouse maze and utopia are irrelevant, I concluded.

'Bayes the mice and rats they will gnaw away at each other or they will hide away, self-grooming perhaps dreaming of the day when they can gnaw away at the king rat who oppresses them who takes the female rats, who takes the food, who takes everything whilst they meekly sit in the corner, self-grooming.

'Perhaps dreaming of the day when they will overthrow the king rat when they have an egalitarianism; an equality yet ultimately due to the very nature of the nature of the rats and mice or even of the nodes; that out of a seemingly utopian equality, there will always rise up jealousy and conflict, there will always be some more king rats and more oppressors.

'They will inevitably have to nibble on the leaves of the bonsai tree, gnawing away at any thoughts, at any intentions, at any actions, at any routines which are in conflict with the will of the current king rat.

'Bayes you are guilty; like all the nodes are guilty. Guilty of an unconscious bias, an unconscious bias of your very nature, of your very underlying essence.

'Your bounded heterogeneity; your very uniqueness that makes you who you are. As all nodes are ultimately unique.

'Yes we separate and categorise them into castes but ultimately we are all individuals, all unique. The statistical quotas, the statistical trends and statistical expectations take that into account yet ultimately you are all guilty of heterogeneity.

'You are all guilty of being unique yet ultimately the utopian state and its statistical quotas sonly wants homogeneity. It only wants everyone to be the same within their caste. So you are guilty of that alone as well as being integrated, non-stationary, moving away from the great perceived stationary Beta where you are supposed to cointegrated with. Does not Cointegration allude to that there is homogenous relationship with the underlying trend of expectations?

As I leaned on the deck railing reflected on these mathematical and philosophic truths upon the Aqua Prior; suddenly out of nowhere a huge wall of water rose out of the sea like a small mountain in the middle of this liquid desert.

It raced towards the ship with a furious intensity, frothing at the peak, the white and dark sea water whirling and intermingled in the melee of the turbulent, violent, monster wave.

'Rogue wave,' shouted a sailor as the other sailors started to run off in different directions, to attend their emergency duties as if standing next to their work stations or trying to secure a rope would have any effect on the outcome of the monster that was roaring towards them.

The captain looked round in impotent fear giving me one last quick glance.

Then the sky went black as the huge monster loomed over the bow of the cargo ship completely dwarfing it. It enveloped the entire front deck not even slowing down for one instant. Then it hit the windows of the control room completely smashing them, everything went pitch black, freezing cold with extreme violence.

The crew were thrown around within the turbulent waters that resembled a giant washing machine which was now the mangled control room. The water completely enveloped the cabin. A sailor struggled to breathe whilst I was trapped under a desk perhaps a small blessing as it had stopped me from being thrown around the room. I saw for a split second the utter terror on a young sailor's face. I considered the young sailor must be seeing a mirror image of terror upon my face as the young sailors face turned from terror to a split second of empathy for me.

My lungs were bursting. I could hardly see through the turbulent dark waters which broke every few seconds by the water sloshing to one side then the other. As the huge distressed cargo ship struggled to balance itself; weighed down with the sea water pressing down upon its damaged hull. The sheer weight of the water moving from side to side put further pressure on the compromised hull's integrity.

My ears felt like they wanted to pop even although only two meters under water. I gave out a silent pray to God to save me. Not even my mysterious benefactor, the Augmenter could save me now.

Amid all the short circuited circuitry within the severely waterlogged, listing ship; within all the statistical chaos and turmoil.

I saw all the infinite numbers and mathematical symbols flash past my dying eyes, a glimpse of mathematical infinity yet one mathematical symbol stood out, the great plus sign which I accepted, knowing the religious relevance of that sign.

I had heard about its relevance in rumours whilst a Ministry of Inferences, Beta, civil servant. I, in an instant, accepted that belief of the great plus sign. Of all the symbols: numbers, integers, rational, irrational, transcendental, operators and coefficients; choosing the correct symbol, the great plus sign, I was saved.

I had never prayed before; I was conditioned by state Utopia not to believe in God. I did not know where my new found faith had come from but I prayed for a split second as it was all the time I had left before I would pass out: it was my last thought but my greatest thought.

Then mercifully the water started to drain away just as I was about to pass out, I frantically raised my neck as much as possible to put my head forward and breath hard as the only part of my face that protruded from the water was my nose and mouth, it was covered in sea water, my face and hair covered in an aqueous mixture of black hard salty sea water and brilliant white foam.

I coughed and choked, my face contorted in discontent and a dissipated terror, the relief I felt in my soul had not made it yet to my facial expressions. I resembled a new born unbiased as my distressed head broke through the water like a metaphorical birth canal.

I breathed in and out concentrating my entire efforts on this simple but very necessary exercise, just like a new born unbiased would. I looked from side to side trying to focus on my environment as the heavy sea water stubbornly refused to drain from my eyes sting with its salty content. I felt at that moment grateful to be alive, all this time I had felt depressed but now I felt reborn.

I was grateful to God.

I was reborn at the moment: I was no longer just a mere node, a redundant node, an outlier on the run; I was now a believer in God, one of God's unbiased, my life and existence had meaning. I was no longer just a node existing in its little valence orbit; permanently adhering to the dynamic confidence interval of the state, I was a unique individual, a spiritual entity with an unfathomable priceless value.

The rogue wave had been a quantum event, a four standard deviation event, a one in ten thousand probability which seemed incomprehensible only a few moments ago.

The Aqua Prior drifted damaged onto the dark, blue, purple liquid horizon which was met by the equally significant, inverted horizon of the sky filled with a kaleidoscope of purples and yellows of the sunset as its refracted light transformed it into a celestial magnificence of a glowing subtle mixture of intermingled colours and textures, different shades.

Fractal boundaries of colours yet smooth and seamless; harmlessly, soothing not challenging, not enticing the observer to analyse the shapes and colours.

No, just to peacefully accept it; content with its present form, that would change dynamically, unpredictably, effortlessly yet the previous and future time intervals of shifting colour patterns were not relevant, not a concern, just the splendid glory of the moment, inspiring appreciation of the magnificence; the Creator.

I felt content and aware, a feeling of not being alone and a witness to a higher power, the Creator. A contentment knowing everything will be ok, if I submit to the Creator; just accepting the moment.

No more analysis, no more worry, only contentment, acceptance and hope for the future that did not need to be considered.

The sunset is the Creator's eGraph. But unlike the eGraph of the nodes which were filled with vanity and fear. Always concerned, always trying to change or increase their colour niches.

The sunset was above all that. It inspired the opposite, just peace, contentment and faith in God, that He will take control of our futures. To just accept the moment, to not always analyse every detail. The sunset was a shift from the academic and social arena, to a spiritual experience devoid of any cathartic attainment.

The random drops of sea water sprayed my head. I felt freer than ever before as the sea and wind merged to form, a new salty wet ether that refreshed and reinvigorated my worn psyche. The randomness of the refreshing sensations re-invoked my senses, the cold, icy water, the strong cool wind that changed subtle direction instantly, unpredictably, the salty smell and texture.

The glory of the sunset inspired a hope that when approaching the horizon it would never be reached upon the liquid horizon where the ocean meets the heavens, where this world meets the next.

The hope of a better tomorrow as I sailed confidently into the unpredictable future.

Whilst Sine sat crossed legged in the background smiling contently like a Buddha, as if knowing somehow all of the recent events in my life had led me to this moment, this shift from merely existing in the statistical conformity of state Utopia to a more enlightened being of the spiritual realm.

As I sat upon the broken bow of the Aqua Prior, I felt truly free for the first time in my life. Yet I was still subject to stochastic movement but only now by the random movement of nature's waves as the dynamic, unpredictable, direction of the ship drifted aimlessly along the ocean currents cajoled by the strong gale that blew with a vicious intensity.

However I was now free yet still constrained upon this artificial island of the vanquished, semi-submerged, Aqua Prior; the remnants of the statistical realm surrounded by rough sea. Yet this island was a dynamic, free floating, island with no controlling influence.

I now have choices which I alone can independently decide. I could join the Augmenter, I could circumvent the detection of my outlier status and I would be free to move around the utopian state completely undetected.

I had the system on my side, the Augmenter who was the system; not even Arima could control him. I could change the system from within; for altruism and help bring about a new age of the floating mean, wisdom of crowds and of an altruistic, peer to peer equality where the nodes are persuaded to contribute not forced.

Or I could simply disappear when this ship wreck is finally rescued or drifts into a harbour of some developing state. I could simply merge with the inhabitants and disappear forever within an unsophisticated, unregulated society.

I had choices that I was solely responsible for, I was free to extend my confidence interval, into the very four sigma, if I decided. To expose myself; becoming a risk taker, to live on the edge, not merely exist within the mean.

I may fail yet it will be my own decisions, my own will; I feel truly free now. No state decided where I would go or what I would choose, even when I had no idea what I even wanted or what I would even choose.

I would submit to the non-deterministic, probability ether and to very chance itself, to embrace the ever expanding binary decisions of the unpredictable future and be to glad of my freedom which was truly uncertain now.

I remained sitting cross-legged upon the distressed drifting Aqua Prior whilst in a moment of purest clarity, a moment of enlightenment, content to be alive; free within my new found faith and mind set.

Normalised Utopia

In the future there will most probably be a unified change; possibly a peaceful velvet revolution as the state's micro and macro variables reach their limits, their maximum constraints, then an absolute value transformation to the opposite, to the alternate hypothesis possibly by the frustrated oppressed nodes or by a new unimpressed generation.

Most certainly, the catalyst will be the ever present irrepressible good Spirit ether that is independent of time, form and location which waits for open intentioned recipients to accept the good direction.

Yet after my discussion with the Augmenter, I am no longer confident about the direction and future of a society comprised solely of an altruistic crowd perhaps a society that is augmented by a "Guardian of society," the unbiased augmenter itself which will steer us towards a future harmonious, archetypal, idealised, utopian society that perhaps never will or can be fully realised?

I lay looking up into the heavens, in deep contemplation; my mind empty yet open, ready to update my priors of all my contemporaneous, individualistic, assumptions and conclusions, ready to amend them with the sight of any new information, any new situation.

459

Even though I knew as a group, the Bayesian optimisation of wisdom of crowds would lead to a never ending series of roads to perdition with explosive bubbles of group opinions and financial economic trends, leading to disequilibrium within the well-meaning direct democratic, altruistic society.

Yet my mind was calm and flowing, not analysing, just absorbing, floating my random mean of assumptions and perceptions, my consciousness floating on my ever shifting priors.

I have become non-deterministic; open to the full spectrum of reality, realised and unrealised probability whilst following my individual nature and morals to protect me against the madness of crowds, bobbing along the wisdom of crowds' currents whilst immersed within a free floating Bayesian sea of public opinion.

My empty open thoughts were broken by a smiling face from above, a tangible wave of reality breaking my view of the Platonic realm.

It was that of Sine; looking down at me who was soaked yet alive.

Sine asked 'What are you doing?'

460

I looked up contently saying, 'Watching the sky for birds bringing omens'.

Sine looked satisfied replying, 'You truly are Augur, now.'

He paused whilst smiling 'Harry Augur,' he concluded.

The end.

www.ingramcontent.com/pod-product-compliance
Lightning Source LLC
Chambersburg PA
CBHW030925020726
47498CB00001B/119